THE
WISHBREAKER

Also by Tyler Whitesides

The Wishmakers

The Janitors series

THE WISHBREAKER

TYLER WHITESIDES

ILLUSTRATED BY
JESSICA WARRICK

HARPER

An Imprint of HarperCollinsPublishers

The Wishbreaker
Text copyright © 2019 by Tyler Whitesides
Illustrations by Jessica Warrick
All rights reserved. Printed in the United States of America.
No part of this book may be used or reproduced in any manner whatsoever
without written permission except in the case of brief quotations embodied in critical
articles and reviews. For information address HarperCollins Children's Books, a
division of HarperCollins Publishers, 195 Broadway, New York, NY 10007.
www.harpercollinschildrens.com
Library of Congress Control Number: 2018947989
ISBN 978-0-06-256834-2 (trade bdg.)
Typography by Jessie Gang
18 19 20 21 22 CG/LSCH 10 9 8 7 6 5 4 3 2 1
❖
First Edition

To all my nieces and nephews

CHAPTER 1

There was a giant robot dinosaur smashing its way toward me.

You might be wondering how I got here, sitting in a pile of peanut butter jars in the grocery store while people ran screaming in every direction.

I'll tell you.

It had been ten terribly lonely days since I lost my genie, Ridge, who disappeared back into his jar once our quest was over. Chasm, the newly freed all-powerful genie bent on world domination, escaped his cave prison—and I got left behind. Luckily, the hole he had blasted to get out of the cave led to the street right outside the Museum of Cans, Crates, Cartons, and Containers, and that strange curator guy was still around. Apparently, he no longer needed to guard the museum, since the undiscovered cave had been, well . . . discovered.

He took pity on me and asked where he could drop me off.

I told him Nebraska, assuming Tina's mom would still be there and that she had the magic trinket I needed to set everything right.

The curator drove me the whole way in the museum van, which was actually a very frightening experience, since he didn't really know how to drive. It shouldn't have taken us so many days, but I was terrible at giving directions since I still couldn't tell left from right.

I went to St. Mercy's Hospital first, made some inquiries, and eventually found the rural town that Tina and her mom called home. From there it was pretty easy to locate the correct house. There really weren't that many to choose from. I thanked the curator and told him that I needed to do this next part on my own. The strange man wiggled his unibrow and drove off into the sunset.

Right as I was about to knock on the door, Ms. Gomez pulled out of the garage. Lucky for me, she wasn't going far. I chased her a few blocks to the neighborhood grocery store and followed her inside.

But how was I supposed to start this conversation?

"Hi, Ms. Gomez. You must be Tina's mom. I know, because I spied on you in the hospital when you were terminally ill. My name's Ace. I'm friends with your daughter. Or at least I was before she got enslaved by an evil genie called Chasm. Anyway,

I'm here to break your favorite necklace. . . ."

No. It would be easier to avoid such a conversation altogether. It would be easier to corner Maria Gomez, take her by surprise, break the chain, and run for it. Tina could explain everything to her mom after I saved her. But first, I needed to get my genie back before Chasm did anything crazy.

I hadn't seen any major catastrophes on the news, so Chasm seemed to be biding his time. I knew the evil genie was somewhere out there. But where? I was sure Chasm had hundreds of nefarious plans cooked up from his millennia of entrapment inside his jar. So, what was he waiting for?

I watched Ms. Gomez pick out a shopping cart, tucking a strand of jet-black hair behind her upside-down ear. As an ex-Wishmaker, she still carried consequences like that from her youth. I could relate. I, too, had a few unfortunate consequences that would be sticking with me forever.

As I looked at her now, it was hard to believe she'd ever been sick. Tina had cured her mom's illness with a wish, and she looked perfectly healthy. Ms. Gomez wasn't very tall, and pleasantly plump, but seemed plenty strong as she yanked apart two shopping carts that had been stuck together.

I crept up behind her as she stopped to pick out a loaf of bread. Tina's note said she had made a wish to turn her mother's necklace into the trinket that would reunite me with my genie.

I saw the thin chain glinting around Ms. Gomez's neck. A sharp tug should easily snap it. Of course, Tina would suffer some kind of nasty consequence in the same moment, but she'd known the risks when she wished for the trinket.

I glanced from side to side to make sure no one was watching. Only then did I realize which aisle we were in. Where fate (or the Universe) had brought me.

The peanut butter aisle.

I moved in as Ms. Gomez stooped to set the bread into her cart. She turned as I leaped toward her, but I was too fast. My fingers brushed her neck as I snatched the chain. My momentum kept me going down the aisle. I heard her gasp, felt the necklace go tight in my grasp.

The chain snapped.

I thought for sure I was safe, but Ms. Gomez whirled with surprising speed, the shopping cart rolling away as she caught me by the arm. I was jerked around, barely getting my feet under me as we came face-to-face.

I probably looked really sick to her. Old consequences meant that my ragged breath smelled like fish, my right eye was yellow, my tongue was green, and my face was smudged with a bit of dried peanut butter.

"Do you have any idea what you've done?" Ms. Gomez whispered, her voice carrying a definite Spanish accent.

"Do you like toast?" I said. Not because I wanted to sound like a smart aleck. The Universe forced me to answer any question with another question. I still had the rest of the year until that consequence let up.

My mismatched eyes fixed on the necklace dangling from my fist. Good. I could see where the chain had broken. Ridge's jar should be on its way.

"You can have it back," I said, opening my fingers and letting it fall from my sweaty hand. Behind me, there was a thump as something fell to the hard floor of the grocery aisle. Craning my neck against Ms. Gomez's iron grip, I saw what had made the sound.

It was a solitary peanut butter jar that had seemingly leaped from the shelf like an anxious volunteer.

A grin spread across my face as the jar wobbled upright. I could see the bright warning label from where I stood. No other peanut butter jar came with a warning. That was it. Ridge! All I had to do was twist off that lid and my genie would be back!

"It's okay," I said. "I'm a Wishmaker. Or, I *was* one. And I'm about to be again."

"That necklace was a trinket," Ms. Gomez cut me off, still holding my arm.

"I know," I answered. "That's why I had to break it. That was the only way to find my genie again."

"That's not what it does!" Her face twisted in confusion, but her grip finally relaxed enough for me to pull free.

"What?" I replied, crossing to pick up Ridge's jar. "The trinket worked perfectly." It felt right to hold the jar again. But my grip also brought back the dreaded responsibility of being a Wishmaker. The power of the Universe at my fingertips . . . in exchange for consequences.

"But the necklace," Ms. Gomez said, pointing at the broken chain on the floor. "I took that trinket from a very bad Wishmaker nearly eight years ago."

What was she talking about? I picked nervously at the edge of the jar's warning label, feeling the edge of the sticker begin to peel up.

Ms. Gomez's eyes suddenly grew wide. "Fudge ripple!" she shouted, stooping to lift the chain from the floor. "It's a double trinket!"

"Double trinket?"

"You wished for this necklace to become a trinket," she said.

"Not me," I replied. Should I tell her about Tina? "It was—"

"What does it do?" Ms. Gomez interrupted me.

"Didn't I already say?" I answered with a mandatory question. "Breaking the chain reunited me with my genie." As proof, I held up the jar of peanut butter, the half-peeled warning label curling up like a scroll.

"Then you better open that quickly," Ms. Gomez stated. "We're going to need a genie to get away from the trinket's original purpose."

"What was its original purpose?"

"The Wishmaker I took this from loved chaos." Ms. Gomez gave a worried glance down the grocery store aisle. "When the chain breaks, the trinket releases a creature capable of mass destruction."

I swallowed hard. "What kind of creature?"

And that's how the giant robot dinosaur got there.

The shelves behind Ms. Gomez erupted. She crumpled to the floor as bagged loaves of bread flew like shrapnel. The force of the impact tossed me backward and I slammed into the rack behind me.

Plastic jars of peanut butter cascaded upon my stunned form, burying me nearly to the neck. I shook my head against the blow and lifted my hands, only then realizing that I had dropped Ridge's jar. No worries. I just needed to find the jar with the warning label on the lid.

Oh, right. The label was stuck to my thumb.

There was another loud crack, and a nearby shelf exploded, sending deadly canned goods flying in every direction. That's when people started running from the store, screaming. I don't know what they thought was going on. The Universe

7

always shielded ordinary people, making magical things seem somehow explainable. But I was no ordinary person. I was an ex-Wishmaker.

So, I think that catches you up on my current situation. Now, any ideas on how to get away from a robot dinosaur?

CHAPTER 2

You probably think dinosaurs are cool. I do too. But I prefer the ones that aren't trying to crush me.

The one in front of me looked kind of like a T. rex, except totally made of metal. Its head scraped the high ceiling of the grocery store as mechanical feet slammed down with enough force to crack the smooth floor.

Robo Rex paused, tilted its head, and let out a roar that sounded like nails in a blender. A row of multicolored LED lights flickered across its razor teeth, and both eyes flashed red and yellow. On a TV show, it would have looked ridiculously cheesy. But in real life it was really quite terrifying.

If it didn't bite me in half, it would stomp me with those iron feet. At least it had tiny, useless arms.

Lasers suddenly shot from Robo Rex's arms, blasting another shelf to bits. Okay, not so useless after all.

It was time to find Ridge and take this punk down.

I grabbed one of the peanut butter jars from the pile around me and twisted off the lid. This time, there was no puff of smoke. But what if Ridge was trapped beneath that papery protective seal? I jabbed my index finger through, feeling it sink in creamy peanut butter up to the second knuckle.

I dropped the jar and grabbed another, repeating the process. The second one was not a genie, either. It was chunky.

A short distance away, I saw a bit of rubble rousing. Ms. Gomez! She pushed aside a broken shelf and painstakingly rose to her knees. Her black hair looked gray with dust, and her movements were slow but determined.

Ms. Gomez looked up at Robo Rex defiantly. Its animatronic eyes fixed on her and I thought I saw the tiny laser arms recharging.

"Hey!" I shouted, leaping to my feet and hurling the ordinary jar of peanut butter at the robot dinosaur. It pinged harmlessly off one of the metal legs. "Pick on someone your own size!"

In response, Robo Rex turned its gaze on me, pointing the lasers in my direction.

"Not me!" I shouted, backing up. "I'm way smaller than you!"

Ms. Gomez looked at me as I tripped on the array of peanut butter jars and fell hard on my backside. "Adios, muchacho!" she said, sprinting toward the store's exit.

"You're not going to help me?" I screamed.

"*I* didn't break the necklace!" I heard her shout as she ducked out of sight.

I managed to stick my fingers into three more jars of peanut butter before the dino's lasers powered up again. It fired and the floor in front of me broke apart, debris flying with a cloud of smoke and the smell of toasted bread. Well, at least Robo Rex had terrible aim.

With the sound of grinding gears, it came toward me. I scrambled away from the pile of peanut butter jars, grabbing two on my way out. I was counting on one of them to house Ridge, because the mechanical dinosaur's foot promptly pulverized the rest of the pile.

That giant stomper came down right where I'd been sitting.

I heard the plastic jars popping like grapes under its metal foot. Peanut butter spattered everywhere. I felt a big gob of it hit me square in the back as I staggered away.

Cleanup on aisle twelve!

I sprinted around the end of the shelf and ran down two more aisles before making a brief stop next to the spices.

Okay, jar number one. Please have a genie inside.

Tucking one jar under my arm, I quickly twisted the lid off the other. I stabbed my finger through the quality seal and came up with nothing but sticky spread.

Grunting in anger, I tossed the useless jar aside. Behind me, I heard the giant robot dinosaur smashing through shelves, coming my way. . . .

Okay, jar number two. It had better be you.

I slipped it out from under my arm, grabbed the lid, and gave it a sharp twist.

Nothing but peanut butter. Organic.

I hurled it down the aisle. Now my only hope was to circle back around to the scene of the peanut butter massacre and try to find Ridge's jar in the mess. I might have stomped my feet in frustration if Robo Rex's head hadn't suddenly appeared over the spice shelf.

As I dove forward, the light-up teeth snapped at the spot where I had been standing. I ran aimlessly, painfully aware that

I was moving away from the peanut butter squish and any hope of finding Ridge.

Hmmm . . . How to stop a robot dinosaur without some magical assistance?

One time, a kid in my class ruined his remote-control car when he dropped it in the toilet. Not sure why he had it in the bathroom, but it was clear that electronics and water didn't mix.

A laser blast went over my shoulder, striking the refrigerated dairy section and melting twenty pounds of butter.

That's it! Milk!

Maybe I could short-circuit Robo Rex with a couple gallons of milk. At least that might slow it down so I could get back to the peanut butter aisle.

I grabbed two jugs of skim milk and turned to face the dinosaur. I really hoped this guy was lactose intolerant.

I threw the first jug, hoping it would break open when it hit, but I missed altogether. Turned out I was just as bad at aiming as the T. rex. And I had full-sized arms!

My second jug got him right under the chin, breaking open and showering the robot. But instead of throwing sparks and slowing him down, the milk bath just seemed to enrage him. Robo Rex's foot came up for a mighty stomp, higher than any one before. And then I saw it.

Ridge's genie jar.

The peanut butter container was lodged in the bottom of the dinosaur's foot like a thorn. The metal was ripped and folded back, and I could just see the plastic lid sticking out.

Any other container would have been smashed to bits, but a genie jar was unbreakable.

I acted out of sheer impulse, leaping forward as the foot started to come down. Dropping to my knees, I slid across the wet, milky floor. My hands came up, scraping the cold metal and groping blindly. I caught the lid and felt the jar fall into my grasp, clearing the foot just as it came down to crack the floor.

I was on my feet, sprinting down the nearest aisle that still had shelves intact. Behind me, the dinosaur's metal tail swiped around, utterly crushing the dairy section.

Gasping for breath, I came to a halt. My fingers were still messy with peanut butter, and I slipped twice while trying to twist off the lid. At last, I felt it turn in my hand.

There was a loud bang and a puff of smoke, and I felt the lid disintegrate in my grasp. I let out a victorious laugh, peering through the smoke to see my long-awaited genie friend.

Across the aisle, I thought I saw his silhouette, but his back was to me. And his voice . . .

"Behold, mere mortal!" cried a gravelly voice. "I stand between you and the power of the Universe. Your wish is my command. But beware the costly consequences that come with . . ."

The smoke cleared and the genie turned around.

"Oh, hey, Ace! It's you!" It was indeed Ridge, and now his voice had returned to the squeaky timbre I was familiar with. "You're my Wishmaker? What are the odds that the Universe would put us together again?"

"The Universe didn't," I said. "It was a trinket. And what happened to your voice a second ago?"

"Oh, that." Ridge scratched self-consciously at his curly hair. "I was trying something new. You see, when I appeared to you the first time, I didn't do a really great job of explaining anything. I figured I should lay down some of the basics for my new Wishmaker. Maybe try out a more intense voice to get some respect."

"It sounded like you had a cold," I pointed out.

"I was going for ominous."

There was a bright flash of lasers and the shelf behind Ridge exploded. He screamed good and loud, but I was past that by now.

"What was that?"

"That's the robot T. rex," I explained. "He's got laser arms."

"Why is there a robot T. rex in the grocery store?"

"Um . . . I blame Tina's mom." I could tell the dinosaur was making its way toward us, demolishing anything in its path. It was wishing time. I held out my arm, waggling my wrist at him. "Don't you have something for me?"

"Right!" Ridge fumbled for a moment before slapping a familiar wristwatch onto my arm. I glanced down at the leather band and smooth face. Hello, old friend.

Robo Rex finally rounded the corner and Ridge got his first glimpse of our enemy. He squealed and turned to run, but I grabbed his arm.

"We run, Ace!" Ridge said. "That's what sensible people do when robot dinosaurs are chasing them."

"We fight," I rebutted. "That's what a Wishmaker does. This thing's purpose is to destroy. If we don't shut it down, there's no telling how much of this town it'll ruin."

A laser blast went over our heads. "Okay," I muttered under my breath, rubbing my hands together and shutting my eyes in concentration. "Wish smart."

My obvious first thought was to wish that Robo Rex would deactivate or fall apart. But that was a direct wish—one that wouldn't require much work from me. During my last quest, I had learned that those direct wishes gave me more intense consequences. Easier consequences came from wishes that still required me to do something.

"He's charging up his bazooka tail!" Ridge shouted.

I cracked my eyes open in time to see the dinosaur's metal tail swing sideways to scatter an aisle display. "He doesn't have a bazooka tail," I replied.

"You don't know that!"

True. I didn't. Maybe Robo Rex was saving the best for last. No matter the case, I didn't want to find out.

"I wish I had metal boxing gloves strong enough to knock this guy out!"

It was my first time wishing in nearly two weeks. The words felt good as they rolled off my tongue. I heard a click and glanced down at my wrist. A magical hourglass had emerged from the face of my watch, standing tall, familiar white sand showing me exactly how much time I had to consider and accept the accompanying consequence.

"It's good to be back!" Ridge shouted, clapping his hands. "If you want metal boxing gloves"—he glanced warily at the slowly approaching dinosaur—"then you'll have to tiptoe everywhere you go for the rest of the day."

"That's not so bad," I said.

"Might even be helpful," Ridge said. "Maybe the T. rex won't hear you coming."

I had plenty of time left in my hourglass watch but significantly less time before Robo Rex reached us. Boxing a T. rex couldn't be too bad. His lasers were still recharging, and it

17

wasn't like he could punch back with those tiny arms.

"I'll take it!" I shouted. But the Universe required me to say the magic word before my wish would be granted. "Bazang!"

The peanut butter jar slipped from my grasp as two large metal boxing gloves formed around my fists. Oh, man, this was going to be awesome. I was going to leap off the shelves and come soaring down with a jaw-shattering superhero punch. . . .

I instantly fell to the floor, pulled down by the incredible weights around my hands.

"Get up!" Ridge shouted, holding his own jar and cowering against the cornmeal. "Get up and punch!"

"I can't!" I had risen to a crouch on my tiptoes. Both my fists were against the floor as I strained against my new mitts. "The gloves are too heavy! Give me a hand!"

Ridge moaned in fear, coming to my side and grabbing my forearm. We heaved together and my right boxing glove lifted about an inch off the floor.

"Maybe you should wish for more muscles," Ridge said.

"Maybe we should run!" How fast could I move on my tiptoes?

Robo Rex was upon us. I slipped my hands out of the metal gloves and jumped back. At the same moment, I saw the dinosaur's lights flicker. The mechanical whirr of its moving parts seemed to slow. Its massive head drooped, and its tiny laser arms powered down.

Then Robo Rex fell uselessly sideways, crashing through a shelf in a tremendous puff of dust and baking flour.

"Woohoo!" Ridge cried, turning to give me a high five. "We did it!"

I stared in confusion at the fallen destruction machine. "We didn't do anything."

"I think we scared it to death," Ridge said. "You know how T. rexes are. Challenge them to a boxing match and they fall right over. Big scaredy-cats . . ."

"There's someone over there," I muttered, peering through the white cloud of flour and dust. A figure was standing atop the crumpled form of the dinosaur. As I watched, he slid down the metal sheeting of the T. rex's side and landed in the aisle in front of Ridge and me.

Now that I could see him clearly, my eyes went wide.

"Jathon?"

CHAPTER 3

It was indeed Jathon Anderthon, my sworn enemy and the son of Thackary Anderthon (who was my even bigger enemy). His blond hair was dusty, and the kid no longer had a beard. That consequence must have worn off. Clenched tightly in his right hand was an empty glass pickle jar. I recognized it from my first quest.

"That's Jathon," Ridge whispered.

"I see that," I said. "Why does he have a pickle jar? Do you think he's a Wishmaker again?"

"That would be highly unlikely," Ridge said. "I'm guessing he carries it around for sentimental reasons."

"Or because he likes pickles," I said.

"I stopped the dinosaur bot," Jathon announced. "You can thank me later."

"You?" I cried. "What could you possibly do against a giant robot Tyrannosaurus rex?"

"It was easy," he said. "I flipped the Off switch on its back."

"THERE WAS AN OFF SWITCH?" I shrieked in frustration.

"Well," Jathon continued, "I had to wish for it, of course."

"So, you *are* a Wishmaker again," I said, pointing at his jar.

Ridge stepped forward, fists clenched. "You monster! Let that genie out of her jar!"

Last time, Jathon had kept his genie bottled up for most of the week. I didn't know what it was like inside a jar. Ridge said it was like a peaceful deep sleep between quests. But putting your genie inside a jar while they were assigned to a Wishmaker was apparently some kind of itchy, unpleasant experience.

"My genie isn't in her jar." Jathon gestured behind him as his genie stepped out from behind the rubble of the T. rex's tail.

"Hey, guys."

"Vale?" Ridge and I cried in unison.

The redheaded genie girl stood with both hands in the pockets of her hoodie, somehow managing to look slightly bored while surrounded by the wreckage.

"But that's . . ." I stammered. "She's not . . ."

"Vale is Tina's genie!" Ridge finally managed.

"You know that's not how it works," Vale said. "The Universe assigns us wherever we're needed."

"I have so many questions right now." I put a hand to my head. "What are you two even doing here?"

"I'm wondering the same about you," said Jathon.

We glared at each other for a moment. "You go first," I said.

"You go first," Jathon replied.

"No. You go first."

"Rock, paper, scissors?" Ridge suggested.

I shot him a dirty glare. Tina had tricked me before with that game. I wasn't going to risk playing it ever again.

"Fine. I'll explain." I took a deep breath. "Tina wished for her mom's necklace to be a trinket that would reunite me with Ridge once I broke it."

"What's with the dinosaur?" Vale asked.

"I've actually been wondering the same thing," Ridge whispered.

"The Robo Rex was a side effect," I explained. "Apparently, Ms. Gomez's necklace was already a trinket. Breaking the chain made two wishes come true. It brought me Ridge's jar, but it also summoned that destructo robot."

"Hmm," Jathon mused. "So you tricked the Universe? You two aren't really supposed to be back together?"

"Yes, we are," I spat. I hadn't thought of it that way. "This was Tina's idea, anyway. We have to help her get away from Chasm."

"That's why we're here," Jathon replied. "The Universe sent me this genie jar yesterday. I was going to have some pickles with my grilled cheese sandwich. I got Vale instead."

"Equally sour," Ridge muttered.

I turned to Vale. "Don't you live inside a little jar of lip balm?"

"That was just how Tina found me," she answered. "The Universe disguises our jars to look like something the Wishmaker would want to open. Apparently, Jathon eats a lot of pickles."

"They're delicious, okay?" the boy defended.

"Calm down," said Ridge. "What's the big *dill*?"

"Is it common for the Universe to send another genie to someone who has already been a Wishmaker?" I asked.

"No," answered Vale. "I've never heard of it happening. But with Chasm on the loose, the Universe must be desperate enough to try something new."

"I have to free Tina from Chasm," Jathon said. "And I only have six more days to do it."

"That sounds like a quest," I said.

"It is," Jathon answered. "My quest is to separate a genie from a Wishmaker. The Universe needs me to save Tina."

"What happens if you fail?"

"If I don't free Tina by the end of the week, then the air is going to turn into chocolate sauce."

"Delicious!" Ridge cried.

"What about breathing?" I asked.

"I think that's sort of the point," Jathon said.

"Another quest with a world-ending consequence," Vale said. "The Universe knows it can count on Jathon Anderthon."

"What about me?" I turned to Ridge. "Do I have a new quest?"

"Yes, you do!" He snapped his fingers. "And I'm so glad you mentioned it. That totally slipped my mind."

"What is it?" I asked, shuffling my feet nervously in the littered aisle. "Am I supposed to find Tina, too? What does the Universe need me to do?"

"You must make a peanut butter and jelly sandwich and feed it to a person named Samuel Sylvester Stansworth," Ridge answered.

"What is it with the Universe and peanut butter?" I cried. "That sounds like the easiest quest ever!"

"Unless the guy hates sandwiches," Ridge pointed out. "Or what if he's allergic to peanuts?"

"What does it matter?" I asked. "I don't see what any of this has to do with saving Tina."

This quest wasn't any stranger than my first, when I'd been told to find Thackary Anderthon and stop him from opening Chasm's jar.

"Neither do I," Ridge admitted. "But that's the quest that the Universe assigned you."

"That's ridiculous!" I shouted, feeling my cheeks turning red with embarrassment. "How's that supposed to help Tina? Make a peanut butter sandwich for some random guy. . . ."

"Samuel Sylvester Stansworth," Ridge reminded me.

I took a deep breath. The quest wasn't what I'd been hoping for, but the Universe had to give me this assignment for a good reason, right? "What happens if I don't succeed?" I asked. "Will the whole world burn up? Will it rain deadly shards of metal?"

Ridge wrinkled his forehead as though trying to figure out a difficult math problem. "If you don't succeed . . ." He paused. "Then all the red roses in the world will lose their smell."

I stared, speechless. But Vale and Jathon both chuckled.

"All the red roses will lose their smell?" I repeated.

"Yup." Ridge nodded. "Really not too bad, considering last time."

"No!" I cleared my throat. "That's dumb. I got you back so I could free Tina. That's what we're going to do."

"What about the consequence?" Ridge asked.

"Who cares?" I threw my hands up. "Unscented roses aren't going to hurt anyone." Insulted by the Universe's lack of trust in me, I turned to Jathon and Vale.

"I assume you're here because you have a lead on how to save Tina?" I asked.

Jathon nodded. "I made a wish to find out if anyone knew

how to separate a genie from a Wishmaker."

"Just wait until the week runs out," Ridge said. "The Universe separates us when the quest ends."

Vale shook her head. "Chasm's different. Tina doesn't have a quest while she's tethered to him. And he said that the two of them would be together until Tina died."

"Is there a way?" I asked. "Some way to cut Tina free and send Chasm back into his jar?"

"We don't know how," Vale admitted. "But the Universe told us about someone who does."

"We're looking for a person called the Trinketer," said Jathon.

"And you thought you'd check the grocery store?" I asked.

"I wished to know where the Trinketer would be at noon today," Jathon said. "The answer led me here."

"How is the Trinketer supposed to help?" Ridge asked.

"Going by her title, she might know about some trinkets capable of freeing a Wishmaker from a genie," answered Vale. "Just what Tina needs."

"Then we'd better find her," I said. "There were a lot of people in the store. Any idea what this Trinketer looks like?"

"I guess we should figure that out," said Jathon, turning to Vale. "I wish to know what the Trinketer looks like."

I saw his watch turn into an hourglass as Vale spelled things out. "If you want to know what the Trinketer looks like," she said, "then every time you look in a mirror, it will break."

"Whoa," Ridge said. "Doesn't that bring you bad luck?"

"How long will it last?" Jathon asked, ignoring Ridge.

"One month," answered Vale.

"I'll take it," he said. "Bazang." His hourglass disappeared and he suddenly had the answer. "The Trinketer is a woman," Jathon said. "About this tall." He held up his hand. "Black hair, dark complexion. She wears a thin gold necklace."

I sighed heavily. "Used to," I corrected.

"Huh?"

"She *used to wear* a thin gold necklace," I explained. "The Trinketer is Maria Gomez. Tina's mom."

CHAPTER 4

I felt pretty bad about the condition of the grocery store. One of the exterior walls had crumbled, and there were only two aisles still standing.

We left the broken heap of robotic dinosaur lying where Jathon had deactivated it. There were bystanders waiting in the parking lot, but we managed to slip past them without attracting too much suspicion. Guess I should thank the Universe for that. We did, however, manage to overhear a snippet of conversation that explained what all the ordinary people had seen.

"Runaway wrecking ball! Must've rolled down from that construction site. Smashed clean through the store. Lucky nobody got crushed!"

I didn't know what they'd make of the lasers. And we weren't going to stick around to find out.

I tiptoed to the street corner and tried to remember which was the way to the Gomez household. I have to admit, I was feeling much more confident with Ridge walking beside me, and that familiar jar of peanut butter in my old backpack.

"We take a left here," I said, gesturing down the street.

"Ace!" Ridge replied with such shock in his voice that I swiveled to see what was wrong. But the genie was grinning. "You knew it was left!"

"Of course I knew. . . ." I trailed off, realizing that I wasn't supposed to know my directions. "Left," I muttered, pointing left. "And right." I pointed right, a smile breaking on my face now.

"Good for you," Jathon said sarcastically. "You know your lefts and rights."

"This is actually a pretty big deal," I said. "I have a consequence. I'm not supposed to know that for a year."

Ridge seemed to get really excited. "Stick out your tongue!"

I raised an eyebrow in confusion. "You're my friend. That's rude."

"You're right," Ridge said. "Stick out your tongue at Jathon. You never liked him much."

I shrugged and stuck out my tongue.

"It's not green anymore!" Ridge shouted loud enough that I thought the neighbors might peek out the windows.

"Seriously?" I went cross-eyed trying to look down at my own tongue.

"Your old consequences . . ." Ridge stammered. "They're . . ."

"Gone," Vale finished. I looked at her for an explanation. As a more experienced genie, she always seemed to have better information than Ridge did.

Vale gestured with her thumb toward Jathon. "Same thing happened to him when he opened my jar."

Now that it had been pointed out to me, I realized that Jathon no longer showed the long-lasting consequences that he'd taken on his last quest. His right eyeball was no longer yellow, and his tongue had also returned to a healthy shade of pink. We were supposed to carry those forever. Now they were gone?

"No more consequences?" I cried. But that couldn't be. My wish against the Robo Rex hadn't been free, and I was tiptoeing to prove it.

"As far as I can tell, the Universe has given you both a blank slate," Vale continued. "It must be an exception that the Universe is willing to make for someone who becomes a Wishmaker twice."

"Makes sense," Ridge supported. "It wouldn't be very fair to make you tackle another quest while you're still suffering consequences from the last one. Tethering yourself to a genie must automatically wipe away all lingering consequences."

I let out a big breath of relief. New quest. New consequences. The Universe was giving me a chance to start over!

"We think that's why my dad was so desperate to find the Undiscovered Genie," Jathon said. "The one free wish actually had nothing to do with removing his old consequences. Since my dad is an adult, Chasm's jar was the only one he could open. We didn't know at the time, but the simple act of opening the jar and tethering himself to Chasm would have deleted his old consequences. He would have still had a free wish after that."

I shuddered, wondering what Thackary Anderthon would have done with a free wish. "Where is your awful dad, anyway?" I asked, tiptoeing down the road to the left.

Jathon shuffled a few steps to keep up, peering anxiously over his shoulder. "My dad . . . I'm not exactly sure where he is."

"Really?" Ridge cried. "You ditched him?"

"Things got kind of ugly after we left Chasm's cave," Jathon said. "My dad was not happy that I gave the jar to Tina."

"Your dad? Not happy?" I mocked.

"Okay, you've got a point," Jathon said. "He's never happy. But he was determined to find Chasm, so we tried to track them."

"Did you see Tina?" I gushed. "Is she okay?"

Jathon shook his head. "We never caught up to Chasm. Without a genie of our own, he was impossible to locate."

"But you got Vale," I pointed out.

"That didn't happen until yesterday," Jathon reminded us. "That's when I ditched my dad."

"And a good thing, too," Vale added. "Last time Jathon had a genie, Thackary demanded that she be kept in her jar unless it was time to wish."

Vale and Ridge shuddered in unison at the itchy thought.

"So I took off," Jathon continued. "My dad messed up a lot of things last time. I thought I'd have a better chance at accomplishing my quest alone this week. Besides, I don't think he'd like my new assignment. Rescuing Tina isn't high on his priorities."

"What do you think will happen when your dad notices that you're gone?" Ridge asked.

"Oh, he already knows," answered Jathon.

"We weren't even a block away when he realized it," Vale added.

"Did he chase you?" Ridge pressed, clearly desperate for the juicy drama.

Jathon sucked in a deep breath. "I didn't know he could run that fast." He checked over his shoulder once again.

"Oh, great," I said. "You think he's coming after you."

"I'm sure of it," Jathon muttered. "He knows I have another genie. My dad will try to use that to his selfish advantage somehow."

"Why not make a wish against him?" I asked. "You could stop him from finding you."

Jathon scowled at me. "Vale and I will just stay ahead of him. I'm not going to wish against my dad!"

"Why not?" I said. "He's a jerk to you. And it's not like you enjoy him all that much, either."

"He's my dad!" Jathon said. "I may not like him, but we're family. You might not know what it's like to have a parent, but I do."

I swallowed half a dozen harsh responses. Jathon had touched on a sensitive subject, and he knew it. I had no parents. No family. Well, I'm sure I did somewhere, but I didn't know about them.

My past was a black hole, without even an inkling of a memory before I was nine. I'd awakened in a hospital three years ago without so much as a name. My hand strayed into my pocket to flick the tattered edge of the folded playing card.

The Ace of Hearts.

I didn't know why I kept the useless thing with me. But I couldn't ever bring myself to throw it away. That card was truly the only link to my mysterious past. Not even a genie could help. Last time, I'd wished to know the truth, but the consequence had been far too severe.

"Are we lost?" Ridge said. "We've already been down this street."

Deep in thought, I might have momentarily wandered in the wrong direction. But I was back on track now. And we were close.

"We're not lost," I answered. "I can tell left from right."

"So can a seven-year-old," Vale said. "It doesn't mean you know where you're going."

"We're not . . ." I muttered. "There! See?"

Everyone looked at the house where I was pointing. It was halfway down the block, a cracked sidewalk running up to the porch.

As we turned in that direction, the front door opened and Ms. Gomez appeared, something rectangular clutched in one hand.

"There she is now," I said. "Maria Gomez, Tina's mom."

"Hello there!" Ridge shouted as we crossed the street. His skinny arm went up in a friendly wave.

Ms. Gomez glanced up sharply, her eyes going wide. Then she leaped down the porch steps and made her way across the yard toward us.

"Hello!" I called. "I just wanted to apologize for what happened at the grocery store. I was hoping we could get to know each other a little bit—"

"We're looking for the Trinketer!" Jathon cut me off. "My friend says it might be you?"

First of all, Jathon and I were not friends. I'd say we were more like archenemies.

Ms. Gomez came to an abrupt halt at the edge of the sidewalk. We were close enough now that I heard her mumble something in Spanish. Then she lifted the item she was holding.

It looked like an ordinary brick. For a moment, I thought Ms. Gomez might hurl it at us. But then she took a cautious step back into the yard and dropped the red brick to the ground.

As soon as it touched the grass, a shimmering blast of magic rippled all the way around the yard. New bricks seemed to form out of thin air, instantly locking together and sealing off the whole property.

At the same time, I saw Maria Gomez duck down and roll forward, setting the top of her head firmly against the grass and rising with surprising agility into a headstand. Her legs stuck straight into the air and she balanced there, face turning red with the exertion of holding herself in such a precarious position.

"The brick's a trinket!" I surmised. And apparently, the consequence for using it was performing a headstand.

Ms. Gomez came down from her balancing act, flushed and breathing heavily as she retreated toward the house. The rest of us sized up the newly formed wall. It was short—not even to my shoulder. I could totally boost myself over it.

Jathon must have reached the same conclusion. He took two quick steps and jumped, putting both hands down on the top of the wall. The moment he touched it, the bricks glowed with another burst of magic. It was like the existing bricks multiplied, laying down mortar and locking the new bricks immediately into place.

As the wall grew, I barely caught a glimpse of Ms. Gomez. Her retreat to the house had been halted as she performed another awkward headstand. Obviously, the trinket required a consequence from her each time its power was used.

The sudden growth spurt of bricks sent Jathon tumbling back to the sidewalk. The wall, quite insignificant before, now stood a good ten feet tall, blocking our view into the yard.

"The brick's a trinket," Jathon repeated, rubbing his bruised hip.

"We got this," I mused, turning to Ridge. "I wish I could jump over this brick wall."

"If you want to clear the wall," said Ridge, "then your teeth will be stuck together for the rest of the day."

"Will I still be able to talk?" It wasn't worth it if the consequence took away my ability to speak and wish.

"I dunno," said Ridge. "Try talking with your teeth clenched."

I bit down, grinding my teeth together as I said, "Can you understand me?"

"Easy!" he replied. "You might not be able to eat, but at least I can understand you."

"Wait a minute," I said. "Why won't I be able to eat?"

"Think about it," Ridge replied. "How can you chew if your teeth are stuck together?"

I felt a little panic coming on. I couldn't go the rest of the day without food. My stomach was already rumbling from missing lunch.

"You'll survive," said Jathon. "Anyone can survive just one day without food."

"I don't know . . ." I said. "I get kind of mean when I'm hungry."

"We don't want a hangry Ace," Ridge said.

"Hangry?" Jathon repeated.

"You know, when being hungry makes you angry." Ridge shook his head. "We shouldn't risk it."

I watched in silence as the last grains of sand slipped

through my hourglass. Jathon and Vale both sighed like they were annoyed with me.

"I don't see you guys coming up with any creative ways to get over this wall," I pointed out.

"Oh, yeah?" said Jathon. "I wish to have a ladder that is ten feet tall."

"If you want a ladder," Vale explained, "then anytime you walk under a tree, all the leaves will fall off."

"What about trees that don't have leaves?" Jathon asked. "Like pine trees?"

"They'll drop all their needles," Vale answered.

"Ouch," I said. "That could be painful."

"How long will this last?" asked Jathon.

"The rest of the week," answered the redheaded genie.

Jathon seemed to debate it for a moment. "Bazang," he finally said.

Well, I guess he wouldn't be enjoying shade anytime soon.

In the blink of an eye, a metal ladder suddenly appeared, conveniently leaning up against the brick wall and reaching almost to the top. Jathon scampered up, Vale holding the ladder steady.

At the top rung, Jathon carefully reached up and placed his hands on top of the wall. Instantly, the bricks activated, a rush of magic causing them to multiply and stack.

Jathon didn't let go. The sudden action lifted Jathon from the ladder and pulled him higher and higher, screaming.

"Uh-oh," Vale muttered. I knew exactly what she was afraid of. There's an invisible tether that connects every genie to their Wishmaker to make sure they stay together. It's only forty-two feet long, which meant that Jathon would be out of range in about three seconds!

Their tether snapped, flinging them both painfully back together. Beside me, Vale sounded like she got the wind knocked out of her. She flew upward, her feet leaving the sidewalk as Jathon came hurtling down from the top of the wall. The two collided hard at the halfway point in midair. But they were still twenty-one feet above the sidewalk, and now gravity was doing its thing.

Tiptoeing into position, Ridge and I managed to form some kind of landing pad. We actually tried to catch them, but the falling kids knocked us all into a heap on the sidewalk.

The four of us lay there, moaning in pain, staring up at the ridiculously high brick wall.

Across the street, a neighbor couple walked past, pushing a stroller. "Check it out!" the man said, pointing to the gigantic wall. "Looks like the Gomezes put in a wall around their yard."

"The brick looks good," his wife replied. "We should do the same at our place, hon."

I watched them round a corner and walk out of sight, amazed at the disguise the Universe had draped over their eyes. Couldn't they see that the brick wall was higher than the trees? The whole town should have been flocking to see what was going on.

I stood up and dusted myself off. "I don't think we can get

over it," I said, pressing my hand against the wall. "Maybe we can blast our way through."

"Be my guest," Jathon said, still doubled over.

"Me?" I said. "You're the one looking for the Trinketer."

"Do you want to help Tina or not?" he replied. Clearly, the kid wasn't in great shape from snapping his tether. I'd have to be the responsible one.

I turned to Ridge. "I wish that I could kick a hole through this brick wall, big enough for us to fit through."

He grinned. "That's going to look epic. You'll be like a superhero!"

"I know, right?" I said. "But what's the consequence?"

"Oh, yeah. If you want to kick through the wall," Ridge said, "then every time you step on a rug, it'll get pulled out from under you."

"Who's going to pull it?" I asked.

"The mysterious magic of the Universe," he answered.

"How long will it go on?"

"Just until the end of the week."

Well, I was sure I could avoid stepping on rugs for a week. "Bazang," I said. I turned back to the wall and struck a karate pose on my tiptoes. "Hi-ya!" I kicked the bricks as hard as I could.

A chunk of the wall exploded under my foot, and it didn't

even hurt! Broken bricks and mortar flew into the Gomezes' yard, and dust rained down over the hole I had just blasted.

"After you," I said politely, gesturing for Jathon to climb through the hole first. It was his quest, after all. Also, I wasn't too anxious to be the first one to pop my head into Ms. Gomez's yard. You know, in case she was waiting with another brick.

CHAPTER 5

Ms. Gomez was waiting for us in the doorway, a bottle of shampoo in one hand. I assumed it was a trinket, since it didn't look too threatening otherwise. She raised her arm to throw it when she saw us on the front step.

"Wait!" I cried. "We're Tina's friends!"

Slowly, the woman lowered her arm, eyes narrowed suspiciously at us.

"How do you know my daughter?" Ms. Gomez asked.

"That's a bit of a long story," I said.

"Tina got a genie in a little jar of lip balm and became a Wishmaker," Ridge began, talking fast. "She had a quest to save the life of an ex-Wishmaker—she thought that was Thackary Anderthon for a while, and he was after an Undiscovered Genie who could grant one free wish without a consequence, so we teamed up with Tina and chased the Anderthons to a secret cave, but Tina ended up opening the genie's jar and used the free wish to heal you and save your life, but then it turned out he was a bad guy named Chasm, and he stole her voice and took her away."

Ms. Gomez's eyes went wide, panicky. It was Jathon who came to our rescue.

"That's why we're here," he said. "It's my quest to save your daughter from Chasm. The Universe told me you could help. You are the Trinketer, right?"

"That's right," said Ms. Gomez. "And you are Thackary Anderthon's son?"

Jathon didn't seem too thrilled to admit it, but he nodded slowly. She stared at him for a long moment. I felt like it got a little awkward. Then Ms. Gomez gestured for us to come inside.

I was almost to the doorway when the ground seemed to shift beneath my tiptoes. I glanced down in time to see the welcome mat getting swept out from under me. I toppled into Ridge and the two of us went down on the front porch.

"Oh, come on!" I griped. "You didn't tell me that the consequence applied to welcome mats!"

"Sorry," Ridge said as we got up. "The Universe must not think there's a difference."

The welcome mat was now safely on the other side of the

porch, so this time I was able to tiptoe inside without any trouble.

The house was a mess. A lot of weird things cluttered the living room: a deflated inner tube, a sprinkler head, one snow boot. And shelves lined every wall, packed with things that a normal person wouldn't usually display. At a quick glance I saw a ball of rubber bands, a roll of toilet paper, a hair clip, and a walnut.

I was careful to avoid another rug as the four of us kids sat down on a lumpy couch. Tina's mom slumped down into an armchair across the room. "Tina is a Wishmaker?"

"Twice now," Vale said.

"You didn't know? Where did you think she's been?" Jathon asked.

"When we were at the hospital," Ms. Gomez explained, "Tina told me that her grandma sent for her. I thought she was in Peru. I've been trying to contact them, but they live in the campo. It's not easy to stay in touch." She was crying at the news, and I shifted awkwardly in my seat. "Now you tell me she is missing? Surely her time will soon be up and she will be free of this evil genie."

"Chasm's different," Vale said. "He isn't bound by the same rules as the other genies. For starters, he's an adult."

"A super-creepy weird one," Ridge said. "Huge. Bald.

Covered in tattoos. But he does have a pretty good singing voice."

"Chasm doesn't assign his Wishmaker a quest," Vale continued. "He stole Tina's voice so he could make the wishes and force her to take the consequences. And he said he can stay out of his jar until Tina . . ." Luckily, Vale was sensitive enough not to say "died" in front of Ms. Gomez.

"Then how are we supposed to save her?" Ms. Gomez sobbed, lifting a hand to her face and muttering, "*mi hija.*" I thought she was doing a remarkable job of keeping it together, considering.

"My quest is to separate Tina from Chasm," Jathon said. "The Universe said the Trinketer would know a way to do that. I'm guessing you have something—a trinket—that will help?"

"I have many trinkets." Ms. Gomez gestured around the cluttered room. "I don't keep these things around because they look pretty."

"Wow! Everything here is a trinket?" Ridge asked. "Who created them all?"

"Lots of different Wishmakers," Ms. Gomez answered, "dating back to the time of the first genies."

"How did you get them?" I asked.

"That's my job as the Trinketer," said Ms. Gomez. "Do you know what happens to old trinkets?"

"Sure," answered Vale. "They continue to work as long as there is a Wishmaker to pay the consequence."

"So, Ace could give himself a wedgie at any moment?" Ridge asked.

Why did he have to bring that up? On my last quest, I had wished for a fridge magnet to become a trinket. Anytime someone used it, I had to give myself an embarrassing wedgie.

"That trinket is long gone," I pointed out. "It got buried when Chasm's cave collapsed." Phew. "Besides, my old consequences don't affect me anymore, right? I thought we decided that the Universe wiped me clean so I could take on a new quest."

"That is true," said Ms. Gomez. "But trinkets are an exception. When you make an ordinary wish, *you* are the conduit for the Universe's magic. But when you wish for a trinket, the Universe fills that *object* with magic. The wish and the consequence remain in effect, even if the Universe has given you a restart."

"Good thing I didn't make too many trinkets," I muttered, glancing at Jathon, who I knew had created several for his dad.

"So, you're a trinket collector?" Jathon asked Ms. Gomez.

"Much more than a simple collector," she answered. "The Trinketer is an important position that was passed on to me when I was a young Wishmaker. It is my responsibility to gather lost trinkets so that innocent bystanders can't accidentally use them."

"You're like the trinket police," Ridge said. "Cracking down on rogue trinkets."

"Like the necklace I broke," I said sheepishly.

"Exactly. I had been safeguarding that necklace for years. When you broke it at the grocery store, the ex-Wishmaker who made it, probably now in his twenties, paid the associated consequence."

"Tina paid one, too," I said, though I had no way of knowing what it was.

"Trinkets are useful," said Ms. Gomez. "But they can be incredibly dangerous."

"What happens when the ex-Wishmaker linked to the trinket passes away?" Jathon asked.

"It goes dormant," said Tina's mom.

"Dormant?" Vale said. "So the power might wake up again?"

Ms. Gomez nodded. "That's the Trinketer's job. When I touch an expired trinket, I have the ability to awaken its original magic."

"Whoa!" Ridge said. "Free trinkets?"

"No!" Ms. Gomez snapped. "No trinket can exist without someone to pay the consequence."

"But if the Wishmaker who made it is gone," said Jathon, "then who pays the consequence?"

"I do," said Ms. Gomez.

"Why would you do that?" I cried. I'd had my fair share of consequences. It made the most sense to leave those expired trinkets alone.

"Like I said," continued Ms. Gomez, "trinkets are useful. Sometimes I need to awaken an old one in order to use its power to find others. Or sometimes I need to defend myself against bad Wishmakers who might come after my collection."

"So, what can your trinkets do for Tina?" Jathon asked.

"The only way I know how to forcefully separate a genie from a Wishmaker is by cutting the tether," said Ms. Gomez.

"Oh, man!" Ridge said. "Jathon and Vale just did that outside. And I remember how it feels from last time. Like an elephant punched me in the stomach."

"Elephants can't punch," I said. "They don't have hands."

"They can punch with their feet," he said.

"That's called kicking."

"Well, it would hurt to get kicked by an elephant, too," Ridge said. "Either way, it was painful."

"You did not cut your tether," Ms. Gomez interjected. "You probably snapped it."

"What's the difference?" I asked.

In response, Ms. Gomez reached onto a shelf and picked up the rubber-band ball.

"What does that trinket do?" Ridge asked.

"Oh, this isn't a trinket," said Ms. Gomez. "It's just a good way to store rubber bands." She carefully plucked one of the bands and stretched it away from the ball. "Let us pretend this is your tether. When you and your genie get too far apart . . ." She let go of the rubber band and it snapped sharply back into place. "The tether springs you suddenly back together. But cutting the tether is something different."

Ms. Gomez retrieved a kitchen knife from the same shelf. The blade sliced through the little rubber band, and it fell limply to the floor.

"So, how do we cut the tether?" Vale asked.

"Well, we can't cut something we can't see," explained Ms. Gomez. "So, the first trinket we'll need is a special spool of string. We can cut a forty-two-foot length and tie one end to Tina and the other to Chasm. Once in place, the string will become a visible tether."

"Then what?" I asked.

"The second trinket we need is an ancient dagger," said Ms. Gomez. "Supposedly, it has the power to cut through a tether."

"Supposedly?" Vale questioned.

"I haven't seen the dagger, personally. It's currently dormant.

Has been for a few hundred years."

"But you can activate it?" Jathon said.

Ms. Gomez took a deep breath. "We'll have to find it first. I have a few clues. And a couple trinkets that should point me in the right direction."

"Maybe there's an easier way," I said. "Instead of wasting time looking for old trinkets, why don't we just make a wish for the tether to become visible? Or just wish for it to be cut?"

"That's basically wishing for my quest to be completed," said Jathon. "Way too direct. The Universe would destroy me with a consequence."

"But it's not *my* quest," I said. "Maybe I could get off with something lighter."

"It's still very direct," said Ridge. "The Universe likes it better when the wish requires you to do something."

"That's why trinkets are so effective," added Ms. Gomez.

"Then let's just create new ones that do the same thing," I suggested.

"I'm afraid that's not an option," Ms. Gomez said. "The spool of string is classified as an exclusive trinket."

"What does that mean?" Ridge asked.

"It means that it's a one-of-a-kind. No other Wishmaker can wish for a trinket to do the same thing."

"Why not?"

"It's part of an old consequence, more than three generations back," Ms. Gomez said. "The particular Wishmaker who created the spool of string had made a wish. The consequence for it was that the next trinket she created would become 'exclusive,' never to be wished for again."

"And she wished for a spool of string to make the tether visible?" I said.

"She tried to think of something fairly useless," explained Ms. Gomez. "A throwaway trinket made simply to satisfy that consequence. At the time, she couldn't think of any reason why a Wishmaker would want the tether to be tangible. Seemed like a tangling, tripping hazard."

I sighed. Of course, the very thing we needed most was something that a previous Wishmaker had deemed a useless throwaway trinket.

"That Wishmaker died of old age almost twenty years ago," said Ms. Gomez. "The Trinketer before me collected the spool for safekeeping."

"Do you have it now?" I asked.

Ms. Gomez nodded. "I do. But it will also need to be reactivated."

"Then let's grab it and get started!" I said. Every minute we sat there talking was another minute for Chasm to inflict consequences on Tina.

"The string is not here," said Ms. Gomez. "My house is not a safe storage place for trinkets. All the ones you see here are just waiting to be moved to a more secure location."

"Where do you keep them?" Vale asked.

"The vault."

"Sounds official," I said. "Where is this place?"

"The entrance to the vault is in Utah," said Ms. Gomez. "The problem is, it can only be entered in the winter."

"What?" we all cried in unison.

"It's barely August!" I said. "Who knows what shape Tina will be in come December." Not to mention that Jathon would have failed his quest and the world would probably be a giant hot-fudge sundae.

"What's so special about winter?" Ridge asked.

"The entrance to the trinket vault only appears when the Powder Peaks Ski Resort is open," explained Ms. Gomez. "You can only get in by skiing."

"Well, I think it's pretty obvious what has to happen," Jathon said, standing up. "I'll just have to wish for the resort to open."

"Will that work?" Vale checked with Ms. Gomez.

"I don't see why not," she said.

All of us looked at Jathon, and he sighed. "I wish it would snow so much at Powder Peaks that the ski resort would open."

"If you want Powder Peaks Ski Resort to open," said Vale, "then your fingers will be cold for a year."

"How cold?" Jathon asked.

"Like you just washed them in ice water."

"Will they be numb?"

"No," Vale said. "You'll still be able to move them."

"Will they hurt?" asked Jathon.

"Not really," answered Vale. "It'll just be uncomfortable."

"What if he wears gloves?" Ridge cut in.

"Then his fingers will be cold inside his gloves."

Jathon checked the hourglass on his wrist. "Well, bazang, I guess."

CHAPTER 6

Snow. So much snow.

In the three years of my life that I could remember, I had never been skiing. It looked like a lot of fun, though, zooming down a steep mountain with two long things strapped to your feet.

I stood outside the lodge with Ridge, Jathon, and Vale, the four of us shivering against the cold. Ms. Gomez had gathered some winter gear from a box in a storage closet before we left her house. Vale fit quite nicely into Tina's clothes, and Jathon sported a hand-me-down coat and pink snow pants. I wore another retired coat, with just my pair of jeans to cover my legs. Ridge's skinny figure was draped in one of Ms. Gomez's old coats, making him look like he was playing dress-up.

It had been a very long drive to Utah. Every time we stopped at a red light, Ms. Gomez would burst into some off-tune opera song. That old, obnoxious consequence had awakened us several times through the night. Tina's mom had kept herself awake using a spray bottle. I wasn't sure if it was a trinket or not, but every so often, she'd spritz herself in the face. As a result, she was soaking wet when we arrived at the ski resort.

There were faster, more magical ways to travel, of course, but they would have required consequences. And it wouldn't have done us much good to arrive earlier, anyway. The way Jathon had worded his wish meant that we had to wait until enough snow fell for the ski resort to open.

According to reports, it had been coming down in a whiteout blizzard all through the night. I opened my mouth, catching a few big snowflakes on my tongue.

Ms. Gomez appeared in the doorway of the lodge, calling for us to come inside. As we stepped into the warm building, a large area rug got pulled out from under my feet. It just so happened that Jathon, Vale, and Ridge were standing on the rug at the same time.

"Not cool, Ace," Jathon said, picking himself up off the lodge floor.

"It's not like I wanted that to happen," I muttered, noticing how the big rug was now wadded up against the wall.

Ms. Gomez guided us over to where a resort employee showed us how to clip into our boots and rental skis. It was nice to travel with Maria Gomez. Sort of like having a mother that

I never knew. She took care of us—finding coats and driving us to Powder Peaks. And she also bought us stuff, like fast-food meals, ski rentals, and lift passes.

As I slipped into my ski boots, a TV mounted above a crackling fireplace caught my eye. It was showing a weatherman who sure had a lot to say.

"Wow, folks! You won't believe what is happening in the Wasatch Mountains right now. An isolated winter storm has struck, shattering records for this time of year with a whopping fifty-two inches of snow. And it doesn't show signs of stopping! Powder Peaks Ski Resort has announced that they will be in full operation today, so dust off your skis and call in sick to work. This is a historic opportunity to hit the slopes in the dead of summer! But remember, it's winter conditions up there, so don't forget your goggles and your balaclava."

"What's a balaclava?" I asked Ridge as he clomped over to me, barely able to walk in his stiff boots, balancing skis in one hand and poles in the other.

"It's a Greek dessert, I think. Shaped like a triangle," he said.

"Why did the weatherman say we should bring dessert?"

"Skiing can work up an appetite," said Ridge. "You want to come prepared."

I tightened down the last clip on my boot and stood up, wiggling my toes. These were uncomfortable.

"Listen closely," Ms. Gomez said, pulling us into a huddle near the lodge exit. "There are a couple of very important things the four of you need to know about entering the vault."

"Wait," I said. "The four of us? You're not coming?"

"Last time I went skiing, I broke my leg," said Ms. Gomez. "My time will be better spent out here, trying to locate the dagger." She produced two big backpacks that I'd seen her bring from the car. She handed one to me and the other to Jathon. I began to unzip mine, but Ms. Gomez reached out and stopped me.

"What? Last time I carried a backpack, it was full of peanut butter and jelly sandwiches," I explained. "Just wondering if you packed any snacks. Maybe some balaclava."

"A balaclava isn't a snack," Vale said.

"Dessert?" Ridge said. "The triangle things?"

"That's called baklava."

"Then what's a balaclava?" I asked.

"It's a cloth mask to keep your face warm," Jathon explained. That made way more sense than dessert. "And I don't think there's one in your backpack."

"The backpacks are full of trinkets that I have been gathering," Ms. Gomez went on. "It's been more than three years since I've been able to get into the vault. You can do me a big favor by depositing them all inside. But the vault will only allow

58

you to withdraw one item. So don't touch anything except the spool of string."

I glanced at Jathon to make sure he heard that. He had a history of taking things that didn't belong to him.

"What will happen if we take more than one trinket?" I asked.

"The vault will close you in forever."

"What?" I cried. "This is the worst vault I've ever heard of." Okay, so it was the only vault I'd ever heard of. But, seriously!

"Hey," Ms. Gomez defended. "I didn't build the vault. It was passed on to me from the Trinketers that came before."

"Now that we've got our skis, how do we get in?" Jathon asked.

"Yellow Snow," she said.

"Never eat yellow snow," Ridge said. "Isn't that a thing people say? I don't really know what it means."

"Think about it, Ridge," I said. "Why would snow turn yellow?"

"Someone spilled their lemonade?" he said.

"Yellow Snow is the name of a run," Ms. Gomez told us. "Very steep. When you see it, you'll be so scared that you might make yellow snow."

"Oh!" Ridge said, wrinkling his nose in disgust. "I get it."

"So, we just ski down that run?" Jathon asked. "Is there a

door or something we should look out for?"

"At the bottom of that run is a sign pointing toward the lodge. You'll have to slide under the sign, passing between the two poles that hold it up."

"That shouldn't be too difficult," Jathon said.

"No," answered Ms. Gomez. "But you could be detained."

"Who's going to detain us?" Ridge asked. "Ski patrol? Can I get arrested for skiing too fast?"

"There are a few safeguards that might try to stop you from getting through the entrance," she said.

"What kind of safeguards?" Vale asked.

"No importa." Ms. Gomez waved a hand. "If you ski fast, you shouldn't run into trouble."

That wasn't a very convincing answer, but I was used to not knowing things that seemed important. I'd just have to keep a sharp lookout.

"We'll see you when we get out," Jathon said, gathering his skis and poles.

"I'll be here," said Ms. Gomez. "Trying to gather information about the old dagger trinket."

Vale grabbed the snowboard leaning against the wall and ducked out into the blizzard. Her movement forced Jathon to follow as quickly as he could, leaving Ridge and me alone with Ms. Gomez for a moment.

"Thanks for all your help," I said.

She stared at me long enough that I started to feel uncomfortable. "Why are you here, Ace?"

"I'm trying to save Tina," I said.

"And I'm grateful for that," she said. "But it's not your quest, is it?"

"Well, no," I mumbled. "But my quest is dumb. I'm not even going to bother with it."

"I do not think the Universe would assign you a 'dumb' quest."

I studied the carpeted floor of the ski lodge, embarrassed to look up, as I muttered, "I'm supposed to find somebody named Samuel Sylvester Stansworth and make him a peanut butter sandwich."

"Samuel Sylvester Stansworth?" Ms. Gomez said.

I looked up sharply. "You know him?"

"Never heard of him," she answered.

I grabbed my poles. "Doesn't matter anyway."

"You never know." Ms. Gomez tapped her chin in thought. "Perhaps feeding this person a sandwich will prevent some grave consequence."

I sighed. "Nope. If I fail, then all the red roses in the world will lose their smell."

"That's really not so bad," Ms. Gomez admitted.

61

"Yeah. That's why I've decided to help Tina instead," I replied.

"That is brave of you, but I'm not sure if it's right to completely abandon your quest." Ms. Gomez took a deep, thoughtful breath. "I'm going to make a phone call while you're gone. I know someone that might have information that'll change your mind."

"Change my mind about helping Tina?" I didn't understand.

"Again, I am grateful for your help," Ms. Gomez said gently. "But this is Jathon's quest, not yours."

I had nothing more to say. I just stared at Ms. Gomez, feeling kind of hurt and insulted.

"Come on, Ace," Ridge urged. The two of us shuffled awkwardly outside, our skis and poles clanging into the doorframe.

It was hard to spot Jathon and Vale in the blizzard, but we finally caught up with them near the chairlift. Jathon's skis were hooked securely to his boots, and Vale had one boot clipped into her snowboard.

My arms were exhausted and I dropped my load of gear onto the snow.

"You'll want to put those skis on," Jathon said.

"Obviously." I tried to step down on the ski, but I just ended up falling over.

"Put your toe in first," Jathon instructed. "Then step down on your heel."

"What makes you the expert?" Ridge asked, clearly having as much trouble as I was. Jathon's advice helped, though, and soon I had one ski on.

"My dad might not be the nicest guy," Jathon said. "But he's taken me skiing a lot."

"Your dad knows how to ski?" I clipped into my second ski, using my poles to stabilize myself.

"He's actually very good at it," Jathon said. "Worked a couple winters as ski patrol in Colorado."

It was hard to imagine that Thackary Anderthon was good at anything other than scowling.

The four of us joined the short line for the lift. The chairs were attached to an overhead cable, and they didn't even slow down for people to get on. Jathon and Vale maneuvered into position just as the chair came around, sweeping them off their feet and carrying them up the mountain into the white storm.

The lift worker beckoned for Ridge and me. We propelled ourselves forward, accidentally crossing each other's skis and bumping heads. Before I was ready, I felt the chair knock me in the back of the knees. I fell onto the padded, snowy seat, using my poles to hold Ridge in place beside me. By the time we untangled ourselves, our chair was thirty feet above the ground.

"Whoa!" Ridge said. "If we fell off right now, do you think we'd survive?"

"Sure," I answered. "Remember when we fell off that roller coaster at Super-Fun-Happy Place? It was way higher than this."

"But we had a big pile of teddy bears to catch us," Ridge said.

"They were trying to tear us apart," I reminded him.

"Yeah, but I morphed into an air shark and chewed them up!"

"That reminds me," I said. "Do you think I should make a pay-as-you-play wish? You know, in case we run into trouble while we're skiing?"

Pay-as-you-play wishes were very convenient. All I had to do was create some sort of trigger word. Something unusual that I wouldn't accidentally say in regular conversation. Every time I said it, Ridge would transform into something awesome. While he was defending me, I'd pay a consequence, but it was easier to make the wish now when we weren't in the heat of the moment.

"Good idea," he said. "But don't turn me into something that'll get cold."

"What do you mean?"

"Like a crocodile," he said. "They're meant for warmer climates. I don't want my teeth to chatter. I could accidentally bite you."

"Do you have something in mind?"

"How about a penguin?"

I let out a laugh. "Somehow I don't think a penguin is going to be very good at defending me."

"What about a humpback whale?"

"What are you going to do? Flop on the bad guys?" I tapped my chin, which was starting to feel a little frosty. And that gave me the perfect idea for a trigger word. "I've got it! I wish that every time I say the word *balaclava*, you will transform between your normal self and a giant polar bear . . . with wings!"

Ridge grinned. "That's way better than a penguin!"

I felt a tug underneath my glove and I knew that my hourglass had just popped up. I'd have to accept quickly since I couldn't see my timer.

"If you want me to transform into a winged polar bear," Ridge said, "then every time I take that shape, you'll have to bear crawl."

That sounded like an appropriate consequence. "What's a bear crawl?"

"It's when you crawl on your hands and feet without putting your knees down," Ridge said.

"That actually sounds easier than slithering on my stomach like last time," I said.

"One more thing," Ridge said. "You can't bend your elbows or knees while you're crawling."

"Wait a minute!" I protested. "Did you just add that because I said it sounded easy?"

"I didn't add anything," Ridge said. "That was the Universe's decision. I'm merely the spokesman."

I grunted. It would be worth it to have a guardian polar bear. Don't you think?

"Bazang," I said, feeling my hourglass flatten under my glove.

I resisted the urge to say *balaclava* and test my new wish. Turning Ridge into a bear might break the chairlift. So we just rode in silence for a minute. Below, a skier wiped out, tumbling through the fresh snow. I thought about Ms. Gomez breaking her leg while skiing. She was probably curled comfortably next to the fireplace, waiting in the lodge. Which reminded me . . .

"I don't know who Ms. Gomez is going to call," I said, "but I don't think anyone can convince me that my quest is worthwhile. It's just the Universe's way of insulting me."

"Just because something seems small," Ridge said, "doesn't mean it's not important."

"How is protecting the world from unscented roses

important?" I countered. "My quest doesn't benefit anyone!"

"Maybe it's supposed to benefit Samuel Sylvester Stansworth."

"By eating a peanut butter sandwich?"

"Maybe he's starving." Ridge shrugged. "I'm just saying that it seems like the Universe has a reason for everything. I don't think it would assign you a quest that didn't matter."

"You're siding with Ms. Gomez on this?" I cried. "It should be my quest to save Tina! Jathon isn't even one of the good guys. Now he gets to rescue Tina and save the world, while I'm supposed to make a sandwich. That's not going to happen. I'm not going to hang out on the sidelines. I'm giving myself a new quest, Ridge."

"That's not really how this works," he said.

"I don't care," I replied. "My new quest is to help Jathon save Tina. Are you with me?"

"Of course. I can't really go anywhere else," Ridge muttered. "You're the Wishmaker, Ace. I don't really get to decide where we go or what we do. I'm just along for the ride."

I stuck out my tongue and caught a few more snowflakes.

Ridge pointed ahead with his ski pole. "Looks like it's time to get off."

CHAPTER 7

"Yellow Snow is this way." Vale pointed left, still seated in the snow from where she had strapped her other boot to her board.

"You've been here before?" asked Ridge.

"Of course not. I'm a genie, not a tourist. I just looked at a map in the lodge." Vale always seemed extra smart. But I knew it was just an act. She only knew things because she took the time to read stuff.

I couldn't see very far through the blizzard, but the slopes already looked steeper than I had expected. Just getting off the lift had been a rather embarrassing experience. As the chair had skimmed across a mound of snow, Ridge and I had pushed ourselves off, fallen flat on our backsides, and slipped down to the spot where Jathon and Vale had been waiting for us.

Vale leaped to her feet now, performing some cool jump

move to reposition her snowboard. At the same time, one of Ridge's skis started slipping and he promptly did the splits, howling in pain.

"Guess we'll see you in the vault," Jathon said. "If you two can figure out how to get down the mountain." He turned his skis, digging in his poles, and the two of them sped off through the snowstorm.

I helped Ridge to his feet and he knocked me down. We accidentally slipped a few yards in the direction we were trying to go. Ridge hit a tree. I face-planted.

And we hadn't even reached the steep run yet!

"This isn't going so good," I pointed out. "I wish the two of us knew how to ski!"

"Thank you!" Ridge called, brushing pine needles off his beanie. "If you want us to know how to ski, then every time you say the word *I*, you'll shiver."

I shuddered at the thought of it. "Will I constantly be shivering?"

"Oh, no," he said. "Just a single chill."

"What about you?"

"I'm a genie, Ace. I don't have consequences."

"But I wished for both of us."

"And I'm very grateful for that," said Ridge. "But you have to experience the shivering alone."

"How long will it last?" I asked.

"Just today."

I sighed. *I* was a very common word. There was no way I could avoid using it. This paragraph alone would have given me a triple shiver.

"Bazang."

Ridge suddenly straightened his skis and zoomed past me, turning sharply to stop just downhill from where I sat. "This is awesome!"

In a moment, the two of us were racing through the snow, careful to stay close as we searched for the run we were supposed to take. My legs were burning from the effort of cutting through the deep snow, and I don't think I looked any less wobbly than Ridge. Apparently, knowing how to ski didn't make us experts. But at least we were getting somewhere.

Ridge pointed to a sign next to a stand of trees. Through the heavily falling flakes, I could barely read the name of the run.

Yellow Snow.

Wow, it was steep. People actually skied down this? On purpose? There was no sign of Jathon and Vale. Maybe they had already tumbled to the bottom.

"You ready for this?" Ridge asked.

"I guess." My answer brought a shiver down my spine. It

passed as quickly as it came, and I took a deep breath, pointing my skis down the terrifying slope.

The two of us made sharp turns, trying not to pick up too much speed. Pine trees lined both sides of the run, and the soft snow billowed around our feet like clouds as we made the steep descent.

I felt like things were going pretty good until someone came careening out of the trees, skis clicking together in midair as the stranger caught some air on a jump. Landing skillfully, he turned sharply, smashing directly into me.

I had no time to move. No time to shout. I went down in a puff of Powder Peaks' perfect powder. One of my skis broke free of its binding and I skidded to a halt just down from Ridge.

Gasping, I wiped snow from my face and sat up to face my attacker. Then I heard his voice and I knew exactly who it was.

"Ahoy there, matey! Ye look to be havin' a frightful time on the slopes."

It was Thackary Anderthon!

He slid toward me, face mostly hidden beneath goggles and a ski mask. Good. I didn't want to see his sneering expression anyway.

"Ace!" Ridge came toward us, but Thackary brought his

71

pole around, catching the edge of Ridge's left ski and crossing it over his right. The genie crashed with an "oof," rolling past us like a snowball.

"I've come a-searching for me little boy! Somethin' tells me ye know where he be!" Thackary pointed a pole aggressively in my direction.

"How did you find us?" I shrieked, reaching uphill to grab my missing ski.

"Ye think I don't know where me own son be hiding?" Thackary answered.

I had forgotten how strange it was to hear him talk like a pirate all the time. Supposedly, that was one of his old consequences from when he was a Wishmaker.

"Jathon's already gone." I had no way of knowing for sure, but with their skill, it wasn't hard to imagine that he and Vale had already passed under the lodge sign and entered the vault.

"I'm sure the lot of ye be working together," said Thackary. "I'll just have to keep ye scallywags hostage until Jathon sails back to find ye."

"Not going to happen!" Ridge shouted. "Ace! Run!" He hurled a snowball at Thackary. But his aim was slightly off and the snowball pelted me in the side of the head, knocking me flat on the slope.

Thackary began to laugh, but as I sat up again, I noticed

something very strange happening right behind the cruel man.

The snow was swirling together into a large ball. A second, slightly smaller ball formed on top of that one, two dried twigs flying from a nearby tree and sticking into the sides. A final ball appeared to complete the stack. I don't know where the carrot came from, but suddenly it was forming a nose, with a collection of pebbles making eyes and a crooked mouth.

"Um . . ." I said to Thackary, who was still cackling like an evil maniac. "There's a snowman behind you."

His laughter faded, and he looked at me like I was an idiot. "I shan't be falling fer that trick. Nobody would stop to build a snowman on a ski run."

"Actually," I said, "I am pretty sure he just built himself." I shivered. Not sure if it was from the consequence or fear.

Wham!

The big snowman slammed into Thackary from behind, sending him facedown in the powder. I leaped up, dropping my ski and slamming my toe into the binding. I felt it click and I swerved down the mountain just as the snowman lunged for me.

"Why is there a demon snowman?" Ridge yelled, swishing through the powder beside me.

"He must be that safeguard Ms. Gomez almost warned us about!"

"He's trying to stop us from getting into the vault?" Ridge asked.

Ms. Gomez had said we wouldn't run into extra trouble if we were fast enough. Sure, we weren't skiing at Olympic records, but I thought we were plenty speedy.

"Jathon and Vale must have triggered him," I said, wondering if those two had already made it through the entrance.

A new snowman materialized right in front of us. He was at least six feet tall, his carrot nose slightly crooked and the pebbles that made up his mouth forming a sneer. Ridge and I swerved, ducking just as his stick arms swiped at us.

"Phew!" Ridge gasped, but this guy wasn't giving up yet.

As I glanced over my shoulder, I saw the snowman's head swivel completely around. Then it leaned forward, using the steepness of the slope to roll after us. The thing should have fallen apart completely, but this snowman was a very skillful roller.

The two bottom snowballs that comprised its body rolled independently. The snowballs managed to stay stacked, stick arms twirling and head bobbing.

"It's getting bigger!" Ridge yelled, risking a peek uphill.

You see, that's what happens when snowballs roll downhill.

74

They pick up more snow as they go, growing bigger and bigger. This usually isn't a problem, unless the enlarging ball is part of a snowman that wants to tear you apart.

I picked up speed, pushing myself to the limit of my skill and seeing Ridge wobble as he kept up. Yellow Snow seemed

to continue endlessly downward. How long was this terrifying run?

If a snowman were alive, what sound do you think he would make? Turns out it was something between a grunt and a demonic laugh. I know, because I heard it right behind me.

I looked back, snowflakes pelting my face. The thing was huge! The snowman must have been twenty feet tall by now, his head (which hadn't been growing at the same rate as his rolling body) looked ridiculously tiny, and his stick arms were like toothpicks on that giant form. Somehow, it made him more terrifying as he positioned himself to roll over both of us.

"Into the trees!" I shouted. It was really our only chance of survival at this point.

I veered, Ridge following closely as we sped off the groomed ski run and into the protection of the forest. Branches lashed at my face and it took all my effort to maneuver my long skis through the tangle of tree trunks.

Behind us, I heard the overgrown snowman smash into the pines. It sounded like an avalanche as he broke apart, snapping branches and bending trees. Clods of packed snow pounded us from behind, the sudden rush pushing us downward with even greater speed.

At last, Ridge and I emerged from the trees, directing ourselves back onto the familiar open runway of Yellow Snow, and coming to a stop so we could get our bearings.

The good news was that our jaunt through the woods had taken us almost to the bottom of the run. Below, I could see the lodge sign we were looking for, two metal poles holding it some five feet above the snow.

But between us and the sign was an army of snowmen.

The white figures ranged in size from knee-high to eight feet. Luckily, none had grown to the height of the rolling guy we'd just ditched. But they had strength in numbers. Most of them were made of three snowballs, although I did see a few figures with additional torsos.

Everybody had a carrot nose, which made me think that somewhere out there was an envious bunny. The stick arms of the snowmen varied from wispy twigs to full-on tree limbs. I didn't care to get whacked by either.

"What are we going to do?" Ridge muttered at my side.

"We've got to ski past them," I said. It was the only way into the vault. And if we waited here too long, Thackary Anderthon might show up again and try to follow us in. Unless he'd been eaten by a snowman . . .

"I'm not good enough!" said Ridge. "You've got to make a wish."

"I already did," I said, feeling a little shiver down my back. Without explaining my plan, I turned my skis and plummeted toward the waiting snowman army.

I swerved around the first one, ducked under the second one, jumped over the third one (he was little), and ran directly into the fourth one.

It was like hitting a slightly soft wall. My skis went flying off and I stuck face-first into the snowman, arms and legs flailing as though I were trying to make a snow angel while standing up. I finally flopped backward onto the slope, craning my neck to see Ridge skiing down toward me. More snowmen were converging on my location, and Ridge wasn't likely to get much farther than I had.

It was time for my secret weapon.

"Baklava!" I shouted, anxious to see him transform and start shredding snowmen.

Ridge teetered unsteadily on his skis, but otherwise nothing happened.

"Baklava!" I called again. Oh, wait. That was the name of the dessert. . . . "Balaclava!"

At the sound of the correct trigger word, Ridge suddenly morphed into a huge shaggy polar bear.

I must say, it was a sight unlike anything I'd seen before—a polar bear skiing downhill, brandishing both poles in his giant paws.

The moment he transformed, I felt my elbows and knees

lock straight as I stooped awkwardly on my hands and feet. My gloves sank into the snow, but I had a good view of Ridge's action as I faced uphill.

Polar bear Ridge flattened the first two snowmen he encountered, skis running them down under his great weight. His poles ripped free of the straps around his hairy wrists and Ridge clobbered three more snowmen.

"Fly, Ridge! Fly!" I shouted.

"I can't!" he answered.

"Where are your wings?" I had specifically wished for wings.

"They're not working right!" he called as he zoomed past me. I glanced at his back.

Seriously? Penguin wings? They flapped uselessly against his hairy back.

I sighed. Sometimes I felt like the Universe was just messing with me.

A nearby enemy plowed into me and I lost my balance, rolling downhill like the big snowman that had chased us. My poles flailed on their straps, accidentally knocking back another snowman.

I skidded to a halt on my back like a turtle, straight legs and arms sticking helplessly in the air. From this ungainly position, I saw the polar bear catch some air on a jump, his ski slicing through a snowman's head. He landed, turning to stop in a spray of snow. By my estimate, the two of us were about as far apart as our tether would allow. But we still had a ways to go before we reached the vault entrance.

"Come on, Ace!" Ridge shouted. It was really quite humorous to hear his squeaky voice coming from the slobbering mouth of a massive bear. He spun, his paw reducing another snowman's head to powder.

A particularly large snowman with a baby carrot nose suddenly loomed over me. His arm lashed out like a cracking whip, and I saw that it seemed to be made of a flexible willow branch.

It wrapped around one of my upright legs and yanked me into the air, releasing me at the apex of my flight. I soared over half a dozen angry snowmen, my scream cutting through the thick falling snow.

"RIIIIIIIIIDGE!"

Have you ever been caught by a polar bear? It was a first for me, too. I landed in Ridge's cradled arms as he made a sharp turn through some moguls.

"You're so soft!" I said, my cheek brushing against his fur.

"Don't announce it," he said. "These guys already want to turn me into a rug." If that happened, he'd get pulled out from under me.

"We're almost to the sign!" I yelled. "You're doing great, Ridge!"

He lowered his blunt head and knocked aside another snowman. "You know, I'm really getting the hang of skiing! I haven't even crashed yet."

We crashed.

Ridge must have crossed his skis, or something. One moment, I was nestled securely in the arms of a friendly polar bear, and the next, I was tumbling recklessly through icy snow.

I popped my head up like a snowshoe rabbit looking for spring. I scanned the area, only to realize that Ridge had made it to the vault entrance!

There he was, maybe thirty feet downhill. But his shaggy white form was *lodged* under the lodge sign! Those broad polar-bear shoulders were too big to fit between the metal poles, penguin wings flapping. In fact, the supports were bending as Ridge tried to wrestle his way through.

"Balaclava!" I shouted.

In the blink of an eye, Ridge transformed into a boy again, tumbling easily under the sign. Gratefully, I could stand upright now, although I quickly found myself alone against the few snowmen remaining between me and the entrance.

"Yarrrr!" called a voice from uphill. "Ye can't shake me so easily, scurvy landlubbers!"

Oh, great. Thackary had caught up to us, skiing between snowmen like an expert on the slalom course.

A snowman leaped at me. Instinctively, I whirled, grasping one of my ski poles like a sword and blocking his stick-arm attack. Hey! These poles were actually pretty useful.

I blocked his other arm and then used my left pole to swing, severing the snowman's head and causing him to slough downward in a lifeless heap of snow.

I sprinted a few feet, slipping my wrist out of the strap and hurling one of my poles like a javelin. It skewered an approaching snowman, knocking him back and staking him to the hillside.

Ducking. Blocking. Thrusting. I ran. Ridge was shouting at me from below, but I was too focused on fighting to hear his words.

A snowman blindsided me, knocking me flat on my back. I raised my pole as he leaped at me, the pointy end ramming all the way through his middle snowball. I rolled aside as his weight came down, bending my pole in half.

I slipped out of the wrist strap, checking the distance to the lodge sign. Ridge was waving at me desperately. From the corner of my eye, I saw Thackary carving around, closing on me with a nautical insult.

I dashed a few steps downhill, my speed and the slope's

steepness proving too much. I tripped on my heavy ski boots, flopping onto my stomach and landing right on one of my lost skis. Headfirst, I slid down the mountain on my stomach, shooting between the bent metal supports and passing beneath the lodge sign. I slammed into Ridge and the two of us tumbled into darkness.

CHAPTER 8

We hit the floor—an actual hardwood floor. What happened to the snow? The mountain? The daylight?

Ridge and I stumbled to our feet, quickly studying our surroundings. I had assumed that the vault would feel ancient and magical, but I must admit, it wasn't at all what I'd expected.

It was an airport baggage claim. If you'd never flown on an airplane before, then it might have seemed unfamiliar. But I recognized it from my brief trip through the San Antonio airport after Tina's private jet had accidentally flown us to South America.

The vault room was very wide, with a high ceiling. There must have been twenty luggage carousels, positioned side by side. Each one was made up of a conveyor belt that came out of a hole in the wall. The mechanized belt made a wide loop, like a racetrack, before disappearing into another hole in the wall.

Usually these carousels were used to display luggage from the flight. Passengers would stand around with bored expressions, waiting to snatch their bags, while workers behind the wall continued to throw more items onto the conveyor belts. The carousels that I'd seen moved at a creaky, slow pace.

But not here. The twenty carousels in the vault were on overdrive! And instead of luggage, the conveyor belts carried a random assortment of items, moving so fast that my eyes could barely make them out.

Among the countless items, I saw a unicycle, a blender, a beach towel, a bottle of soda pop, a measuring tape. . . . At least, I think that's what I saw appearing from one hole in the wall, whirring along the conveyor, and disappearing behind the wall again.

Jathon and Vale were standing to one side, zipping out of their snow gear and discarding it in the corner next to their skis and snowboard.

"I thought you guys weren't coming," Jathon said.

"We would have been here sooner," I answered, "but your dad slowed us down."

"My dad?" Jathon's eyebrows raised. "He's here?"

I looked around the room. "Well, not here," I said. Thackary probably didn't know about the secret vault entrance, and he must not have seen us go under the sign. Understandable, since he was being attacked by snowmen in a blizzard. He probably thought Ridge and I simply disappeared.

"But I'm sure this means he'll be waiting for us when we get out," Ridge said.

"What happened to your boots?" Jathon gestured at Ridge's ski boots. The hard plastic was shredded and the clasps hung loosely, barely keeping his feet in place.

Ridge easily stepped out of the clunky things. "My polar bear feet were a lot bigger than my human feet," he said, as though that answer should make sense.

"Welcome to the vault of trinkets." The sudden announcement caused the four of us to whirl around in surprise. No one had magically appeared, but the disembodied voice sounded like it was right behind us. "I hope you enjoy your visit." The voice didn't sound evil or scary. In fact, it sounded like a little girl. Which was actually kind of creepy in its own way.

"Did you hear that?" Ridge asked me.

"Who are you?" I asked the voice.

"Where are you?" asked Jathon.

"I'm the speaker of the vault," answered the voice. "I'm here to answer any questions you might have."

"Okay." I slipped the backpack from my shoulder. "The Trinketer gave us a bunch of trinkets to deposit. Where are we supposed to put them?"

"Oh, just toss them on the conveyor belts with all the others," said the voice.

"Those things are all trinkets?" Ridge exclaimed.

Not only were there more items than I had suspected, but they didn't seem to be very carefully stored. For some reason, I had imagined that the vault would keep each trinket securely locked in its own case.

I stepped up to the nearest luggage carousel. An illuminated sign marked this one as number 10. I couldn't figure out how the trinkets were staying on the conveyor belts. At this speed, they should have all flown off.

I cautiously unzipped my backpack and peered inside. Time to see what Ms. Gomez had packed.

"Don't worry about accidentally setting off any of the trinkets," said the voice. "None of them work inside the vault. That's sort of the whole reason the Trinketer keeps them here."

That made me feel a little better about sticking my hand into a backpack full of unknown magical items. I pulled out the first trinket.

It was a little two-pound dumbbell weight—the kind I'd seen old folks carrying on their morning walks. I held the weight above the luggage carousel and dropped it. The dumbbell struck the conveyor belt with a thud and was instantly whisked away, moving so fast that I immediately lost track of it.

Next up was a small journal. I resisted the urge to see if anything was written inside, instead donating the mysterious trinket to the conveyor belt.

It didn't take long to empty the backpack. There was a stapler, a jump rope, a lemon, a paintbrush, a little bottle of pink soap, a shoelace, a candle, a spoon, some fingernail clippers, and a ping-pong ball. I wondered what each trinket did, knowing that behind each seemingly ordinary object, somebody had made a wish and accepted a consequence.

I swung the empty backpack onto my shoulder once more, Ridge's peanut butter jar now the only thing inside. Glancing over, I saw that Jathon had just finished emptying his backpack onto luggage carousel number 9.

"Your deposit is greatly appreciated," said the voice, sounding like a little girl who had memorized words that were too big for her. "Thank you for keeping unclaimed trinkets off the streets. You may exit out the door behind you. It will lead you back to the ski resort."

"Wait a minute!" I shouted. "What about our withdrawal? We came here to get an important trinket."

"That's fine," said the voice. "You may take one trinket off the conveyor belt."

"We want the spool of string," said Jathon. "The one that makes a tether become visible."

The voice giggled. "Good luck grabbing it!"

"We're just supposed to snatch it off the conveyor belt as it passes?" I shrieked. "This thing's moving way too fast!"

"We should spread out and see if we can spot it," Ridge suggested, positioning himself at carousel 12.

We each watched a different conveyor belt, my eyes trying to take in the blur of objects. It was giving me a headache. And what was I supposed to do if I did manage to see a spool of string? My reflexes weren't nearly fast enough to grab it before it was whisked away.

"Oh, forget it!" Jathon cried after several minutes. He turned to his genie. "Vale," he said. "I wish to know which luggage carousel the spool of string is on."

"If you want to know where the string is," said Vale, "then anytime someone says a word that rhymes with *belt*, you will have to spin around in a circle."

"Luckily, there aren't too many words that rhyme with *belt*," he said.

"*Belt, felt, dealt,*" Ridge started to rhyme, "*melt, pelt, welt, smelt, knelt.*"

"How long will this last?" Jathon asked, ignoring my genie.

"A year," said Vale.

"What about the word *belt* itself?" Jathon asked.

"That counts, too," said Vale.

"*Helt, relt, velt,*" Ridge went on, "*jelt, zelt, telt . . .*"

"Those aren't even real words!" Jathon yelled.

"She didn't say they have to be real words," I pointed out. "Just anything that rhymes with *belt*."

"You guys aren't making this very easy," Jathon said.

"Sorry," I said. "It's a good wish. I think you should do it." I shivered.

Jathon shut his eyes and sucked in a deep breath. "Bazang!" His eyes snapped open. "It's on carousel six!" he shouted. "No, wait. It's on seven."

Ridge and I turned to the one he had indicated when Jathon cut in again. "Now it's on eight!"

"Make up your mind!" I shouted.

"It's just moving so fast," he answered. "All the conveyor belts must be connected behind the wall." He spun in a quick circle. "It's making its way through. Now it's on eleven!"

Ridge and I scrambled forward, eyes darting across the trinkets. But by the time we were in position to grab anything, Jathon said it had moved on to carousel 12.

The four of us raced across the vault as Jathon continued to call the numbers. There was no time to stop and search. We could barely keep up while running along.

"It's on number twenty!" Jathon cried. "The last one!"

I sprinted around the side of the carousel, my eyes fixed on the spot where the conveyor belt disappeared into the wall. Rubbery plastic strips hung over the opening, blocking my view of whatever was beyond.

"Oh, come on!" Jathon shouted. "It's gone!"

"What do you mean, gone?" Vale asked.

"It must have gone behind the wall."

"Well, is it coming back?" I asked.

It was the little girl's voice that answered. "Yep! It'll circle back around in about a minute."

We all took off running across the room, finally positioning ourselves beside the first luggage carousel, gasping for breath from our sprint.

"Now what?" Ridge said. "We just keep chasing it around? I don't think we're going to get any faster."

"Not without a wish," Vale seconded.

The genies were right. Jathon had done his part to locate the spool of string, but it wasn't enough. Now it was my turn to make a wish.

"Ridge," I said. "I wish that the conveyor belt would slow down." I shivered and Jathon spun in a circle.

"Good one," Ridge encouraged. I would have rather wished for the spool of string to fall into my hands, but that was too direct. Slowing down the conveyor belts would still require effort to retrieve the right trinket.

"It's back!" Jathon shouted, his focus returning to the conveyor belt. "Already on carousel three!" Jathon and Vale moved after it, but I stood still, waiting to hear the consequence attached to my wish.

"If you want the conveyor belt to slow down," Ridge said, "then time outside the vault will speed up until we leave."

"How fast will it go?" I asked.

"Well, every minute that passes in here will be an hour out there."

I thought about the usefulness of my wish. Once the conveyor slowed down, we could grab the string and leave. At most, we'd be inside the vault for another five minutes. That would be five hours outside, but it seemed totally worth it to me.

I nodded at Ridge. "Bazang."

Beside us, the conveyor belt slowed significantly. It was still moving way faster than the normal airport luggage claim, but at least I could see the items gliding past. A potted plant, a fake bird, a little toy drum, a toilet plunger . . .

"Hey!" Jathon shouted from the middle of the room. "What just happened?"

"I made a wish," I said, feeling another shiver down my back as Ridge and I jogged over to them.

"The spool of string just came onto carousel nineteen," Jathon said. The four of us fanned out, actually feeling hopeful. But there were still a lot of trinkets to sort through. Maybe I should have wished for the conveyor belt to come to a full stop.

"Nope," Jathon said. "It's on twenty now."

We hurried into position, Jathon and I racing toward the last stretch of conveyor belt.

"There it is!" Vale stood at the bend in the carousel track, pointing. "It's coming your way!"

Jathon and I spotted the trinket at the same time, gliding swiftly toward the opening in the wall. The spool of string looked old and weathered. The whole thing was about the size of my fist, wrapped around a short piece of wooden dowel.

"You've got this, Ace!" Ridge shouted. "We'll be back to the ski resort before the snow even has a chance to melt."

At the sound of a word that rhymed with *belt*, Jathon performed a quick spin, knocking me back. My knees struck the floor as Jathon steadied himself. But it was too late. The spool of string had passed through the opening in the wall.

The minutes passed like hours—quite literally for everyone outside the vault.

Last time the string had gone behind the wall, it had taken only a minute or so before cycling back around. But my wish had slowed down the conveyor belt, and now there was nothing to do but wait. I tried not to think about how much time was passing outside, and I certainly didn't tell Jathon and Vale what my consequence had been.

"I wish the conveyor belt would speed up again," Jathon finally said, spinning in a circle as we all sat around carousel 1.

"Can't wish that," said Vale, her voice bored. "That would be wishing to undo a wish that Ace made."

So we waited. It was very boring with nothing to do. We watched the assortment of trinkets go by. The weird little-girl voice shared some poems with us. We felt bad that she didn't have a name, so Ridge and I decided to call her Beatrice.

After what seemed like forever, Jathon leaped to his feet. "It just came out on carousel one!" he announced. I saw him stoop down, and when he stepped away, Jathon was holding the much-desired trinket.

"Aha!" said the voice. "You picked the spool of string."

"Duh!" Jathon said. "We've been sitting here talking about it for at least an hour!"

"Thank you for visiting," said the voice. "Come again soon."

"Before we go, I've actually got a couple questions for Beatrice," Ridge said. "Do you talk to yourself when no one is in the vault? Do you go into a deep sleep like how I do between quests? Is it possible for you to get a sore throat?"

"No time for that, Ridge!" I said. "Why didn't you ask her those questions while we were sitting around?"

"I didn't think of them till now," he said. "I'm bad at good-byes!"

We moved toward the exit she had told us about, and I yanked open the door. The four of us hurried onto the hillside of Powder Peaks Ski Resort.

But there was no snow.

The August sun shone through the trees, and a few birds chirped happily. Behind us, the crooked poles of the lodge sign jutted out of the mountain soil. We stepped forward and a tree dropped all its leaves on Jathon.

Ms. Gomez rose from a large rock where she'd been sitting. Tina's mom looked very tired, and her expression was like that of an upset parent waiting to scold a child for staying out past curfew.

"Ay! Raspberry swirl!" she shouted. "It's about time. What happened in there?"

"We got the spool of string." Jathon held up the trinket triumphantly.

I swallowed, afraid to ask the question. "How long were we gone?"

Ms. Gomez put her hands on her hips. "Three days."

CHAPTER 9

"We were gone for three days?" Jathon shouted as we followed Ms. Gomez down the dirt path toward the ski lodge. "I don't understand. We were only in there for a few hours at most."

Ridge began to say something, but I subtly elbowed him in the ribs to keep quiet. Okay, maybe it was not as subtle as I had meant, since it left him gasping for air.

"I don't know what happened," I said. "We don't know anything."

"There must have been some sort of time warp," Ms. Gomez said. "Making time pass faster outside the vault."

"So, now it's Thursday?" Vale asked.

"*Sí,*" answered Ms. Gomez, heading up the lodge steps. "Almost suppertime."

Jathon moaned. "What about my quest? Oh, this is bad."

"When did you open Vale's jar?" I asked.

"Last Saturday afternoon," he answered. "Now I've only got two days to finish my quest! And we don't even know where the next trinket is!"

"Give me a little credit," said Ms. Gomez. "I haven't just been sitting around waiting for you kids. Three days gave me plenty of time to figure some things out."

So, accelerating time outside the vault hadn't been totally bad. As an added bonus, I realized that some of my short-term consequences had gone away. I no longer shivered when I said *I*.

Ms. Gomez pulled open the lodge door and we all stepped inside. It was very different now that it had returned to summer. The fireplaces were cold, and the skiers were gone. The fluke day of winter weather had been short-lived, and now the place was totally empty. I didn't know if Ms. Gomez had permission to be in there, but it looked like she'd been living in the lodge the whole time we'd been gone.

I saw blankets piled in one corner like a makeshift bed, and several of her belongings spread across a table where skiers would normally stop for lunch. Only one thing in the room made me feel nervous. Sitting in a stuffed armchair near one of the empty hearths was a familiar figure.

Thackary Anderthon glared at us, his greasy dark hair combed to one side. "Ahoy there, buckaroos. Did ye think ye could maroon me so easily?"

I scrambled backward, bumping into Jathon, who was also scrambling backward. The four of us were desperate to get away from the man. Could you blame us? We didn't have a great history with him. He'd stolen from me, pushed Ridge off a cliff, manipulated Jathon, and a whole lot of other cruel things.

But we couldn't escape through the lodge door because Ms. Gomez was suddenly blocking our way.

I felt my heart sink. Had she tricked us? Like mother, like daughter, I guessed. Ms. Gomez had led us right to Thackary. So, now what? I was going to have to make a wish or unleash polar bear Ridge to help us escape.

Thackary Anderthon stood, thin fingers steepled in front of him. His pants were too short, and his T-shirt looked dirty and tattered. "Jathon, me boy," he said. "Ye must be punished fer runnin' away from yer ole dad."

"Thack!" Ms. Gomez shouted, like they were on a nick-name basis. I had learned at the end of my last quest that the two had known each other when they were Wishmaker kids, although I didn't imagine that they'd stayed in touch over the years.

"Get ahold of yourself and sit down," Ms. Gomez fumed at him. "Caramel cashew!"

"Why do you always do that?" Ridge asked. "Whenever you get mad, you yell something that sounds delicious."

Ms. Gomez was rubbing her forehead. "It's an old conse-quence from when I was a kid," she said. "Instead of yelling swear words, I have to yell the name of ice cream flavors."

"Har har har!" laughed Thackary. "I can say all the swear words!"

Thackary didn't sit like Ms. Gomez had demanded, but he stopped advancing on Jathon. Instead, he gave a patronizing bow toward Tina's mom. "Yar! Whatever ye say, Cap'n Maria."

"What is going on?" I finally said. "You two partnered up while we were gone?"

Ms. Gomez sighed. "Something like that. I saw Thackary just after you entered the vault. He was setting traps to catch you when you came out."

"And the traps would've worked, too!" said Thackary. "I would've had the lot of ye!" He swung his arm, closing his bony fingers as though he were wringing the neck of a small animal.

"Why were you trying to trap us?" Ridge cried.

"I want to join ye on yer journey," he answered. "But ye keep trying to ditch me."

"I have explained the situation to Mr. Anderthon," said Ms. Gomez. "He knows about Jathon's quest to save Tina and he has offered to help in any way he can."

"Why?" I asked, eyes narrowed in suspicion.

"That poor girl . . ." said Thackary. "I felt a wee bit bad

about what happened in Chasm's cave."

Jathon stood and spun in a circle. Oh, because *felt* rhymed with *belt*.

"I don't believe it," I said. "How do we know you're not just using us to get what you want?"

"I would neverrrrrr!" said Thackary. "Me dreams were shattered when I missed me chance to open Chasm's jar. All I want now is to help free Maria's daughter."

"I don't trust him," Ridge muttered.

"Neither do I," I said. "He's one of the bad guys!" Last time, my whole quest had been centered around stopping Thackary from carrying out his selfish plan.

"He can't be trusted," Vale agreed.

Everyone looked at Jathon to see who he would side with. The boy was shaking his head, eyes wide.

"You're not coming, Dad," Jathon finally said.

Thackary slowly turned to look at his son. I thought his expression seemed kind of scary. "What was that, sonny?"

Jathon clenched his teeth. "I ran away for a reason." His voice started out small, but it grew louder as he continued. "You always treat me like garbage. And you almost ruined my last quest—which would have ended the world. I don't want you to come with us."

I held my breath, hearing Ridge gasp at my side. Jathon was

finally standing up to his mean old dad! But the boy looked like he was about to collapse in fear. I could see his legs shaking.

"Vale is right," Jathon said. "You can't be trusted."

"No, he can't," Ms. Gomez said, suddenly stepping between them before Thackary could say anything. "We shouldn't trust him. We shouldn't even listen to a word he says. But if you want my help, then your dad comes with us."

"What?" the rest of us moaned.

"Why are you defending him if you don't even trust him?" I asked.

"Thackary begged me to let him come along," she said. "I don't have the heart to turn him down."

"Find the heart!" shouted Ridge.

"He's only going to cause trouble," I said. "Leave him behind. You don't owe him anything."

"You're wrong," said Ms. Gomez. "I owe Thackary a lot. We were Wishmakers together. Many years ago. He finished his quest early, but he stayed by my side to help me complete mine in time."

"That sounds too nice," Ridge said. "Must have been a different Thackary Anderthon."

Ms. Gomez glanced sadly at the thin man. "He was a different person back then." To that comment, Thackary snarled. I thought only animals snarled. But in that moment, Thackary didn't seem much different from a savage raccoon.

Ms. Gomez sighed. "Thackary stays. End of conversation." She gestured to the soft seating around the hearth where Thackary had been. "Why don't we all sit down? We have a lot to discuss."

Reluctantly, like mice sniffing out suspicious bait, the four of us drew closer to Thackary. We sat down on a couch as Ms. Gomez plopped into an armchair. Thackary remained standing, probably just to spite her invitation to sit.

"You got the spool of string?" Ms. Gomez asked.

Jathon held it out, looking much less enthusiastic than he had when we'd exited the vault. Ms. Gomez took it ceremoniously from his hand. As soon as she touched it, she began to speak.

"The Wishmaker that created this trinket wished that the string could be tied between the wrist of a genie and another person to create a visible tether between the two."

"Phew," I said. "Glad we got the right thing."

"Do you know the consequence?" asked Jathon.

"I can sense it just by touching the trinket," replied Ms. Gomez. "It is one of my gifts as the Trinketer."

"Well, what is it?" I finally dared when nobody else asked.

"Every time the string is used to make a connection," Ms. Gomez said, "my ankles will be tied together."

"Well, that's going to make it hard to get around," I said.

"How long will it last?" asked Jathon.

"For a whole day after the string connects genie to Wishmaker," she answered.

"Hopefully we won't need to do any running away," I said. "The plan is to cut Tina free as quickly as possible. Won't that send Chasm back into his jar for good?"

"It should," answered Vale. "A genie can't stay in this world without being tethered to a Wishmaker."

Ms. Gomez nodded. "Now I must reactivate the trinket."

"Okay," I said. "How long is that going to take?"

"Bazang," said Ms. Gomez. The string twinkled magically for just a moment before returning to its ordinary look. "It's done."

"Oh, so, just like two seconds," I said. "For some reason I thought that would be more of a process."

"How do ye even know if there be enough string to reach between Chasm and Tina?" Thackary asked.

"It looks like there's plenty," I said. "Way more than forty-two feet."

"We should measure," suggested Vale.

"Will it hurt the trinket if we unspool some?" Jathon asked.

Ms. Gomez shook her head. "The magic of the trinket will only activate when the string is tied between two people." She handed it back to Jathon. "You can unspool it, study it, even cut off a forty-two-foot piece without any effect."

Jathon stood up, unwinding the loose end of the string from the spool and handing it to Vale. "Let's find out how much we have," he said.

Jathon held the ends of the wooden dowel loosely, while Vale carried the end of the string across the huge lodge. She stopped on the far side of the room and turned to look at her Wishmaker.

"This is about forty-two feet," she called.

"You're a pretty good judge of distance," Ridge said.

She glanced at him. "I've been a genie for a long time. I've got an eye for it." Then she called to Jathon, "How much do you still have?"

"Lots," Jathon replied. "Here, Ace. Hold on to the string right here."

I stood up and grabbed on to the spot where he indicated, pinching the string where it came off the spool.

"Stay there," Jathon instructed as he walked toward Vale, letting the string continue to unwind from the spool in his hands.

"So, that's forty-two times two," Vale said, holding on to the string as Jathon looped back toward me.

Jathon continued like this, unspooling the string and

delivering it between Vale and me, over and over again. Each time he came around, the spool grew smaller until I finally saw bare wood.

The thin white string made only a few more wraps around the wooden dowel. Jathon didn't go any farther, but instead began rewinding it.

"That's a lot of string," Ridge said, looking at the lines draping back and forth between Vale and me.

"Enough to go between them thirteen times," Jathon replied.

"So, five hundred and forty-six feet of string," said Ms. Gomez. "Thirteen times forty-two."

"Arrr!" said Thackary, who clearly wasn't as impressed with her math skills. "What good does it do ye to know that useless fact?"

"It's not useless," I said. "It tells us exactly how many tries we have to save Tina."

"Is that so?" said Thackary.

"If something goes wrong the first time we tie Tina to Chasm," I explained, "then we can cut off another length of string and tie on again." I didn't actually know if that would work, but it made me feel a little better to know that we had plenty of extra.

"Yarrr." Thackary scowled. "It don't matter if ye have

thirteen tries or a hundred. Ye will never beat the mighty Chasm."

"Whose side are you on?" Ridge shot Thackary a glare.

"Jathon should keep the spool of string with him," said Ms. Gomez. "His quest will depend on using it."

"What about the second trinket?" I asked. "The dagger that is supposed to cut the tether?"

Ms. Gomez sighed. "While you were gone, I learned the general location of the ancient dagger. But it's going to be nearly impossible to retrieve without a wish."

"Where is it?" Vale asked.

"Somewhere on the bottom of the Atlantic Ocean," she said.

"Yar!" added Thackary. "It be sunken like pirate treasure!"

"So, we're going to have to dive?" I asked. On my last quest, I had swum to the bottom of Lake Michigan. A helpful wish allowed me to hold my breath for an hour. But this sounded way deeper.

"Even if you dived," said Ms. Gomez, "you'd never find it in time. It could take years to search the bottom of the ocean."

"That's why ye must wish fer the dagger to wash ashore," said Thackary. "Narrow the search to a single beach."

I didn't want to admit it, but the pirate man actually had a pretty good idea.

"Why don't you wish for this one, Ace?" Jathon said. "I opened the ski resort and got us to the first trinket. I think it's your turn."

I sat down, shrinking into the couch cushions. "But . . ." I stammered. I'd been doing pretty good so far. I didn't want to take on any consequences that could be avoided. "It's Jathon's quest. Shouldn't he make the wish?"

"Really?" Vale cut in. "You're so busy bragging about how you abandoned your quest to help us free Tina, but you're not doing your part. If you are truly as committed as you claim to be, you'll give Jathon a break and make the wish."

Well, she had me backed into a corner now. I really did care about Tina. She'd paid some kind of consequence for me to be reunited with Ridge's jar. It was the least I could do to make a wish to help us find the dagger that could save her.

I sighed. "Fine." Then turning to Ridge: "I wish that the dormant trinket dagger capable of cutting a tether would wash up . . ." I hesitated, not sure where. Then I remembered a postcard that my foster parents had on their fridge. "At Myrtle Beach." I didn't actually know where that was, but the postcard made it look like a nice sandy place. "But not until we get there."

"If you want the trinket dagger to wash up on Myrtle Beach," said Ridge as my hourglass watch popped open, "then whenever you shout, smoke will come out your ears."

"Will I catch on fire?" I asked.

"It's just smoke, not fire."

"How do you have smoke without fire?"

Ridge shrugged. "You'll have to take that up with the Universe?"

"How long will it last?"

"A year."

"What if I set off a smoke alarm?"

"Just don't shout indoors," Ridge said. "That's not polite, anyway."

"Okay," I said. This was for Tina. "Bazang."

Thackary clapped his hands, moving toward the lodge exit. "We best set sail fer South Carolina."

Well, at least Myrtle Beach was in the United States. Nobody seemed too upset about the location I had picked for the dagger to wash up.

"That's all the way across the country," Ms. Gomez said. "And we need to get there quickly." Everyone turned to Jathon and me.

I held up my hands in defense. "Not it."

Jathon sighed. "I guess I'll take this one." He scratched his head in thought for a moment. "I wish that everyone in this room would teleport to Myrtle Beach, South Carolina."

I glanced down at his wristwatch, but I was surprised to see that the hourglass didn't appear.

"Umm . . ." Vale said. "Sorry, but apparently you can't wish that."

"What do you mean?" he asked. "I didn't think there were limits to wishing."

"There are really only two," Vale said. "No wishing away old consequences. And no wishing away other people's wishes."

"But Jathon's wish was fine," I said.

Vale shook her head. "Obviously not."

I turned to Ridge. "I wish to know what is stopping Jathon's wish from coming true."

"If you want to know that," said Ridge, "then whenever someone laughs, you will hiccup."

"How long will that last?"

"Until the end of the week."

Well, that was only two more days, anyway. "Bazang."

"Interesting . . ." I mused as the information flooded my brain. "Chasm made a wish against us. He must know we're going to try to stop him eventually, and his wish was meant to slow us down."

"What was it?" Jathon asked.

"He wished that current Wishmakers wouldn't be able to wish for any magical means of transportation," I explained.

"How are we supposed to get anywhere?" Jathon cried.

"Sounds like we can still take cars, trains, buses, bicycles, airplanes, jets, subways, boats, horses . . ." Ridge said. "Basically any man-made, nonmagical methods of transportation."

"But nothing fast!" I said.

"Aeroplanes be swift enough," said Thackary. "Jathon, me boy, will wish for us to get tickets to Myrtle Beach. We can be there by dawn."

"Ugh," muttered Jathon. "I guess that's our best option." He turned to Vale. "I wish we all had plane tickets to Myrtle Beach."

"If you want tickets," said Vale, "then every time someone says your name, you have to laugh. For the rest of the week."

Oh, great. That meant hiccups for me.

Jathon nodded. "All right. Bazang."

Instantly, airline tickets appeared in everyone's hands. I glanced down, a little disappointed to see that mine wasn't first-class.

"Flight leaves in an hour," said Vale.

"Yar, we'll have to do a bit of speeding on the roads and a bit of wishing to get through security lines," Thackary said with a smile, as though the idea of Jathon taking extra consequences pleased him.

"Hurry out to the car," said Ms. Gomez. "I need just a minute to talk to Ace."

"Come along, Jathon, me boy," said Thackary.

At the sound of his name, Jathon laughed. I hiccuped. And then they were gone. I turned nervously to Ms. Gomez, feeling like I'd been sent to the principal's office.

"I want to talk to you about your quest," she began.

I shook my head. "We've been over this. There's nothing you can say to convince me that my quest is worthwhile."

"I made a phone call while you were gone," said Ms. Gomez. "I learned something very interesting about Samuel Sylvester Stansworth."

"What?" I said flatly. "He likes his peanut butter creamy?"

"He was a Wishmaker," Ms. Gomez said. "But Samuel Sylvester Stansworth disappeared three years ago, on the morning of July twenty-first."

I felt my body start to tingle with shock. Three years ago . . . That was exactly when I showed up in a hospital, the ace of hearts card stuffed in my pocket.

Mint chocolate chip!

Was *I* Samuel Sylvester Stansworth?!

CHAPTER 10

"Tell me more." I moved closer to Ms. Gomez. "Where is he from? Does he have a family?"

Tina's mom waved a hand at me. "I thought you weren't interested in your quest." She was turning my words against me.

"Well, I am now!" I shouted. Smoke suddenly came curling out of my ears, reminding me to calm down. "What else did you learn?"

"Nothing else," she said. "But the person I called can give you more answers."

"Who?" There was a giddiness inside me.

"He is called the Genieologist," Ms. Gomez said. "He works at the Library of Wight and Wong."

"The Library of Right and Wrong?" Ridge said.

"Wight and Wong," she corrected. "My contact's name is Eli Wong. After you went into the vault, I called him to ask if he'd ever heard of Samuel Sylvester Stansworth. He only told me a little, but he'll share more information with you because it has to do with your quest."

"How does this Wong guy know so much?" Ridge asked.

"It's his responsibility," said Ms. Gomez. "Like the Trinketer, the Genieologist is another position that has been passed down for generations. His job is to keep a record of all the Wishmakers and their genies. He also catalogs each quest, wishes made, consequences accepted, and whether the Wishmaker succeeded or failed. Once you get to Mr. Wong, you'll need to tell him this password." She paused to make sure we were listening. "It's a nice day to shave a chipmunk."

"Technically, wouldn't that be a passphrase?" Ridge said. "It's more than one word."

"Fine," she said. "It's a passphrase."

"Where is this library?" I asked.

"New York City," she replied.

I grabbed Ridge's arm. "Let's go!"

"What about Myrtle Beach?" he asked. "The dagger?"

"Oh, come on! All this time you've been telling me not to give up on my quest," I said. "Now that I actually want to do it, you're doubting me?"

I decided not to say anything about my suspicions yet—that I might be the Stansworth kid we were supposed to be looking for. Something inside me was afraid that speaking it out loud would somehow make my hopes fall apart, leaving me extra-disappointed. I needed more information.

"We'll go to the Library of Wight and Wong," I continued, "learn more about Samuel Sylvester Stansworth, and then meet up with everybody in South Carolina."

"I've got something that will help you," Ms. Gomez said. "Follow me."

Ridge and I followed Ms. Gomez like ducklings over to a table. She picked up an old book and handed it to me.

I read the title. "*One Thousand and One Nights.*"

"That's a long book," Ridge said. "What do you think it's about?"

I glanced at the title again. "It's probably about a thousand and one nights."

"Yeah, but do you think they win the war?" Ridge asked.

"What war?"

"I dunno." He shrugged. "Whatever war the knights are fighting."

"Not those kind of knights," I said, showing him the book title. "Nights. Like when the sun goes down."

"Well, that doesn't sound nearly as cool."

"Technically, it sounds exactly the same," I said. "That's probably why you were confused."

"It's a collection of folktales from the Middle East," Ms. Gomez cut in. "Some call it *Arabian Nights*. Stories about Sinbad, Aladdin, genies . . ."

"Oh, yeah!" I said. "I've heard those stories. Three wishes, magic lamp . . ."

Ridge chuckled. "They were way off."

"Anyway," said Ms. Gomez, "it doesn't matter what the book is about. It's a trinket."

I suddenly froze, holding the book carefully as though it might explode at any second.

"What does it do?" Ridge asked.

"It will transport you to the Library of Wight and Wong."

"Won't Chasm's wish stop us from using it?" I asked.

Ms. Gomez shook her head. "His wish only stopped you from wishing for magical transportation. This trinket already existed."

She reached out and opened the book's front cover. Glued inside was a little envelope with an open top. An index card was stuffed snuggly into the envelope, yellowed top poking out about an inch.

"What is this? Some kind of bookmark?" I reached up to pull out the little card, but Ms. Gomez grabbed my hand in a viselike grip.

"That is a checkout card," she said.

"Who glued it into the book?" I asked.

She looked at me like I was ignorant. "The librarian. You use it to check out. Every library book has one."

"Not in the libraries I've been to," I answered. "We just check out with a little scanner on the computer."

"How do you think people used to check out books?" Ms. Gomez asked. "They used that little card to write down your name. The librarian would stamp the due date and slip the checkout card into the envelope."

"Sounds like a lot of work when they could've just used a computer," said Ridge.

"Lemon custard," Ms. Gomez muttered, taking a deep, steadying breath. "This is a very useful trinket. When you remove the checkout card, you will be transported to the Library of Wight and Wong. You can give the card to Mr. Wong and he'll stamp it for you. Slide the card into the envelope again, and you'll be transported back to the Trinketer. Me."

This was going to save us a lot of time! "Where did you get this?" I asked.

"It was made by the Trinketer, three generations back," Ms. Gomez said. "From time to time, it's helpful to consult with the Genieologist's records. He has a lot of information on quests, which means he knows about trinkets that may be lost or dormant. I keep the book now, but I haven't seen Mr. Wong in years."

I studied the book in my hands. "What's the consequence for using this?"

"Don't worry about it," she answered.

"No, seriously," I said. "If it's going to be horrible for you, then we can find another way."

"Anytime you remove or replace the checkout card," said Ms. Gomez, "I will be stuck talking like a barnyard animal for an hour."

"Which animal?" asked Ridge.

"It changes each time," she said. "It's really not so bad. Just very inconvenient."

I nodded, my attention turning back to the book as I prepared to use the trinket.

"One more thing," said Ms. Gomez. "Mr. Wong is very old, and he's got a few lingering consequences of his own. Whatever you do, don't say the word *meanwhile* around him."

"Meanwhile?" I said.

"Don't say it," she warned. "And don't lose the book or the checkout card, or you'll have to find another way to meet up with us." Ms. Gomez pointed at Ridge. "The book will only teleport the person holding it. So you'll get a nasty tether snap if Ridge isn't in his jar for transport."

Ridge did a little shiver and started some preemptive scratching. I pulled the peanut butter jar from the backpack beside the couch and gave the command. "Ridge, get into the jar."

He vanished, a wisp of smoke trailing into the peanut butter container. I stowed Ridge in the water bottle pocket and shouldered the backpack.

"Good luck," Ms. Gomez said. "I hope you find the answers you're looking for."

"We'll see you at the beach." I grasped the tip of the checkout card and pulled it out of the little envelope.

I suddenly felt very flat and two-dimensional. Some unseen force folded me up like a piece of paper and I seemed to drop into the very book I was holding. I heard Ms. Gomez call out, but her voice sounded like a distant "baaaaaa!"

Then it was dark. The only sound was the whirring of pages, like someone was thumbing through a giant book, of which I was a part. Then it was evening and I unfolded, standing in the middle of a busy sidewalk, holding the book in one hand and the checkout card in the other.

Someone bumped into me. A chorus of cars honked.

This was New York City!

Tall buildings loomed overhead in the most dramatic contrast from the mountains I'd just left behind. There was a dark wooden door in front of me, with a sign that said *Open*. I glanced up at the little umbrella awning to make sure I was in the right place. The name was printed in bright lettering.

The Library of Wight and Wong.

It didn't look like much, nestled between a pizzeria and a nail salon. The flat brick wall extending above the library displayed rows of apartment windows.

I reached back and grabbed the peanut butter container. "Ridge, get out of the jar." I wasn't worried about all the people passing by. The Universe would shield them from the genie's magical appearance.

A businessman bumped into Ridge as he materialized in a cloud of smoke. "Watch it, kid!" He skirted around us, muttering. Wordlessly, I moved to the door, pushing it open with a little chime of a bell.

It was dim inside the library, and my eyes took a moment to adjust. When they did, I realized that the place looked more cluttered and cramped than a regular library. The space wasn't very big, and bookshelves lined the walls and divided the room like a maze. From this angle, I didn't see anyone browsing the shelves.

The only person in the library was an old man sitting at the front desk. He must have been ninety, with pure white hair, and a thick pair of glasses resting on his nose. A chain dangled from the horned rims, drooping to form a loop behind his wrinkly neck. His hands looked gnarled with arthritis as he turned the page of a paperback book.

"Excuse me?" I said. He didn't seem to hear me, so I leaned forward. "It's a nice day to save a hamster."

"Um, Ace," Ridge said. "I think it was 'shave a chipmunk.'"

"Oh, yeah," I said. "I thought that sounded wrong." Clearing my throat, I began again. "It's a nice day to shave a chipmunk."

The old man slowly looked up from his book. "And a nice night to bathe a squirrel." He reached across the desk to a dark lamp with a green glass shade. He grabbed the hanging chain and gave it a tug. As the light bulb turned on, all the books in the library suddenly changed. It was as if the regular novels and resource books suddenly fell out of sight, and a collection of new books popped up in their place, filling the shelves.

"Welcome to the Library of Wight and Wong, young Wishmaker," the man said.

"And you're Mr. Wong?" I verified. "The Genieologist?"

"Of course," he said. "Who else would I be?"

"Well," said Ridge. "You could be Wight."

"I'm always right," he answered.

"I thought you were Wong," Ridge said.

"I'm never wrong." A slow smile broke across his face. "Ha! That joke never gets old!" He began to laugh, and I hiccuped. But his laugh quickly turned into a cough that lasted a full three minutes. Just when I thought the old man might croak, he seemed to recover.

"Ruth Wight was the Genieologist before me," said Mr. Wong. "I was the young Wishmaker who helped her found this library to store our records."

"Let's hope the next Genieologist goes digital," I muttered, glancing around the dusty shelves.

"Ace," said Mr. Wong. His eyes, hugely magnified behind those glasses, studied Ridge and me.

"Umm . . . you know me?" I said.

"The Trinketer told me you were coming." His speech was slow and slightly accented. "Once you gave me the password, I knew it was you."

"Passphrase," Ridge muttered under his breath.

Mr. Wong slowly rose to his feet and hobbled across the library. He opened the front door and flipped the sign from Open to Closed. Then it took him about five minutes to shuffle back to his desk and lower himself into his seat.

"There," Mr. Wong said. "Now we can talk privately without anyone barging in."

"Do you get a lot of visitors?" Ridge asked.

"Oh, no," said Mr. Wong. "No one cares about libraries anymore. Something called the *internets* have ruined me. Have you heard of them?"

"The internet?" I chuckled. "I've heard about it."

"Still, I'm glad to see that you have a book." Mr. Wong pointed at the heavy volume I was holding.

I dropped it on his desk and handed over the checkout card. "The Trinketer gave this to us," I said. "She said you could stamp it so we can get back."

The Genieologist's magnified eyes studied the card through those thick glasses. Then his bent fingers scooped up a pen and he scribbled my name onto a blank space. It was only three letters, but it took Mr. Wong a long time. After that, he rummaged in a desk drawer for a good five minutes, finally producing a pad of ink and a strange-looking stamp.

The stamp had a bunch of numbers and some little letters, abbreviating the names of the months. Mr. Wong fiddled with it, rotating the right combination into place until today's date was the only one showing.

"I've met sloths faster than this guy," Ridge whispered.

"You've met sloths?" I asked. "When?"

"It's just an expression," he replied. "I haven't actually met any in person."

Mr. Wong removed the cover of the ink pad and dabbed the date stamp onto the dark surface. Then, ever so carefully, he pressed the stamp on a blank space beside my name, rocking it gently back and forth.

"*One Thousand and One Nights*," he said. "Have you boys read this one?"

"We didn't really have time," I said. "We only got it like a half hour ago."

"It's full of stories," Mr. Wong said.

"Aren't most books?" asked Ridge.

"She told stories for more than a thousand nights," said Mr. Wong.

"Who?" I asked.

"Scheherazade."

"Bless you," Ridge said.

"That wasn't a sneeze," said Mr. Wong. "That was the name of the young girl who told these stories to the king of ancient Arabia. Like Scheherazade, it is my responsibility as the Genieologist to keep and tell stories. Stories of quests, and genies, and Wishmakers. True stories that the common person would take as fiction."

Mr. Wong handed me the stamped checkout card and I slipped it into my pocket.

"Now, you have come to the Library of Wight and Wong seeking answers for your quest," said Mr. Wong.

I nodded excitedly. "What can you tell me about Samuel Sylvester Stansworth?"

"I will tell you his story," said the old Genieologist. "I will tell you about his quest, and his fate."

"Can you tell me about his family?"

"I'm sure I've got that information on file here." Mr. Wong gestured at the books behind him.

My heart was hammering. Did this guy really know as much as he claimed?

"Pull up a chair," said Mr. Wong. "It's story time."

CHAPTER 11

Ridge and I had just hauled a couple of heavy chairs over to the desk when Mr. Wong began the long process of standing up. "Follow me," he said.

"But I thought you just told us to pull up some chairs," I said.

"I only said that for dramatic effect," he said, leading Ridge and me into the cluttered library. "I have to look up the information on Samuel Sylvester Stansworth. My memory isn't what it used to be."

Mr. Wong ran his fingertips along the outward-facing spines of the books. "This is the special collection," he said. "My trinket lamp replaces all the common novels with these books. As the Genieologist, it's my duty to write down everything I can about each young Wishmaker."

"What's the purpose of keeping a record?" Ridge asked.

"What's the purpose of history?" he shouted. "The Universe likes things organized. If there is ever a question about wishes made, or consequences accepted, the Universe can send a young Wishmaker to me for answers." He moved to another bookshelf, squinting through his thick glasses. "Much like what you're doing here today."

"So, the Universe tells you about every Wishmaker?" I asked.

"The knowledge comes into my mind as each quest unfolds," he answered. "I then have three days to write it down before it is lost from my memory."

"So, you know that Ace just took a consequence that makes smoke come out his ears?" Ridge asked.

Mr. Wong nodded. "Yes. He accepted that consequence in order to have the trinket dagger wash up on the beach."

"Oh, he's good," Ridge said to me.

"Does that mean you know what Chasm is up to?" I asked. Maybe Mr. Wong could give us a glimpse into what our enemy was planning. Maybe he could tell me how Tina was faring.

"I'm sorry," said Mr. Wong, "but I cannot sense the actions of the Wishbreaker."

"Wishbreaker?" I'd never heard that term before.

"The one you call Chasm," said Mr. Wong. "The Universe named him the Wishbreaker because he can take control of the human he is tethered to. I know that he has stolen Tina's voice, and with it, her ability to make her own wishes. But that information was only made known to me because it was part of your last quest."

"We're going to save Tina," I said.

"I believe that is Jathon Anderthon's quest," said Mr. Wong. "The Universe has trusted him to save the world again. It is very unusual to see a Double Wishmaker."

"I'm a Double Wishmaker, too." This was another new term, but I had a good idea of what it meant.

"Are you really, though?" asked Mr. Wong. "With Tina's trinket, you found a way to forcefully get your genie back. At great personal sacrifice for the girl."

"What was her consequence?" I had wondered before, with no way to find out.

"Tina wished for that trinket necklace when she was with the genie named Vale," answered Mr. Wong, still perusing the books. "When the jewelry snapped, a great chain of iron would suddenly tighten around her neck."

"Yikes!" Ridge cried. "That could kill her."

Mr. Wong shook his head. "If she had died, the Wishbreaker would have returned to his jar. I sense his presence in the world, so Tina must have survived the consequence."

I took a deep breath, suddenly feeling really guilty for

breaking the necklace and bringing that kind of pain to Tina.

"Likely, the Wishbreaker saved her life," continued Mr. Wong. "He is said to be very strong. He probably stopped the chain from strangling her. The Wishbreaker needs the girl alive in order to stay free."

Mr. Wong finally pulled a book from the shelf. "Oops. Wrong one." He put it back and kept scanning.

"It's a hard book to find?" I guessed.

"Well, the trinket desk lamp has a way of shelving the books in a random order every time I access the special collections," answered Mr. Wong. "I expect it'll take me several hours to find what I'm looking for."

"Several hours?" I cried, a bit of smoke venting out my ears. "I can't wait that long."

Ridge looked at me. "Yesterday you didn't even want to think about your quest."

"Something changed," I said.

"Like what?"

Should I tell him? Ridge knew how badly I wanted answers about my past. As Mr. Wong pulled out another book, I leaned closer to Ridge and lowered my voice to a whisper. "I think I might be Samuel Sylvester Stansworth."

"What?"

"It's just a theory," I said. But I was growing more sure of it with every minute. "That's why we're here." I glanced at Mr. Wong. "But the old guy's taking forever. We've got to speed up this process." I took a deep breath. "I wish Mr. Wong would find the book he's looking for in the next minute."

"If you want him to find the book," Ridge said, "then every time you reach into your pocket, a rat will crawl out of it."

I shuddered. I knew people that kept rats as pets, but they always creeped me out. Now I'd have to deal with furry rodents crawling out of my clothes. . . .

"Seems kind of steep, just to have Mr. Wong find a book," I tried.

"A book about Samuel Sylvester Stansworth," replied Ridge.

"How long will I have rats in my pants?"

"Only for a month."

"Okay," I said. "I guess I just won't reach into my pocket." It was that or wait painstaking hours while Mr. Wong searched for the book. "Bazang."

"Ah." Finally, Mr. Wong pulled a book from the shelf. "Here we are, at last."

The old man opened the front cover and scanned over the volume as he turned pages. I tried to peek over his shoulder, but the handwriting in the book was really squiggly and hard to read.

"Oh, yes," Mr. Wong said after a few painful minutes. "I remember this story. . . ."

My story. I was about to get the answers I'd been craving for years!

"Three years ago," Mr. Wong began, "on July fourteenth, a boy named Samuel Sylvester Stansworth opened a jar of salsa."

I liked salsa.

"Was it spicy or mild?" Ridge asked.

I reached over and whacked him on the arm. "Don't distract him!"

"The salsa, as you might have guessed, was a genie jar," said Mr. Wong. "Upon opening it, Samuel Sylvester Stansworth became a Wishmaker to a genie named Dune."

"Because his jar was first opened on a sand dune?" Ridge guessed. That was the usual way for genies to get their names.

"Yes," said Mr. Wong. "Dune was an experienced genie and he quickly explained the rules of the Universe. He gave Samuel a quest."

"What was it?" I asked. Maybe I was a Triple Wishmaker! Had I really been a Wishmaker before opening Ridge's jar? I was desperate to know how I'd worked with this Dune genie on my first forgotten quest.

"Samuel needed to find a specific saltshaker and empty it into the Grand Canyon," said Mr. Wong.

"Well, that's random," I said.

"More random than poking a statue of Roosevelt in the eye?" Ridge reminded me.

"The Universe has a reason for everything," Mr. Wong explained.

"What was the reason for emptying the saltshaker?" I asked.

The old man shrugged. "The shaker was a trinket, but we'll never truly know what purpose it would have served since Samuel failed his quest."

"What?" Maybe I was a better Wishmaker now than I'd been with Dune. "What was the consequence?"

"When Samuel failed," said Mr. Wong, "every silver car that was parked on the street at the end of his quest was swallowed up by the asphalt."

"Every silver car in the world?" I asked.

Mr. Wong shook his head. "In the United States."

"What if there were people inside?" Ridge asked.

"The quest only threatened vehicles," said Mr. Wong. "The Universe spit anyone inside the car onto the sidewalk."

"But I don't remember hearing anything about silver cars getting swallowed up by the streets," I said. Not that I'd ever spent much time watching the news.

"It happened," said Mr. Wong. "On the morning of July twenty-first, three years ago."

Well, that would explain why I didn't remember it. If Mr. Wong had his dates right, then I would have still been asleep in the hospital. I wasn't due to wake up for another three days.

"The media reported a massive string of automobile thefts," Mr. Wong said. "The Universe's shield stopped anyone from being too suspicious about the fact that all the cars were silver."

"Why did Samuel fail his quest?" I finally asked.

"Sometimes Wishmakers fail. Let me see. . . ." Mr. Wong turned the page of his book and scanned the text. "Oh, yes. Here we are."

I leaned forward, hands feeling suddenly sweaty. "Go on," I urged.

"The saltshaker that Samuel was trying to find belonged to a dangerous ex-Wishmaker who kept an unauthorized collection of active trinkets," Mr. Wong said. "Samuel and Dune discovered the ex-Wishmaker's hideout—a little diner on the interstate in western Iowa. Time was running out and Samuel felt overwhelmed with consequences."

"I know the feeling." Toward the end of my last quest I had wanted to give up more than once.

"Samuel and his genie made it into the diner, but the ex-Wishmaker had a number of trinket defenses safeguarding the building," Mr. Wong continued. "The two boys ended up trapped in the diner restroom, Samuel forced into making several wishes in a very short space of time, piling more consequences onto his already burdened shoulders. The restroom door was blockaded to buy them time, but it was only a matter of minutes before the angry gorilla chefs broke through with their fiery spatulas."

"Whoa," I said. "How did they get there?"

"Summoned by a trinket," said Mr. Wong. "To defend the ex-Wishmaker's hideout."

"Sounds like a bad situation," Ridge said.

"Indeed," the Genieologist answered. "And with only minutes left before his genie disappeared, Samuel tried to make a direct wish for his quest to be completed, but he couldn't bear the consequence. He made a trinket that he thought would help, but it turned out to be useless. So, Samuel Sylvester Stansworth gave up."

"Just like that?" I cried. "He let the evil spatula-wielding gorilla chefs get him?"

"Not quite," said Mr. Wong. "He made one more wish. A wish for no more wishes. No more choices. No more responsibility. And that was the end of Samuel Sylvester Stansworth."

Ridge and I sat in stunned silence, knowing exactly what that meant. I had made that very wish on my last quest with Ridge. I had been overwhelmed with consequences, betrayed by Tina, and I had been so tired of it all. I hadn't accepted, of course. The consequence was . . . unknown.

"He accepted the Unknown Consequence," said Mr. Wong. "And he was never heard from again."

"What is that consequence?" I asked. "What does it do?"

"I do not know," Mr. Wong said. "For me, Samuel's story ended when he said *bazang*. I know nothing more."

Ridge shuddered. "I'm glad *I* don't have consequences."

"You shouldn't be so happy about it," the Genieologist said. "Having consequences means having choices. And that is what makes us human."

"So, that's it?" I shouted, smoke shooting out my ears as I felt the disappointment settle in. "That's all you can tell me?"

"I think you know enough for your quest," said Mr. Wong. "I can tell by the look on your face that you believe that *you* are Samuel Sylvester Stansworth."

Well, it made sense! Samuel's quest fit with the timeline of my memory loss. The Unknown Consequence must have done something to me!

I stared at Mr. Wong, finally getting the nerve to ask it out loud. "Am I Samuel Sylvester Stansworth?"

"I do not know," he answered. "I only know his story. I never actually met the boy. But if you are correct, perhaps now is the time to make yourself a peanut butter sandwich and complete your quest."

"If I finish my quest early," I said to Ridge, "what happens to you?"

"Nothing," he stated. "You're stuck with me until the week ends, no matter what."

"So, I could test my theory by eating a sandwich," I went on. "If it completes my quest, then I'll know that I really am Samuel Stansworth."

Ridge made a glum face. "There's no way to know for sure until the end of our time together."

"That's cruel," I said.

He shrugged. "Just the Universe's way of keeping you guessing until the end."

"I don't care about my quest," I said to Mr. Wong. "I came here to find out if I am really Samuel. If you don't know, then I'll have to find someone who does. You said you could help me find Samuel's family?"

"Yes," he replied. "Written in these pages will be the names and address of the Stansworth family. Or at least their last known location. This information will be three years old, since I would have written it when Samuel first opened the jar of salsa and released Dune."

Mr. Wong flipped a couple of pages and peered down through his thick glasses. His fingers scrolled over the hand-written text at the same speed that a snail moves across the sidewalk.

Ridge and I looked on with growing impatience as he turned to the next page and began the same slow reading.

"Maybe I should make another wish to speed him up," I said to Ridge.

"Or at least wish for some dinner," replied the genie. "I mean, while we're just standing around, we might as well have something to eat."

Mr. Wong suddenly turned to stone.

Seriously, *stone*! The transformation started at his feet and spread through his entire body in the blink of an eye. His clothes, his hair, even the book in his hand now looked to be chiseled from smooth marble.

"What the heck?" I jumped back in shock, smoke venting through my ears.

Ridge stepped forward and knocked on Mr. Wong's head. "Seems like solid rock!"

"I don't get it," I muttered.

"Is he, you know . . . dead?"

"I hope not." I carefully grabbed the book and tried to pry it away from him. Yeah, right. That thing was fused tightly to his stone hands, as though they had been carved out of the same piece of marble.

"Did we do something wrong?" Ridge asked. "The only thing Ms. Gomez told us not to do was say . . ." He trailed off. "You remember."

"*Meanwhile*," I said, the truth of what had happened dawning on me.

"Shhh!" Ridge covered Mr. Wong's stone ears.

"You already said it," I explained. "You said *meanwhile*."

"No, *you* did," said Ridge. "Twice!"

"Before that," I answered. "What was the last thing you said before he turned into stone?"

"I wanted you to wish for something to eat," said Ridge.

"'I *mean, while* we're just standing around.'" I quoted him directly.

"Ohhhhhhhh," Ridge said sheepishly. "I don't think that should count."

"Well, I'm guessing it did, since Mr. Wong is now a statue." I tried to turn a stone page, but there was no chance. "Maybe I can make a wish to turn him back."

Ridge shook his head. "Not if this is one of his old consequences. You can't wish to undo a consequence."

I knew that. But what else were we supposed to do? And I thought he moved slowly when he *wasn't* made of rock! "How long is he going to be like this?"

"No idea."

Behind us, I heard the library's front door open.

"Oh, of course," I said. "Now that Mr. Wong's a statue, his library finally gets a visitor."

I peered around the corner of the bookshelf to see who had arrived. My heart stopped.

It was Tina.

And filling the doorway behind her was the hulking form of Chasm.

CHAPTER 12

Tina looked terrible. I know that's not something you're supposed to say about your friend, but it was true. In fact, she was so weighed down with consequences that my eyes had a hard time believing it was her.

Tina's mouth was agape, and her black hair was soaking wet. One eye was covered with a green Post-it note, and there was an old banana peel draped over one shoulder. Her left arm was tucked behind her back, and her right hand was covered with a dirty sock.

She wore a belt that looked to be dripping with sticky honey, and a few bees were buzzing around her. Tina had a small plant tucked in one pocket and Chasm's crimson jar protruding from the other. Her left foot had been replaced with a roller skate, which caused her to stand a bit lopsided.

Chasm, too, looked a little different from the last time I'd seen him. Instead of a shirtless chest webbed with tattoos, he wore a classy button-down linen and a gingham bow tie. Suspenders looped over his massive shoulders, fastening to a pair of skinny jeans with rolled ankle cuffs. He reached up and perched a stylish fedora on his bald head.

I ducked behind the bookshelf, covering Ridge's mouth as I pulled him into a crouch. At the library entrance, I heard Chasm draw in a long sniff.

"Oh, don't you just love the smell of old books? Dusty, woody, with subtle notes of printers' ink." He clapped his hands. "Mmmm! Makes my nose hairs stand up and salute the sad little librarian who stocks these shelves."

Beside me, I saw Ridge's expression change as he recognized the frighteningly chipper voice of the evil genie.

The Wishbreaker.

"What do you say, Teeny?" said Chasm. "Should we make a few painful wishes until we get what we want? Or should your old pal Ace just step out from behind that bookshelf so we can have a little chat?"

At the mention of my name, I, too, turned into a statue. At least that's how I felt. My outsides were as motionless as stone, while it felt like someone was popping popcorn in my stomach.

"We're going to die," Ridge mumbled. "We're so dead right now."

"Alrighty!" said Chasm. "I guess we'll start wishing! Sorry, Teeny. Friends can really let you down sometimes."

I stepped out from behind the bookshelf. It was an impulsive decision, but I wasn't going to let Chasm start manipulating Tina into careless wishes. She obviously had enough horrible consequences.

"Acey-poo!" Chasm's face showed mock surprise. "So good to see you again, bud. For reals."

Ridge stumbled out next to me, visibly trembling at the confrontation. "This would be a good time to be a polar bear," he whispered. But I held up my hand. Chasm had called me out for a conversation. Letting Ridge attack would only spur the evil genie into striking back.

Tina was staring at me with her one open eye, looking helpless and desperate. "What do you want, Chasm?" I shouted, trying to sound brave as smoke came out my ears.

"Oh, you're taking my order?" He smiled. "I'll have a double cheeseburger, extra ketchup, hold the pickle. A large order of fries and a soda. Do you have cookies? I'll take a cookie."

"We don't have cookies!" It was kind of a strange thing to shout at the bad guy. But he was kind of a strange bad guy.

"I know what you're up to," said Chasm. "A little tip that I got from the Universe."

"The Universe told you our plans?" I cried.

142

"Well, I mean, the girl and I had to wish for it," Chasm said. "I actually knew about your plans long before you did," answered Chasm.

"What?" I said. "How?"

"Well, right after Teeny and I left that cozy little cave in Texas, I said to myself, 'Self, what if those bratty little Wish-makers come looking for you? What if they somehow get new genies and try to spoil your fun?' And myself said, 'But Kaz, how would they do it?' Of course, I didn't know the answer to that, so Teeny had to make a fancy wish so I could figure it out. As it turns out, some of your plans could be kind of helpful to me, so I've been making a few preparations of my own."

"Helpful?" I said. The trinkets were designed to take Chasm down. What good would they be to him?

The big man turned to Tina. "Teeny, honey. I've got a bit of explaining to do. Can you lay down a beat for this next part?"

Tina reached out with her sock hand to stabilize herself against the checkout desk. Then she began stomping her non-skate foot to a steady pulse. Surprisingly, the sound came out with all the booming resonance of a drum, with faster rhythms making an interesting beat.

Chasm grinned. "Special beatbox shoe," he said. "We wished for it a few days ago. I was just so sick of performing without backup, you know?"

Ridge and I looked at each other. It was official. Chasm was insane.

And then he started to rap.

"I'm not a friend of the Universe,
But sometimes I turn there for better or worse.
The Teeny and I made a couple of wishes,
We learned of some plans that sound awful suspicious.
Yeah! I know that you're looking for trinkets!
Yeah! I think that you better rethink it!
But kid, I've discovered a great silver lining,
The thing that you got from the vault is aligning
With all of my plans for world domination.
Your first little trinket will lay the foundation.
Wait till you see what I do with that twine.
I'll conquer the world! Don't worry. It's fine.
I admit that the second one gives me concern,
A trinket with power to make me return
Into the jar where I can't hurt a fly,
Where I can't conquer cities from here to Shanghai.
No! You never will make it that far.
No! You won't get me back in the jar.
I'll stop you from finding the trinket you're seekin',
The world will be mine by the end of the week, and

The people will bow before Kaz the almighty,
And yes, I will dance on your graves in my nightie.
Uh! Yeah! Chasm's on fire!
Uh! Yeah! I'm here to inspire!
Uh! Yeah! I'll never retire!
Y'all take a knee, it's okay to admire!"

I didn't know if I should applaud or run. Tina's beatbox shoe fizzled out as she realized that the Wishbreaker genie had finished his rap.

Chasm rubbed his big hands together. "Honest feedback, guys," he said. "Too forced? I just want to make sure I'm getting my point across."

"Which point?" I asked. "The one about you taking over the world? Or the one about you taking over the world?"

He pointed at me with finger guns. "The one about me taking over the world."

"Not going to happen!" I shouted through a cloud of smoke. "We're going to find that second trinket and stop you."

"You're probably too late already," added Ridge. "The others will find the dagger—"

"Oh, so it's a dagger?" Chasm cut in. "The Universe didn't specify about the trinket that would take me down. I found that odd, since it clearly mentioned the spool of string. While we're on the topic . . ." He held out his hand and beckoned. "Give it up, Ace-face."

Chasm thought I had the string! That was why he'd come to the library. He wanted that trinket for some reason. Apparently, the Universe had told him that the spool of string would further his plans for world domination.

"You're not getting the string!" I clenched both fists at my sides. If I could stall him for a while, it might give Jathon and the others time to find the dagger before Chasm fulfilled his vow to stop them.

"Why do you insist on doing this the hard way?" Chasm looked at Tina. "Teeny, you wish that Ace would give us the spool of string trinket that he took from the vault."

So direct! A wish like that was bound to have a terrible consequence. But Chasm didn't care since Tina would be the one who had to pay for it.

It didn't matter that I currently didn't have the string. If Chasm wished for it, and Tina received the consequence, then the Universe would make it happen, even if I had to travel back to Jathon, steal the string, and deliver it to the evil genie.

Chasm's hourglass watch popped up, red sands spilling from the top chamber. "If you want Ace to give us the spool of string," said Chasm, "then a dozen snakes will constantly be slithering over your body. Are they venomous? No. Will they bite you? Sometimes. How long will it last? Forever."

"Whoa! Whoa! Wait!" I shouted, holding out my hands as smoke came out my ears. "You don't have to make that wish. I'll cooperate." I couldn't let Chasm do that to Tina. It was my best option to tell Chasm the truth and try to stop him later.

"I don't have the string," I confessed.

"Who does?" asked the big genie, holding up his wrist threateningly, so I could see how much sand was in his hourglass.

"Jathon Anderthon," I answered.

"Ah, the boy that helped Teeny open my jar." Chasm grinned. "I think I like him. Where is he?"

"I don't know." Technically, it wasn't a lie. Chances were good that Jathon and the others were on an airplane by now, traveling from Utah to South Carolina. They might be anywhere across the United States.

"If you don't know where they are, how did you plan to meet up with them again?" asked Chasm. I tried to resist, but he gestured to his hourglass again, the sands almost gone. "Don't make me say the magic word!"

My eyes flicked to the checkout desk. Ridge swallowed hard as Chasm followed my gaze to the trinket. "The book!" I blurted.

Chasm watched the last grains of sand fall through the

hourglass. "Phew!" he gasped as it folded away. "I'm so glad you decided to talk. Did you really think I'd let Teeny take that consequence?"

"You were bluffing?" Ridge cried.

"The girl already has a hard time keeping up without snakes tripping her," he said. "Soon, I'll be able to wish and not care about my weak little Wishmaker. But for now, I need her in working order, or I won't get anything done. Teeny's mortality is really the only thing slowing me down."

Chasm crossed to the checkout desk and scooped up the heavy book. "*One Thousand and One Nights*," he read. "Feels like a trinket." He opened the front cover and took a big sniff. "Smells like a trinket. Let me take a stab at this one—the book has some kind of magical feature that will transport you back to Jathon." He must have known he was right from Ridge's moan and the drained expression on my face. "Boom, baby! Am I good or am I good?"

"Actually," whispered Ridge, "you're bad. Very, very bad."

"Clever little work-around, finding an old trinket like this," said Chasm. "It must be the pits not being able to wish for magical travel." He thumbed through the book as if trying to figure out how to use it. "I'm not forbidden, like you, but the Universe doesn't seem to give me what I want. I wished to transport the string to me. I wished to transport myself to the string. Had to turn down both options since the consequence would have left Teeny completely useless to me. I was ecstatic when I finally beamed over to your location. But I guess the Universe was just lowering the cost of travel since you don't actually have the spool." He lifted the book. "This will help me bypass all those pesky consequences and transport for free!"

"Ridge," I said, tensing. We had to stop Chasm before he used the book. "Balaclava."

The skinny kid beside me suddenly morphed into a massive polar bear, easily matching Chasm for height as he reared up on hind legs. I barely glimpsed his little penguin wings as I went down on all fours, my stiff arms and legs planting me in a bear crawl.

Ridge sprang forward in an impressive display of courage, knocking the big genie onto his back. It was hard to see with my head down, but it seemed like Ridge had him pinned, hairy paws swatting at the bad guy.

"Stop! Mercy! Please!" Chasm shouted. But wait a minute. Was he laughing? Yes, because I suddenly had the hiccups. "It tickles! Oh, it tickles! Make him stop!"

Ridge's polar bear attacks were tickling him? Could nothing hurt this guy? Still, his pounce had caused Chasm to drop *Arabian Nights* next to the front desk. I had the checkout card in my pocket. If I ordered Ridge into his jar, I could slip the stamped card into the cover envelope and we'd be out of here!

But in my current state, I couldn't possibly reach back to access the peanut butter jar in my backpack. I'd have to turn Ridge back into a boy.

"Balaclava!" I shouted, smoke puffing out my ears.

"Not now!" Ridge replied as he morphed into a boy again. Then I saw him go sailing across the library, his skinny figure getting wedged in the top shelf of a bookcase.

"The polar bear was a nice touch," Chasm said, leaping to his feet. "A little pay-as-you-play wish? I like it. It's classy." He turned to Tina, who had ducked behind the checkout desk.

"Teeny," he said. "You wish that anytime I say the word *abracadrizzle* I'll transform between my current form and a fire-breathing dragon."

Yikes! Why hadn't I thought of that? His hourglass clicked into sight.

"As a consequence," said Chasm, "whenever I'm in dragon form, you will be surrounded by a wall of fire ringing tightly around you. Will it be uncomfortably hot? Absolutely! Will it burn you? Not much."

Ouch! Maybe that's why I hadn't wished for something as big and powerful as a dragon.

"Very well," said Chasm. "Not super convenient for me, since you won't be able to move while the fire surrounds you.

But I guess it'll have to do." And then he sang the magic word. "Ba-ba-bazang!"

Oh, man. We had to get out of here! Reaching back, I gripped the side of the peanut butter jar and shouted, "Ridge! Get into the jar!" He disappeared from his precarious perch, leaving a wisp of smoke in his wake, and my shout leaving a wisp of smoke next to my ears.

Chasm tilted back his head and yelled/sang, "Abracadrizzle, baby!"

Fire suddenly sprang up around Tina, and I saw her pull her arms close to her sides to avoid getting singed. At the same time, Chasm underwent a sudden transformation.

The dragon was about the size of a minivan, not counting his long tail that snaked around by the library exit. His scaly skin was red, with Chasm's familiar spiderweb of tattoos laced across his torso. His face was downright terrifying, with tendrils of smoke wafting up from his nostrils, and teeth as long and sharp as kitchen knives.

Chasm's dragon wings were kind of pathetic, though I didn't feel inclined to point that out. They were obviously too small to carry him, which left them looking useless and ornamental. Ha! I guess even the Wishbreaker didn't always get his wishes granted as perfectly as he wanted.

But then there was the whole fire-breathing thing. Chasm

opened his mouth and spewed flames directly at me. They went over my head, igniting one of the bookshelves behind me.

I plunged my hand into my pocket, but withdrew it with a yelp. There was something hairy wriggling its way out. Oh, yeah. Rats. Bracing myself, I reached in again, feeling the rodent climb out. As the rat scampered across the floor, I fumbled between my familiar ace card and the stamped library checkout card. Behind me, I knew the fire was spreading. I could feel the heat on the back of my neck and hear the crackling flames. I thought of how terrible it must be for Tina, who was even closer to the fire.

"Abracadrizzle!" Chasm shouted as I pulled out the card I needed. I saw Tina collapse onto the desk, sock hand wiping at her sweaty forehead.

I lunged for the trinket copy of *Arabian Nights*. Just as I reached it, a suede loafer shoe stepped on the hard cover. Chasm reached down with one hand, gripped the front of my shirt, and lifted me completely off the ground.

Chasm swiped the stamped checkout card from my grasp with his free hand and then tossed me to the floor. I hit hard, rolling over to grip the peanut butter jar. I whispered the command.

"Ridge, get out of the jar."

My genie friend appeared at my side, giving a yelp of terror at seeing the spreading flames. "What about Mr. Wong?" he shouted.

As long as the Genieologist remained a stone statue, he had a chance of surviving the fire. The books, on the other hand . . . Would there be anything left of the Library of Wight and Wong?

"It's been a pleasure, boys," said Chasm, scooping up *Arabian Nights*. "But it's time to find that spool of string. So, if you'll excuse us . . ." He opened the front cover of the book.

I knew the trinket wasn't going to work correctly unless Chasm put himself in a jar. If he teleported across multiple states, the tether would snap, flinging Tina and the Wishbreaker together again. Over such a great distance, there was no telling what kind of damage that would do to my friend.

I needed to wish for something to stop him. I could turn him to stone, like poor Mr. Wong. But then Tina would be trapped in a burning building with her genie. Maybe I could just turn the book to stone, like the one Mr. Wong had been holding!

I reached out and grabbed Ridge's arm to make sure he was listening. "I wish that all the books in the Library of Wight and Wong would turn into stone until the fire goes out."

I was proud of this wish, since it would kill two birds with one *stone*. By turning *Arabian Nights* into rock, it would prevent

Chasm from immediately using the trinket. And turning the Genieologist's special collection would protect it from burning up.

"If you want the books to turn to stone," said Ridge, talking fast, "then anytime you step on the sidewalk, you'll have to dance."

I didn't have time to debate my options or ask any questions. I was a horrible dancer, but Chasm was only inches away from placing that checkout card in the envelope!

"Bazang!" I shouted with more smoke escaping out my ears.

The checkout card skidded across the stone cover of *Arabian Nights*, deflecting off the envelope that had changed with the rest of the book. Chasm looked up, his face twisted with rage.

"You two will burn!" Chasm yelled. "And the only reason I feel bad about that is because you won't get to see me debut my rap musical on Broadway." He stuffed the checkout card into his shirt pocket and maneuvered the petrified book into a more comfortable position. Then he tipped his hat to us and turned to exit, calling over his shoulder, "Keep up, Teeny! Snapping that tether hurts you a lot more than it hurts me."

"Tina!" Ace cried.

I raced toward her, but what could I do? Tina was a slave to the Wishbreaker, even though her decision to open his jar had saved the world three times over.

Tina's uncovered eye locked onto mine and she reached out her sock-clad hand. Sweat dripped down my forehead as I reached across the checkout desk to take her hand. But it wasn't just a farewell handshake.

Tina was passing me a note!

Her hand slipped away from mine and she turned, coasting out the door on her single roller skate.

Through the open doorway, I heard sirens. Fire trucks were almost here, but the flames were spreading fast.

I glanced at the scrap of paper in my hand. The edge was blackened and burnt, and Tina's writing looked rushed and sloppy. I wondered when she had found time to write anything. Probably during Chasm's lengthy rap.

Chasm's hideout: Wish-Come-True Mini Golf Park, Nashville.

Beneath that, Tina had written the address.

"Ace!" Ridge shouted. "We've got to get out of here!"

He pulled me toward the library exit, both of us coughing on smoke as we burst onto the New York City street.

CHAPTER 13

The morning light glinted off the Atlantic Ocean as Ridge and I made our way toward the beach. The summer day was already very hot, and I took a drink from my water bottle.

Ridge and I had been pretty shaken up after Chasm's surprise attack in the library. Eventually, I'd made a simple wish for an airplane to pick us up and fly us to South Carolina. It wasn't very creative, but Chasm had grounded me from wishing for magical travel. Besides, the flight had given us a few hours of needed sleep. As a consequence, until the end of the week all I would have to do was walk into a cobweb every time I went through a doorway.

"Popular place," Ridge said as we stepped onto the sand. He was right. People were spread up and down Myrtle Beach. The piers were bustling, and I saw lots of surfers and swimmers. We took off our shoes and loaded them into my backpack as we headed toward the water.

"Do you think we beat the others here?" Ridge asked.

"I don't know," I answered. "Hopefully they already found the dagger and got out of here before Chasm figured out how to use the trinket book."

"How will we meet up with them if they're already gone?" asked Ridge.

It was a worrisome question. I needed to tell Jathon and Ms. Gomez what I had learned from Tina's note so we could locate Chasm's hideout and use the two trinkets to cut Tina free.

Jathon only had another day and a half to complete his quest. I'd stay with him till the end, since I had one extra day with Ridge to try to find my parents. The Genieologist had been so close to giving me their address, but I hadn't been able to stick around and see if his stone statue consequence would wear off. I'd have to make a wish to find the Stansworths on my own.

"I don't think we're going to find them without help," Ridge said, scanning the crowd.

He was right. We didn't really have time to search around. "I wish to know where Jathon and the others are right now."

"Good idea," said Ridge. "If you want to know their location, then you have to wear an eye patch for the rest of the day."

"Which eye will it cover?"

"It'll randomly switch throughout the day," Ridge answered.

"Weird," I said. "But, okay. Bazang."

Something clapped over my left eye, causing everything to go dark on that side. I reached up and felt the patch, an elastic band holding it tight around my head like a costume piece.

"They're over there." I pointed. "Under the pier."

We set off across the beach. I was completely blind on the left side and my depth perception was a little off. In a moment, we saw the four familiar figures huddled in the shade of one of the pier's pylons.

No sign of Chasm yet. I figured that was a good thing, but we needed to warn them quickly. He could be there any minute!

"Hey!" I shouted, smoke coming out my ears as Ridge and I sprinted over to them. They came out to meet us. As soon as we got within speaking range, everyone started talking at once. It took me a few moments to realize that my warning was too late.

Chasm had already been there.

Ridge and I fell silent, letting Jathon explain. "He showed up out of thin air! We had no chance to defend ourselves."

"Yarr!" said Thackary. "That be a stylish patch, Ace. What did ye do to yer eye?"

"My eye's fine," I answered, waving him off. "How did Chasm find you?"

"He was holding that book." Vale gestured to Ms. Gomez, and I saw that she was gripping the familiar copy of *One Thousand and One Nights*.

"How?" I muttered. "Chasm shouldn't have been able to use that book. It would separate him from Tina, unless she put him in his jar."

"But she doesn't have a voice to do that," Ridge stated.

"Chasm was carrying Tina in his shirt pocket," Vale said.

"Huge pocket?" Ridge asked.

Jathon shook his head. "Tiny Tina," he corrected. "Must have been a wish. Chasm pulled her out once they appeared, and Tina returned to full size."

"Bawk bawk!" said Ms. Gomez.

"We don't right know what happened to herrrrr," said Thackary. "Started cluckin' like a chicken the moment Chasm dropped in."

"She did something like this yesterday, too," said Vale. "Right after you guys left, she made sheep sounds for about an hour."

"That's the consequence tied to using that trinket book," I explained.

"Bagawk!"

"How long ago did Chasm show up?" Ridge asked.

"About fifteen minutes," said Vale. "Ms. Gomez knocked

the book out of his hand while he was distracted. He didn't seem interested in fighting her for it."

Jathon leaned forward and lowered his voice. "Tina looked like she was barely hanging in there."

Ms. Gomez gave a sad-sounding squawk.

"I know," I replied. "We ran into them last night. We tried to get here before him so we could warn you that he wanted to steal—"

"The spool of string," Jathon finished. He looked down, ashamed.

"He already got it?" Ridge cried.

"I couldn't stop him," said Jathon.

"I don't understand what he's up to," I said. "He told me that he needed the spool of string in order to complete his plans for world domination."

"That doesn't make sense," said Vale. "Why would it help him to make Tina's tether visible?"

"'Tis not what he meant," said Thackary. "'T'would only help him by stopping us from succeeding."

"No," I said. "He specifically said that the spool of string would help him, but the second trinket we were seeking had the power to bring him down."

"The dagger," said Jathon.

"He didn't know what the second trinket was," I said. "But

Ridge might have let that part slip."

"An honest mistake," Ridge said. "It was hard to tell exactly what he knew, since most of our conversation was a rap."

"Rap?" Vale said.

"He didn't rap for you guys?" Ridge asked.

"There wasn't much time for that," said Jathon. "He grabbed the spool of string and took off."

"After he stuck our heads in the sand," Vale said.

"Ouch," I muttered.

"Yeah," said Jathon, using his little finger to pick at his ear. "It's not fun to be at the receiving end of Chasm's wishes."

"We have to find that dagger," I said. "Hopefully we can catch up to Chasm and Tina before he has a chance to use the string for his evil plans."

"Ye don't know that the string be helpful to him!" insisted Thackary.

"He told us!" I shouted with a puff of smoke.

"All ye know is that he didn't want us to be having it." Thackary squinted at me in the morning sun. "If I had a purpose fer stealing a trinket, ye could bet I wouldn't blab me plans to me enemy."

"Chasm was caught up in the moment," Ridge said. "Stuff rhymed."

"Bawk!" said Ms. Gomez.

"But what benefit would it give Chasm to see the tether?" Vale asked again.

"Bawk! Bawk!"

"I can only see how it benefits us," said Jathon. "Since we can only use the dagger to cut it once it's visible."

"Bawk! Bawk! Bagawk!"

"Umm," said Ridge. "I think Ms. Gomez would like to say something. Does anyone speak chicken?"

"Bagawk! Bagawk!" This time she pointed frantically, and we all turned to the ocean behind us.

Something was rising out of the water. Waves crashed as the creature stood taller and taller.

What was it? A seaweed monster.

Stringy ribbons of aquatic vegetation twisted together, forming long legs, whiplike arms, and a slimy-looking head. It stood a good ten feet tall, dripping salt water from its dark green body.

The seaweed monster slogged forward, spraying salt water as it advanced onto dry land. The common people strolling the beach began to scream, running every which way. I had no idea what they thought they were seeing. The Universe would be shielding their non-Wishmaker eyes from the magical threat.

"I'm guessing Chasm wished for this?" I said as the seaweed's kelp arms stretched out, pounding the beach aggressively. Sand flew in all directions as the strands of kelp retracted.

"Bawk!" said Ms. Gomez.

"We must not have heard him with our heads in the sand," Vale said. "That guy isn't going to make it very easy to find the dagger."

"We should spread out and start searching," said Jathon. "Chances are good that the seaweed will be guarding the spot closest to where the dagger washed up."

"Ridge and I can circle around," I said. "You guys search this side."

Without waiting for a response, Ridge and I took off running, bare feet churning through the sand. The beach was mostly cleared of bystanders by now, which made us the obvious target.

Mr. Seaweed stood completely on dry sand, turning its slimy head this way and that as if searching for something to hit. Ridge and I veered sharply, splashing through the edge of the water as we tried to move behind the sea monster.

We were almost past when the creature turned, bringing its seaweed arms together. In a flash, the long green strands had woven together like a net. Mr. Seaweed lunged, bringing the webbing down on Ridge and knocking him flat on his back, completely under the shallow waters.

"Ridge, get into the jar!"

The genie disappeared from the entanglement, causing the seaweed monster to whirl in surprise. A strand of kelp whipped me in the chest, knocking me backward. Water went over my head, but I held tightly to the peanut butter container.

"Ridge, get out of the jar!" I gasped as soon as my mouth

found air. The two of us were up in a heartbeat, scrambling out of the shallows and back onto wet sand.

"Watch out!" someone shouted. I didn't even know if the warning was for me, but I ducked anyway. Good thing, too! A streamer of slimy seaweed swiped right over my head. I backed up, observing the new technique Mr. Seaweed was using.

The creature had rooted both feet in the sand, arms lashing out at anyone who stepped within range. Jathon and Vale were attempting to get close, with no success.

I glanced to where Thackary and Ms. Gomez were combing frantically through the sand a short distance away. They were obviously coming up empty-handed.

"Doesn't look like the seaweed guy is interested in moving from that spot," I pointed out. "If he's guarding the dagger, then we must be close."

"What do we do?"

"I need a distraction," I said. "Do you think a polar bear could bite through those seaweed arms?"

Ridge shook his head. "Yuck. I don't want to eat seaweed."

"Just think of it like sushi," I said.

"I don't like sushi."

"But maybe polar bears do," I answered. "Besides, crawling on my hands and feet will put me at the perfect angle to search the sand." I took a breath. "Balaclava!"

Ridge transformed. I went down on all fours.

"Phew, it's hot," Ridge said. "I'm really not meant for this climate, you know. Even my fur is sweating."

"Charge in there!" I encouraged.

As Ridge leaped forward, the arms of kelp whipped around, lassoing the polar bear around the middle. More ribbons of seaweed surged from the creature's body, wrapping around Ridge like a dozen pythons. His hairy arms were now pinned at his sides, sharp claws useless. With a heave, Mr. Seaweed hoisted Ridge into the air. He dangled, kicking his paws and screaming at me to make a wish.

As uncomfortable as it was for Ridge to be waved around like a flag, the distraction opened the way for me. I tromped forward on all fours. With my hands down in the sand, it was easy to dig. I felt like a scavenger, rummaging desperately through the area where the creature had planted its feet.

"The seaweed's got me in a bear hug!" Ridge shouted from above. "It's squishing my insides!"

"Hang on!" I shouted, my ears suddenly smoking.

Mr. Seaweed shifted sideways. Its feet had burrowed to form a very deep hole. As a ray of sunlight shone down, I saw something at the bottom of the pit. It wasn't shiny, but I could tell it was metallic.

It was the dagger!

But there was no way I could reach it without climbing into

the hole blocked by the monster's feet.

Behind me, I heard Jathon shout "bazang!" I hadn't heard what he'd wished for, but it seemed pretty obvious as a huge wave abruptly roared higher than the rest, knocking into Mr. Seaweed and dragging him from his mark.

"Ace!" Ridge screamed. The creature was still holding him aloft, but my genie was about to get swept out to sea!

"Balaclava!" I called, returning Ridge back to his original form and jumping to my feet. Reducing so rapidly in size, the skinny boy instantly slipped through the slimy strands of kelp, landing in a heap on the sand as Jathon's big wave retreated.

"It's here!" I shouted, ears smoking again. "The dagger is right here!" But as I looked down, I realized that the same wave that had removed our enemy had also filled the hole in the sand.

I dropped to my knees and began digging for the buried dagger as water and sand sloughed inward. Ridge tapped me on the shoulder. I paused long enough to see that Jathon, Vale, Thackary, and Ms. Gomez had all gathered behind me. But that wasn't what the genie was pointing at.

Apparently, Mr. Seaweed wasn't the only Mr. Seaweed. More than a dozen creatures stood surrounding us on the sand, blocking our way off the beach. Their arms twisted and snaked as they moved threateningly toward us.

"Bagawk!" cried Ms. Gomez.

CHAPTER 14

"Arrr! We'll never get around 'em!" said Thackary. "Best if we sacrifice Ace and Ridge to the monsters so the rest of us can sail past."

"That's a horrible plan!" Ridge said. "There are too many of them, anyway. It wouldn't even work."

"Maybe not," he replied. "But at least we'd be rid of ye."

"Nobody's getting sacrificed to the evil seaweed today!" My ears smoked as I shouted. "But we need to start digging!" I dropped to my knees again, hands clawing through the hot sand.

"Bawk!" said Ms. Gomez, joining me.

"The seaweed's moving in on us," Vale said. "This would be a great time for a Wishmaker to make a wish!"

She was right. My first thought was to wish for the dagger to resurface, but that was probably too direct. We needed some kind of protection to buy us time. I glanced at Ridge, who had also started digging. He was using his hands to pack the wet sand as he dug it up, forming it into a tidy mound. That gave me the perfect idea!

"Ridge," I said. "I wish there was a giant sandcastle surrounding us while we dig for the dagger!"

"If you want a sandcastle," he said, "then anytime someone greets you, you'll be forced to take a knee and say, 'I am at your service, my liege.'"

"*Liege?*" I said. "What does that even mean?"

"It's just something servants said to their lords in the Middle Ages," answered Ridge.

"But what if I don't want to be a servant to the person that greets me?" I said. "What if we meet Chasm again and I have to pledge myself to him?"

"Oh, you don't actually have to serve them," said Ridge. "You just have to say the phrase. It won't mean anything."

"Do I have to say it the way you said it?"

"How did I say it?" Ridge asked.

"It was pretty melodramatic," I said.

"You can say it however you want, Ace."

The seaweed monsters were closing in on both sides. If I debated the consequence any longer, my sandcastle might become useless. One more quick question.

"How long will this last?"

"For a year," he said.

Okay. It would probably be worth the awkward greetings if the sandcastle gave us enough time to find the buried dagger.

"Bazang!" I said.

At once, a spectacular castle was constructed around us. It must have taken up a good fifty yards of the beach, with walls that rose well over thirty feet high, forcing back the approaching seaweed monsters. We seemed to be in some kind of central courtyard. The blue sky could be seen overhead, but the damp sand walls instantly cast a comfortable shadow across the spot where we'd been digging.

There were a few enclosed rooms around the courtyard, complete with sand doors and everything! I could see flights of stairs leading up to walkways at the top of the wall where medieval lookouts would be able to see anyone approaching the castle.

Pleased with my wish, I returned to helping a clucking Ms. Gomez dig for the dagger. The others joined in, pulling sand away as we delved deeper in the spot where I had seen the old blade.

Something slammed into one of the castle walls, causing it to bow inward, sand sloughing down. Could the seaweed monsters break through? The sandcastle was just supposed to surround us. I had no idea how strong it would be! I mean, it was only made out of sand.

I stepped away from the hole we were digging. "We've got to get up there and check the castle defenses." Made me feel pretty heroic to say that line.

Ridge shook the sand off his hands and joined me as I sprinted across the courtyard. The stairs looked like they might collapse under our feet, but they turned out to be pretty sturdy as we made our way to the top of the wall.

From the upper walkway, we were able to appreciate the true scope of my wish. The wall had that cool castle edge, with square blocks that looked like jack-o'-lantern teeth. The front gate faced toward the ocean. There was a deep moat surrounding the sandcastle, the crashing waves delivering water to fill it. I even saw a drawbridge, though it was held in the upright position since we were apparently at war.

The seaweed dudes appeared to be less impressed by my massive sandcastle. Instead of admiring its construction, they seemed bent on tearing it down. Several of them had already made it across the moat. They stood close against the castle wall, using their kelp whips to lash at the structure.

"Why isn't the moat keeping them back?" cried Ridge.

"They're made of seaweed," I pointed out. "I don't think they're afraid of the water."

A little ways down the wall, one of the seaweed monsters was growing its arms. The kelp snaked up the castle wall like slippery vines, groping for something to hold on to at the top.

Ridge and I raced over to the spot, desperate to prevent the enemy from pulling itself up. I stepped on a strand of kelp that had stretched across the walkway, feeling the aquatic vegetation squish between my sandy toes.

Ridge grabbed a handful of the castle wall and leaned over the edge. "Eat sand!" he yelled, hurling it down at the creature's head.

But our defenses were weak. Mr. Seaweed was hoisting itself at an impressive rate. Its dark green head popped over the edge of the wall, and Ridge let out a little squeal of fear. I stumbled backward on the narrow walkway, unsure what to do.

A knight in shining armor suddenly appeared.

Okay, his armor wasn't actually shining. It was made of sand. In fact, the entire knight seemed to be made of sand. He leaped forward, drawing a longsword made of (you guessed it) sand. With a deft slice, he cut the arms off the rising kelp monster, causing it to free-fall, flailing, before it struck the moat below.

"Thanks," I said to the knight.

He bowed slightly to me and Ridge. "You should return to the courtyard," he said. "Help the others dig."

"You can talk?" Ridge said.

"We are the knights of the sand," he said. "Of course we can talk."

"There are more of you?" I cried. What a great bonus! My sandcastle was populated with helpful sand knights!

"We have sworn to defend the Wishmakers within these castle walls," the knight said. "Go. Dig in peace."

Grinning, Ridge and I sprinted along the walkway and down the stairs. We passed another pair of sand knights guarding the front gate. One of them had an awesome battle-ax.

We rounded the corner and came into the courtyard. Thackary and Ms. Gomez were still digging. Vale was standing beside them, but I didn't see Jathon. No matter: he couldn't be more than forty-two feet away.

"We should be safe in here," I said, dropping to my knees beside the hole in the sand. "My sand knights have sworn to protect us."

"*Your* sand knights?" Vale put her sandy hands on her hips.

"Yeah," said Ridge. "Apparently, they came with the castle. I did *not* see that coming."

Jathon suddenly appeared around the corner. But there was

something different about him. Oh, yeah. He was riding a horse.

Unlike everything else around, the horse wasn't made of sand. It looked like a real stallion, big and black, with a leather saddle.

"Where did you find a horse?" Ridge asked him.

"I didn't find it," answered Jathon. "What do you think? There's a bunch of stray horses wandering along this beach."

"Not a bunch," said Ridge. "You only got one."

"It's a consequence," Vale answered.

"For what?" I asked.

Just then, one of the sand knights entered the courtyard. He approached Jathon, taking a knee, helmeted head bowed, with the point of his sword touching the ground in a reverent pledge.

"Lord Jathon," the sand figure said. At the sound of his name, Jathon laughed. At the sound of his laugh, I hiccuped.

"The south wall is holding," the sand man continued. "We have knights stationed at every access point. We await your commands."

"Uh . . ." Jathon said. "Just keep doing what you're doing. Don't let the bad guys in."

The knight nodded. "Wise orders, sire. I am at your service, my liege."

Hey! That was my line.

The tall knight rose, sand armor grinding together as he retreated from the courtyard.

"*You* wished for the knights?" I asked Jathon.

"Had to come up with something more helpful than a sandcastle," he replied. "As soon as you guys went up those stairs, one of the seaweed monsters punched a hole through the wall. I had to make a quick wish for something to keep them back."

"And you got to ride a horse as a consequence?" Ridge said. "That's way better than what Ace usually gets."

"It's actually really uncomfortable," said Jathon. "My legs are already hurting, and I can't help dig. In fact, I can't even get off this thing until tomorrow morning."

"Have you ever ridden a horse before?" I asked.

"No," Jathon said as the animal tromped backward, causing him to lurch in the saddle. "They make it look so easy in the movies."

"Well, at least you can't get bucked off," Ridge pointed out.

"Quit yer gabbing and start diggin'!" shouted Thackary, who was now standing waist-deep in the hole.

"Bawk!" added Ms. Gomez.

"We should hurry," I admitted. "We have no idea how long

the sand knights will be able to stand against those seaweed monsters." I had less faith in them after learning that they answered to Jathon.

I focused on scraping sand out of the deepening hole. The shade from the walls was nice, and the sand felt cool the farther down we got. Everyone helped dig except for Jathon, whose big horse pranced around the courtyard.

From time to time, a sand knight would come into view, bowing to Jathon and giving him updates on the castle defenses. It sounded like they were doing a pretty good job, until one guy with a tall shield made his report.

"Sire! The west wall is barely holding. A dozen knights have already been crushed to dust."

"See?" Vale yelled at Jathon. "I told you to wish for knights made of granite!"

"Bagawk!" Ms. Gomez, who had been taking a turn in the hole, suddenly stood upright. Clutched tightly in her raised hand was the dagger we had been searching for.

The blade was tucked into a rusted, dingy-looking sheath. Years underwater had not been kind to it. The hilt didn't look much better, with grit from the ocean's bottom clinging to the ornamentation on the handle. The dagger was longer than I had expected, the whole thing measuring about half the length of her arm.

"This is glorious news!" cried the knight. "I shall bear this hopeful omen to the defenders at the west. . . ."

Two strands of tough kelp suddenly lashed around the knight like deadly ropes. The streamers tightened, and the warrior collapsed in a heap of useless sand.

The seaweed monster whose arms had done the damage came flailing into the courtyard. From the shadows, two more sand knights appeared, swords slicing through kelp and driving the creature back.

But the seaweed wasn't our only problem now. All around, the castle seemed to be falling apart. It was most noticeable at the inner rooms around the courtyard. The walls sagged, and wind off the ocean caused the sand to swirl as it collapsed.

"What's happening?" Jathon called.

Ridge suddenly slapped a hand to his forehead, and I knew that he had some bad news. "You wished for a sandcastle to surround us as we dug for the dagger."

"I know!" But I didn't understand why my wish was failing!

"We're done digging," said Ridge. "We found the dagger. That means the castle won't protect us anymore."

I grimaced, realizing that my specific wording of the wish was coming back to bite me.

"That's a problem," said Vale.

"Duh!" I replied.

"Not just because the castle is falling apart," she said. "Jathon wished that the knights would defend us while we were in the sandcastle."

Jathon laughed at his name. I hiccuped.

"So the knights are going away with the castle?" Ridge shrieked. "We'll be defenseless."

I whirled at Jathon. "Why didn't you wish for the knights to escort us off the beach?"

He glared back at me. "Why didn't you wish for the

sandcastle to last until the seaweed went away?"

"Arrr!" cried Thackary. "Ye both be terrible Wishmakers!" He hurled a handful of sand in my direction. It probably would have gotten in my eye if it weren't for that convenient patch covering my left side.

Another portion of the castle crumbled into dry sand. It wouldn't be long before the outer walls completely fell.

"We've got to get out of here!" Ridge shouted.

Ms. Gomez scrambled out of the hole, ancient dagger gripped tightly. "Bawk!" she said. There was a sincere look in her eyes, but it was really hard to take her seriously when she sounded like a chicken. "Bawk, bawk, bawk, bagawk, bawk, bawk, and we can meet up with you later."

"I think I'm finally understanding her!" Ridge said.

"That's because you're a chicken," Vale said with a sly grin.

"Mocha almond!" cried Ms. Gomez. "It's about time that consequence ran out!"

"It's good to hear you say something other than *bawk!*" I admitted.

"They were real words to me," she said. "Mostly ice cream flavors. You guys have no idea how frustrating it is when nobody can understand you."

"Could other chickens understand you?" Ridge asked. "You could have talked to them."

"Do you see any chickens on this beach?" Ms. Gomez cried.

We all jumped as another wall by the courtyard turned into a pile of sand. Jathon's horse reared on its hind legs, but magically, he didn't fall out of the saddle.

"Your Majesty!" shouted an approaching knight. The horse had barely settled enough for Jathon to carry on a conversation. "The castle is collapsing!"

"We noticed!" Jathon replied.

"What are your orders, sire?"

Jathon struggled to keep his horse under control in the chaos. It was Ms. Gomez who answered the knight.

"Lower the drawbridge and open the east gate," she said. "Jathon and Ace can take the dagger and escape on horseback."

Jathon laughed, causing me to hiccup as we pondered Ms. Gomez's plan for a moment. Then he turned to the knight. "Do as she says."

The sand knight nodded. Turning eastward, he shouted, "Lower the drawbridge!"

"Lower the drawbridge!" the call was repeated.

"Open the gates!"

"Open the gates!"

At the top of the east wall, I saw a few knights spring into action, heaving against a huge crank and pulling some sand chains.

"What about you?" I asked Ms. Gomez. Strangely, I didn't worry so much about Thackary.

"The seaweed monsters are obviously after the dagger," she explained. "You need to take it as far away as possible. Maybe you can outdistance them."

I studied Jathon on his big black horse. The animal was impressive, but I felt like I needed to point something out. "There's no way four of us will fit on that horse."

"You'll have to put your genies in their jars," said Ms. Gomez.

Ridge and Vale moaned in unison.

"Ridge could go polar bear," I suggested.

"What would that do to you?" asked Ms. Gomez.

"Good point," I replied. "I don't think I'll be able to stay on the horse if I have to bear crawl."

I cast an apologetic glance at Ridge. The least I could do was wait until the last possible second to stow him. "Let's get into position." I crossed to Jathon's horse.

It was ridiculously hard to climb onto the stallion. I put my bare foot on the strap that dangled from the saddle and hoisted myself up. The horse shied away and I fell flat on my back in the sand. I eventually managed to get into the saddle, but it took Ridge, Vale, and Ms. Gomez boosting me up while Thackary stood by, laughing. That made me hiccup, which made the task even harder.

I didn't want to hold around Jathon's waist, but I grabbed on to him with all my strength when the horse lurched forward. The others followed our trotting stallion as we maneuvered into position at the east wall.

"Sire," the knight said to Jathon. "We cannot protect you outside the walls of this castle."

"Well, in a few minutes, there won't be any walls left," Jathon said. "We'll have to take our chances on the beach."

The thick gate was open, and the drawbridge had just settled into place, spanning the deep moat that surrounded my castle. A couple of armored sand knights were still raising the latticework grate that covered the entryway.

Beside us, the knight reached to his belt and drew his longsword. Carefully gripping the sandstone blade, he offered the handle up to Jathon. "Take my sword," the knight pledged. "May it serve you well on your daring ride."

"Nah," said Jathon. "I think I'll need both hands to hold the reins."

"I'll take it!" I said. Wicked-looking longsword? Yes, please!

"Yeah," Jathon said. "Give it to Ace. He's more likely to need it since he might get bucked off."

The knight turned, swinging the hilt of the sand sword over to me. It felt . . . sandy. And heavy. As soon as he let go of the blade, I nearly dropped the weapon. Still, it felt better to have some kind of defense against the seaweed monsters.

Behind us, the south and west walls of the castle had totally disintegrated. The seaweeds that had been waiting charged forward in a frenzy. Ahead, I saw two more creatures moving onto the drawbridge.

I saw a glass pickle jar in Jathon's hand as he commanded Vale inside. Reaching back, I gripped the peanut butter jar in my backpack and did the same to Ridge. I must have looked pretty epic, sitting on a black stallion with a longsword in my hand, residual smoke from the disappearing genies swirling around us.

"Ride, boys!" Ms. Gomez said. She stepped forward and tucked the old dagger into Jathon's belt. "Ride like you've never ridden before!"

"I haven't," Jathon croaked.

"I don't think that's what she—" I started to say.

Our horse saw that the way was finally open and took off at a full gallop, sand churning under its hooves. I barely managed to hold on to Jathon with one arm, while my sand sword dangled in my grasp.

Overhead, I heard the twang of bowstrings as arrows flew from the knights on the crumbling wall above us. The arrows found their marks, cutting into the pair of seaweed monsters on the drawbridge. They were knocked back as we rode on. I attempted to swing my sword at one of them, but we were past by the time I got some momentum behind it.

There were more seaweed creatures waiting for us where the waves lapped at their feet. Our horse turned hard, splashing through the shallows and dodging streamers of kelp as it moved westward for the city. It didn't seem like Jathon was doing much steering at this point. Our trusty steed was as desperate to get off the beach as we were.

A seaweed monster lunged from the side. I acted on pure instinct, heaving my sword into a horizontal position. The speed of the horse did the rest. As we galloped past, the edge of my sand blade caught Mr. Seaweed in the middle, shearing it into two wriggling tangles of aquatic vegetation.

Ahead, two seaweed monsters reached out for each other, intertwining their kelp arms to form a sturdy trip wire. I braced myself to be thrown from the saddle, but our stallion jumped. Like a prize rodeo horse, it cleared the hurdle of seaweed and landed with a jarring jolt. I spun my sword around, cutting down one more enemy.

All at once, the sword in my hand turned to soft sand. It slipped through my fingers, caught on the ocean breeze. Glancing over my shoulder, I saw that the final wall of my castle had collapsed.

With the fallen fortress, Jathon's knights must have also

disintegrated, which explained the sudden loss of my sword. A huge mound of sand now stood where my castle had once been. I worried about Ms. Gomez and Thackary, but there was no way we could turn back now.

This was the final stretch!

Suddenly, I heard the horse's hooves touching down on something other than sand. I looked ahead to see that we'd made it off the beach! We were galloping on a paved street, heading into town.

"We should probably stop now!" I said to Jathon.

"That would be nice," he replied. "But I think my horse has other plans."

And so we rode on.

CHAPTER 15

By the time Jathon's horse stopped running, we found ourselves in an outlying neighborhood. I couldn't bear to leave Ridge in his jar any longer, so I climbed down from the saddle and called the genie out. Jathon did the same for Vale, although he had to stay on horseback. My legs were aching from the ride, and I wondered how uncomfortable it must have been for Jathon.

"Where are we?" Ridge asked, glancing down the street.

"No clue," I responded. "But we should make our way back and try to find Ms. Gomez and Thackary."

"Forget them," said Vale. "Let's try to find Tina."

"We need Ms. Gomez to reactivate the trinket," Jathon said, holding up the ancient dagger.

"Why didn't she do that at the beach?" I asked.

"We were in a collapsing sandcastle, getting attacked by seaweed monsters," Jathon said. "I'm guessing she didn't think of it in the moment."

Probably true. Survival had been the main thing on my mind.

"Well, I don't think the four of us are going to fit in that saddle," said Ridge. "And I'd rather not go back into the jar."

"We can walk," I replied, heading on to the sidewalk. Instantly, I broke into a wild dance move.

"Apparently, he's really excited about walking," said Vale. I did a quick little jig to get myself into the gutter.

"Hey, how long is this going to last, anyway?" I had accepted the dance-on-the-sidewalk consequence without learning much about it.

"It's just for a month."

"Guess I'll stick to the road," I said.

"That's dangerous," Ridge warned.

"I'll be careful."

Ms. Gomez and Thackary Anderthon weren't at the beach by the time we got back there. I was glad to see that the seaweed monsters had fallen apart, their body parts strewn all over the sand. Chasm's wish must not have been able to hold itself together once we got far enough away with the dagger.

We headed back into the city, wandering aimlessly in search of the adults while the hot afternoon crept on. We finally stopped under a small tree. I was grateful for the shade until Jathon's consequence made all the leaves fall off. That was the last straw.

"I wish Ms. Gomez would find us," I said to Ridge.

"Okay," he answered. "If you want her to find us, then every time you hear a car honk, you'll have to do a jumping jack."

"Just one?" I asked.

"One per honk," Ridge answered. "For the rest of the year."

I listened down the street. Not too many pushy drivers here. I just needed to make sure I didn't go back to New York City. "Bazang," I said.

Ridge, Vale, and I sat down under the leafless tree, while Jathon's horse carried him a few yards away to graze on some scrubby grass. I thought my wish would be answered promptly, but I hadn't specified *when* she would find us, so it ended up taking several hours.

We waited impatiently in the shade. My eye patch switched from the left to the right. Every so often, the Universe forced me to leap to my feet and perform some jumping jacks as a passing car honked.

"Don't wear yourself out," Vale said to me after a near collision caused two drivers to have an angry conversation with their car horns. "I'd hate for you to slow us down any more than you already are."

"Hey!" Ridge cut in. "That's not nice."

"She's right." I sighed as my jumping jacks ended. "You'd think I'd be better at this since it's my second time around."

"Still," said Ridge, "Vale shouldn't be so hard on you. She's had a lot more experience."

"That's true." I turned to her. "It must be really frustrating for you to watch Wishmaker after Wishmaker stumble around trying to complete quests."

"It can be," she admitted. "They don't always do things the way I would."

"With all your experience, I bet you'd be a great Wishmaker," I said.

She simply scoffed and rolled her eyes.

"I'm serious," I followed up.

"That's a ridiculous idea," Vale said. "Genies don't make wishes. We aren't in charge of making the decisions, just carrying them out."

"Do you guys like being genies?" I asked them.

Ridge shrugged. "We don't know anything else."

"Well, I don't think you're missing out," I said. "All the pressure is on Jathon and me."

"So is all the freedom," said Vale. "We're just pulled along because we have to be here."

Although she didn't say it, I thought Vale looked a little bit sad in that moment. I'll be the first to admit that I didn't love being a Wishmaker, but talking to Ridge and Vale made me realize that they actually had it worse. Like Ridge had said on the ski lift, they were really just observers along for the ride, stuck with some inexperienced kid in charge of making all the decisions.

At last, Ms. Gomez arrived in a rental van. I was kind of disappointed to see that Thackary was in the passenger's seat. They acted so relieved to have finally found us, completely unaware that it was a fulfillment of my wish.

The fast food that they brought was a nice bonus, though. Soon, the six of us were chowing down, anxious to make a plan now that we were all reunited with the dagger.

Ms. Gomez turned the weathered weapon over in her hands and finally slipped it out of the dirty metal sheath. The blade was rusted and corroded, the once-sharp edge dull and rough.

"Are you going to reactivate it?" I asked.

Ms. Gomez nodded grimly. She held the dagger lightly across both open palms, the sheath in the grass beside her. "Bazang," she said.

Like the string had done in her living room, the dagger twinkled magically for just a moment, before returning to look like the rusty blade we had dug up on the beach.

"This dagger now has the power to cut through anything," said Ms. Gomez. "Including a visible tether between genie and Wishmaker."

"What happens to you when we use it?" Jathon asked. "You know the consequence?"

She nodded solemnly. "Every time the dagger is used to cut something, I will shrink."

"But you'll get big again, right?" Ridge asked, dipping his fries in ketchup.

Ms. Gomez shook her head. "This consequence is permanent."

"How tiny will you get?" I had shrunk down to three inches once. It wasn't too bad, but I wouldn't want to stay that way.

"I'll get one inch smaller for every item that the dagger cuts through," she said.

"That's not so bad," I said with a relieved sigh.

"Maybe not so bad for a tall person," she said. "I'm only five foot four inches."

"Luckily, we only need to cut through one little piece of string," said Jathon.

"How does five foot three sound?" Ridge asked her.

"Worth it," said Ms. Gomez, "if it means setting my daughter free from Chasm and sending him back into his jar." She picked up the protective sheath and slipped the old blade safely inside.

"But the dagger isn't going to help us at all unless we get that spool of string back from Chasm," I said.

"Unless he already used it for whatever evil plan he's cooking up," said Ridge, sipping his soda through a straw.

"I don't know what he's planning," said Ms. Gomez, "but Chasm definitely hasn't used the string to tie onto Tina."

"How can you be sure?" Ridge asked.

"Consequences," she said. "If he had used the string, my ankles would be tied together."

"Yarr!" exclaimed Thackary. "Ye be our very own alarm system."

"We're running out of time," said Jathon, who looked terribly uncomfortable eating a hamburger on horseback. "I've got less than twenty-four hours to complete this quest. Tomorrow makes a week from the time I opened Vale's pickle jar."

"Really?" Ridge said. "Man, this week really flew by."

"That's what happens when you spend three days in a vault," said Vale.

"Oh, yeah," said Ridge. "That consequence really bombed us."

"Consequence?" Jathon wadded his hamburger wrapper into a ball. "What consequence?"

"Nothing!" I snapped. "Nothing at all."

"Umm . . ." said Ridge. "I meant to say *fonsequence*."

"*Fonsequence* isn't a word!" Jathon said.

Vale squinted suspiciously at me. "Something happened

when you wished to slow down the conveyor belt."

At the mention of the word, Jathon somehow managed to spin in a circle while seated in the saddle.

I could tell that my secret was about to come out. "It would have been fine if the spool of string hadn't gone into the back room."

"What happened?" Jathon asked.

"Time outside the vault sped up," I finally confessed.

"Blackberry cherry!" cursed Ms. Gomez. "It makes so much sense now."

"I was going to tell you guys," I said. "I was just waiting for the right time."

Jathon had a hand to his forehead. "I'm going to fail my quest," he muttered. "The air is going to turn into chocolate sauce and everyone is going to choke because you made a stupid wish."

"To be fair, my wish was pretty smart," I said. "It was the consequence that was stupid."

"We need more time!" said Jathon. "We don't even know where to start looking for Tina and Chasm."

"Actually, I might be able to help with that." I dug my hand into my pocket for Tina's note. A rat crawled out, startling everyone. It grabbed one of Ridge's fries and ran off.

I held out the crumpled note that Tina had passed me in the

Library of Wight and Wong. "This is the address to Chasm's hideout."

Ms. Gomez snatched the little paper out of my hand, studying her daughter's strained handwriting. "A miniature golf course outside of Nashville," she said. "We can get there by morning if we drive through the night."

"I see a problem with that plan," Jathon said. We all turned to him and he patted his horse on the neck. "I'm stuck in the saddle until morning."

"What be the problem?" asked the boy's dad. "If ye don't fit in the car, we sail away without ye."

"That doesn't make any sense," I said. "It's Jathon's quest. He has to be the one to save Tina."

I hiccuped when Jathon laughed at the sound of his name.

"There be no harm in getting there before the boy," continued Thackary. "Give me a chance to look things over."

"That sounds awfully suspicious," said Ridge. "I still can't believe we trust this guy."

"We don't," I said. "He almost ruined our quests last time, and I wouldn't be surprised if he tries to ruin them again."

Thackary burst into laughter, causing me to hiccup. "Ruin yer pitiful quest?" he said. "Ye aren't even serious about completing it!"

"I wasn't," I admitted. "But I learned something that

changed my mind." I glanced at Ms. Gomez. "The Universe wouldn't give me a useless quest. Sure, I might not be saving the world, so it probably doesn't matter to any of you guys. But I know that my quest matters to one person."

"You?" Jathon asked.

"Samuel Sylvester Stansworth," I answered. So, yeah. Me.

"Did you find this Samuel?" Ms. Gomez asked.

"Mr. Wong was this close to telling us his family's address." I held my fingers an inch apart.

"But then he turned into a statue," added Ridge.

"I told you not to say *meanwhile*," she said.

"It was an accidental compound word," said Ridge. "Besides, turning into stone probably saved his life when Chasm burned the place."

"Unless turning into stone killed him," I pointed out.

"Mr. Wong will be fine," said Ms. Gomez. "He only stays that way for twenty-four hours."

"I'll have almost a full day after Jathon's quest ends," I said. Jathon laughed and I hiccuped. "Hopefully that's enough time to complete mine."

"It's not going to be easy to feed a sandwich to Samuel . . . *whatever-his-name-is,* if you don't know where he lives," Vale said.

"You're right," I said, looking at Ridge. "Guess it's time to find out, so I'll be ready. I wish to know where Samuel Sylvester Stansworth's parents live." I glanced down at my wrist as my hourglass came into play.

"If you want to know their address," said Ridge, "then anytime you meet a new adult, you'll only be able to see their feet."

Ah. I see what the Universe did there. I was wishing to find my parents, but I wouldn't be able to see their faces. Still, they'd be able to recognize me.

"How long will it last?" I asked.

"For the rest of the year," answered Ridge.

Find my parents, but only be able to study their feet? Totally worth it.

"Bazang."

It was silent for a moment as the Universe filled my mind with new information. The Stansworths' address came into my mind as though I'd known it for years. Probably because I had.

"Well?" Ms. Gomez asked.

"Atlanta," I said. "Georgia." I even knew the street name and house number.

"Hey," said Ms. Gomez. "We have to drive right through Atlanta on our way to Nashville."

"Maybe we could stop along the way," I suggested.

"We don't have time for Ace to make a social call," Jathon said. "My quest is far more important."

"But wait," I said, an exciting idea dawning on me. "Maybe you can drop me off and I can catch up before you reach the mini golf park."

"How would you do that?" Vale asked. "Chasm stopped you from magical travel."

"*One Thousand and One Nights*," I said. "If Ms. Gomez leaves me with the book, I can find the Stansworths, complete my quest, and use the book to teleport to the library, and then to you."

"Arrr!" cried Thackary. "Multitasking."

"It's a good idea, *muchacho*," Ms. Gomez said. "I think your plan might work."

CHAPTER 16

"Sure you don't want me to drop you at the house?" Ms. Gomez asked as the rental van pulled to a stop in the grocery store parking lot. My eye patch was finally gone, and I squinted against the bright sun.

"This will be fine," I said. "The Stansworths are just down the street." I felt like I needed to make the approach on my own. Besides, I needed a few supplies in order to complete my little quest.

Ridge yanked open the sliding door and jumped out into the hot mid-afternoon. We'd been driving for hours, after spending the night in a decent hotel. The hotel's free breakfast had been pretty good, and we'd taken leftovers to cover our lunch in the car.

I glanced at Jathon as I climbed out of the minivan. He and Vale were fast asleep in the backseat. It was incredible that they hadn't awakened with Ms. Gomez singing off-tune opera at every stoplight. But those two were totally wiped out, having spent last night in the parking lot because the hotel had a strict "no horses allowed" policy.

As I slid the door shut, Thackary leaned out the passenger window. "'Bout time we be getting rid of ye meddling boys."

"Yeah, we'll miss you, too," I said sarcastically.

"Ye always be hindering me plans."

"Plans?" I said. "What plans?"

Thackary quickly rolled up his window just as Ms. Gomez came around the front of the minivan.

"I'm worried about Thackary," I said to her. "I'm afraid he's planning something. Something that could cause the rest of you trouble."

"I'm sure he is," said Ms. Gomez. She glanced at the backseat of the minivan where Jathon and Vale were sleeping. "Thackary's angry. He's mean, and he can't do anything good."

"That's what we've been saying," I said.

"You need to dump that guy on the roadside," said Ridge.

"I can't," said Ms. Gomez. "Thackary Anderthon was one of the nicest boys I ever knew."

Ridge and I stared at her as though she'd just said the moon was made of cheese.

"Him?" Ridge pointed through the car window at the man in the passenger seat. "Nice?"

"I have to believe that he can be kind again," she whispered.

"What aren't you telling us?" I asked. Ms. Gomez clearly knew something about Thackary that the rest of us didn't.

"I can't say," she answered.

Thackary knocked on the passenger window, his sneering face an inch away from the glass as he gestured for Ms. Gomez to hurry up.

"I should go," she said. "Tina is lucky to have you as a friend. And I believe that you can complete your quest and still be there to help us take down Chasm."

"Thanks," I said.

Ms. Gomez reached out to press something into my hand. It was a twenty-dollar bill.

"What's this for?" I asked.

"Buy yourself a nice loaf of bread," she answered. "Samuel deserves the best sandwich you can make."

The minivan peeled away from the parking lot, and Ridge and I headed into the grocery store. I had a little freak-out as I stepped through the entrance. Sputtering, I slapped at my own face frantically.

"Are you okay?" Ridge asked.

"Just walked through a cobweb," I answered, regaining composure. "It didn't get you?"

He shrugged. "Nope. Wasn't my consequence."

We wandered around the store for a moment before finding the bread aisle. "Do you think Samuel likes white or wheat?" Ridge asked.

"Let me ask him." I paused. "He said white." I grabbed a loaf of soft-looking bread.

"You're sure about this?" Ridge asked.

"About white bread?" I replied.

"About you being Samuel Sylvester Stansworth."

"Yeah," I answered, stopping in front of a shelf lined with jars of peanut butter. There were chunky and smooth. So many brands. I knew which one I liked best, so I grabbed it off the shelf. Grape jelly would be tasty, too, so I picked some that came in a convenient squeeze bottle.

"You heard Mr. Wong's story," I said as we headed for the checkout line. "The dates line up perfectly with my memory loss. And I've decided that magic is the only thing that could wipe my mind like this. It must have had something to do with the Unknown Consequence."

I handed my sandwich supplies to the cashier. She must have been only seventeen years old, since I could look her in the face. She scanned the items and halfheartedly announced my total. I handed her Ms. Gomez's twenty-dollar bill, and she gave me change.

"You know, you might have already completed your quest," Ridge said.

"What do you mean?" I asked as the cashier bagged my purchased items.

"Well, we ate a ton of peanut butter sandwiches on your last quest."

We exited the store, cobwebs assaulting my face as I danced my way across the sidewalk.

"I thought about that, too," I said, once I got control again. "But those sandwiches wouldn't have counted. First, I hadn't been given this quest yet. And second, none of those sandwiches would've counted because, technically, the Universe made all of them. In order to complete the quest, I have to put the sandwich together myself."

I stopped in the parking lot and placed my supplies on the hood of a random white car. Opening the plastic bread bag, I pulled out two slices, laying them on the hot metal hood.

"What are you doing?" Ridge asked.

"I'm making a peanut butter sandwich," I said.

"Here?"

"The Stansworths' house is just down the block. I want to be prepared." I grinned at him. "We're going to meet my family, Ridge. I've always wanted to have lunch with my mom and dad."

I opened the ordinary jar and swiped my index finger through the sticky peanut butter, smearing the glob onto one of the bread slices.

"That is *not* how you make a sandwich," Ridge said, looking away with disgust. "That's called finger painting. Besides, that's too much peanut butter. It's going to be so dry!"

"Since when did you become the PB and J expert?" I squeezed some of the purple jelly on top of the peanut butter. Then I picked up the other slice of bread, nicely warmed from sitting on the hot car, and set it in place, finishing the sandwich.

"I'm disappointed in your peanut-butter-to-jelly ratio, Ace," Ridge said.

"Would you relax?" I placed the finished sandwich back in the plastic bread bag and tied it closed. "I'm the one who has to eat it." I zipped all the supplies into my backpack, and dusted a few crumbs off the car I had used as a table.

"Good thing you didn't make extra sandwiches for the Stansworths," Ridge muttered. "They'd never accept you as their son if they tasted your creations."

It was less than a block to the address that my wish had given me. We approached slowly, reverently. The house wasn't huge or fancy, but it looked like home to me. I took in every detail as we moved along the street.

A couple of large trees dotted the yard. The grass was well maintained, and I saw a little vegetable garden on the side of the house. The garage door was closed, but there was a blue car parked in the driveway.

Lying on the lawn was a small bicycle with plastic streamers attached to the handlebars. Did I have a younger sibling?

My heart was hammering as I danced my way up the walkway toward the front door. Luckily, the dance moves stopped once I moved onto the porch. There was a welcome mat. I felt so welcome here! I just needed to make sure I didn't step on it.

Ridge and I stopped side by side before the green front

door. Green was my favorite color!

"What are you going to say to them?" he asked.

A million things went through my mind. Would they believe me if I told them where I'd been? Would the Universe shield them from the truth about my genie and me? But then, maybe I wouldn't have to say anything. I was counting on them being overcome with joy when they saw my face.

"What if nobody's home?" Ridge asked.

I glanced at him with a look of mild annoyance. Ridge was kind of spoiling the moment. I'd dreamed of this for years, and I suddenly felt like I needed to do it alone.

"Ridge?" I said. "Can I ask you a huge favor?"

"Anything," he answered. "Literally, the only reason I'm here is to do what you ask."

"Would you mind hanging out in your jar for a minute?"

He sighed, shoulders slumping a little.

"Just until I get inside," I explained. "I've got to do this on my own."

Ridge reached out and slipped the peanut butter jar from the side pocket of my backpack. "I understand," he said. "Just don't forget about me in there."

"Never." I took the jar from him. He nodded at me and I spoke the words to command him out of sight. "Ridge, get into the jar."

I waved my hand through the wisp of smoke that lingered on the front porch. Maybe I should have jarred him sooner. Oh, well.

Taking a deep breath, I reached out and rang the doorbell.

CHAPTER 17

Nothing happened.

I rang the doorbell again, but I couldn't even tell if it chimed since all I could hear was my own heartbeat. I was just about to knock when the front door opened.

I gasped, trying to look at the person who had answered. Instead, my eyes snapped downward and all I saw was a pair of shoes. Women's tennis shoes with white laces.

"Hello, there," she said. The voice of my mother! It was like music to my ears. What did I want my first words to her to be?

I dropped to one knee on the porch. "I am at your service, my liege."

Oh, yeah. That.

And my knee happened to touch down on the welcome mat, which was instantly whisked away, sending me toppling to my side. Kind of an embarrassing first impression.

She chuckled as I rose to my feet once more. "Are you selling something?" she asked. "Peanut butter?"

I glanced at the jar in my hand. "Oh, no. This is . . ." I trailed off. "Are you Mrs. Stansworth?" Why hadn't she recognized me yet?

"I am," she said. "What can I do for you?"

"It's me," I said, growing frustrated. "I'm . . . I'm home."

A second pair of shoes arrived in the doorway. These were nice leather business shoes.

"Who's our visitor?" the man asked, his voice low and rumbly. They were both here! Both my parents had come to the door! But why didn't they know me? Maybe they couldn't see my face while I stared down at their feet.

"Must be a neighbor boy," said Mrs. Stansworth.

"NO!" I shouted, smoke coming out my ears. "I'm not a neighbor. It's me! See?" I closed my eyes and looked up, giving them a plain view of my face. I held that strange position until I heard them both snickering.

"Are we supposed to recognize you?" Mr. Stansworth asked. "Are you a movie star or something?"

"But . . ." I stammered, opening my eyes as I looked down again. "You said you were the Stansworths."

"We are," he replied.

"Then shouldn't you be happy to see Samuel Sylvester Stansworth?" I shouted. More smoke.

It suddenly went very silent. I wished Ridge was out of his jar so he could tell me what expressions were on their faces. But I couldn't pull him out now. I was committed to finishing this awkward conversation alone.

"Please leave," said Mrs. Stansworth. I saw their feet shuffle backward as the door began to close.

"Wait!" I called, reaching forward to stop the door with my arm. "I didn't mean anything. . . ." I felt my dreams slipping away from me. Something had caused my parents to forget all about me. I needed more information, even if it upset the Stansworths.

"I just wondered . . ." I faltered. "Is Samuel home?"

More silence. I saw Mrs. Stansworth's tennis shoes disappear into the house as her husband stepped forward. "Samuel hasn't been home for three years."

"But you remember him?" I asked.

"Of course we . . ." He trailed off, voice angry. "What is this all about, kid?"

"And I don't . . ." How was I supposed to ask this? "Do I look like him?"

I heard Mr. Stansworth suck in a bitter breath. "Please don't come back."

The green door slammed in my face. Green was such an ugly color.

I stumbled away from the Stansworths' porch, dancing

down the sidewalk until I hit the street running with the peanut butter jar tucked under one arm like a football. I heard Ridge's voice calling out to me, but I didn't want him to see me crying, so I left him in there until I got control of myself.

I was angry, disappointed, sad, frustrated, hurt, confused, devastated, upset, and hungry. And that's a lot of feelings to feel at the same time. But through this cloud of emotions, it was suddenly very clear what I needed to do.

"Ridge, get out of the jar."

He appeared beside me, placing a hand on my shoulder for comfort. But I didn't need comfort anymore. Something had snapped inside me, and the result gave me more clarity than I'd ever felt before.

"I'm sorry about the Stansworths," whispered the genie.

"Me too," I admitted. "But I think they were finally the straw that broke the camel's neck."

"I think it's supposed to be the camel's back," Ridge corrected.

"Does it matter which part of the camel broke?" I said.

"Probably matters to the camel," said Ridge.

"The point is," I continued, "I'm not Samuel Sylvester Stansworth. Or, if I am, no one remembers me. Not even my own parents. Maybe it's an old wish or part of the Unknown Consequence. It doesn't really matter. Having the Stansworths turn me away taught me a lesson I should have learned a long time ago." I looked Ridge right in the eye. "My past doesn't matter."

"What?" he said. "Of course it does."

"It's ruining my life," I said. "I worry so much about who I *was* and what I *did*, that I don't even know who I am now. I don't know why the Universe assigned me this pointless quest. I don't know who Samuel Sylvester Stansworth is. But after his parents slammed the door in my face, I realized that I don't care anymore!"

"Are you all right?" Ridge said slowly. "You've got a crazy look in your eye."

"I've never felt better!" Smoke streamed out of my ears.

"So, you're giving up on your quest again?"

"The peanut butter sandwich quest was nothing but a decoy," I said. "The Universe was trying to distract me from what really mattered. Meeting the Genieologist, hearing Samuel's story . . . Those clues made me think I could find my family. But the whole thing must have been a test, Ridge."

"What are you being tested on?"

"Do I care more about learning my past?" I said. "Or do I care more about Tina?"

"That's a tough question."

"No, it's not!" I cried. "Not anymore. From now on, nothing can distract me. It's time to face Chasm, cut Tina's tether, and send the Wishbreaker back into his jar!" I gripped the magical peanut butter container. "Ridge, get into the jar."

He disappeared, but his voice floated up to me. "What was that for, Ace? *I'm* not the evil genie."

"Oh, sorry," I said, unzipping my backpack and withdrawing *Arabian Nights*. "I just had to stick you in there while I use the trinket book."

I opened the front cover and gripped the stamped checkout card tucked into that little envelope. I tugged it free and instantly felt that strange folding sensation. I plunged headfirst into the pages of the big book, and when I unfolded, I was standing on that same New York City sidewalk.

I started to dance, my groovy moves punctuated by jumping jacks as car horns echoed down the streets. It was quite the workout.

There wasn't much left of the Library of Wight and Wong. Even from where I was dancing on the sidewalk, I could see that the building had taken serious damage from Chasm's dragon fire. The front door was hanging ajar. Yellow caution tape was strung across the entryway, forbidding anyone to come in.

"Ridge, get out of the jar," I said between jumping jacks.

He hopped around on the sidewalk for a second, scratching himself. Then he noticed the charred building. "I have a feeling Mr. Wong isn't going to be inside."

"Then we'll have to stamp the checkout card ourselves," I said. Assuming the desk and ink pads hadn't burned up, too. "The trinket book is the fastest way to get back to Ms. Gomez."

I lifted a streamer of plastic caution tape and ducked under, pushing past the damaged door. "Ugh!" I cried, swiping at my face. "Cobwebs!"

Inside, the library was an even greater mess. Everything was black and charred. Not a single bookshelf remained upright. The books, which had once been stone, had returned to paper. There were heaps of them strewn across the floor, but none of them were burned. Guess my trick had worked!

I shuddered at the memory of what had happened here. In my mind, I saw Tina's tormented face and I wondered how I had ever let myself become sidetracked with my own little quest.

Ridge moved over to the checkout desk and brushed off a bit of rubble. "We might be in luck," he said. "The desk looks okay."

I picked my way to the other side, bumping into the remains of Mr. Wong's swivel chair. I remembered seeing him pull the ink pad from one of the drawers on the side. Miraculously, they looked intact.

I grabbed the soot-covered handle of the bottom drawer and pulled it open. It slid easily—too easily! The drawer knocked me back and kept rolling out, somehow becoming wider as it went. It finally slammed to a halt, sticking some six feet out of the desk.

Ridge looked down and screamed a high-pitched shriek, shying away and covering his eyes. Before I could stand up and peer into the unusual drawer, I saw a wrinkled hand reaching up from the depths. Then slowly, like a corpse rising from the grave, Mr. Wong sat up.

"Ah, you boys again," Mr. Wong said. "You've got a lot of nerve, coming back here!"

"Why are you in a drawer?" I asked.

"This is where I sleep," he answered. "Here, give an old man a helping hand."

Ridge and I stepped over and took his arm, hoisting Mr. Wong carefully out of the drawer.

"How did you even fit in there?" I asked.

The Genieologist gave the drawer a good kick and it became small again, sliding easily back into its place. "The desk comes with the job," said Mr. Wong. "I wished for it back when I was helping Mrs. Wight build this place. As the Genieologist, I don't like to leave the library. Middle drawer is the refrigerator. Bottom drawer is the bed. Quite comfortable, actually."

"What's the top drawer?" Ridge asked. "The bathroom?"

"Top drawer is just a drawer," said Mr. Wong. "Bathroom's

down the hall." He sighed. "Or it was before you maniacs let an evil, fire-breathing genie inside!"

"We didn't let him in," I said.

"Well, at least it makes for an interesting story," Mr. Wong said. "To think that I was in the same room as the Wish-breaker . . ." He shuddered.

"Looks like the books survived," I said.

"Yes," he replied. "Somehow, most of them were untouched by the fire."

"That's because I made a wish that turned them into stone," I said. "I got the idea from you because you were, well . . . stone."

"Yes. One of you boys must have said *meanwhile*."

Ridge jumped forward like he might try to cover the old man's mouth. "Don't say it!" he shouted.

"*I* can say *meanwhile*," he said. "The consequence only happens if I hear someone else say it. Ha! What kind of a storyteller would I be if I couldn't say *meanwhile*?"

"We're glad you survived," I said. "But right now we need you to stamp the checkout card so we can get back to the Trinketer." I held out the little paper.

"You completed your quest?" asked Mr. Wong. "You found the missing Stansworth boy?"

"No," I answered. "But that doesn't matter anymore."

"Perhaps you should—"

"Don't try to talk me into it," I cut him off. "I've finally come to terms with who I am."

"And who is that?" asked Mr. Wong.

"I'm Tina's friend," I answered. "The Universe tried to distract me with a useless side quest. But I'm going back to what I should have been doing all along. Saving Tina Gomez."

"Another interesting story for the Genieology books," Mr. Wong said. "But I won't mark your quest as a failure just yet. There is still time."

"I don't need time," I spat. "I don't care!"

"And that is precisely why you might succeed."

"That doesn't make any sense," Ridge muttered.

"The Universe does not always make sense," said Mr. Wong. "Sometimes, if you give up what you always wanted, the Universe gives you what you truly need."

"You, old man, are full of baloney." I was tired of this conversation. "Would you just stamp the card so we can get going?" I waved the checkout card at him until he took it.

Mr. Wong opened the top drawer and withdrew that same alternating date stamp and ink pad. They looked to be in perfect condition, despite the fire that had raged around the desk.

The old man took his sweet time, applying just the right amount of dark ink to the stamp and pressing it onto the checkout card.

"How do you expect to take down the Wishbreaker?" Mr. Wong asked, passing the card back to me.

"We've got some trinkets," I said.

"Yes," said Mr. Wong. "I could still hear while I was a statue. Chasm said the spool of string would be helpful to him if he got his hands on it."

"I don't know what it'll do for him," I admitted. "But he took it from Jathon Anderthon. They're headed to Chasm's hideout right now to steal it back."

"You are still seeking the second trinket?" asked Mr. Wong. "The one that can bring him down?"

"We found it," I said. "A dagger capable of cutting a tether."

"That will merely send the Wishbreaker back into his jar," said Mr. Wong. "But it will not destroy him. Chasm's story will go on. How long will he be locked away? How long before another unsuspecting victim opens his all-powerful jar?"

I'd always thought if we trapped Chasm in his jar, he'd lose. But the Genieologist had brought up a valid point. Our plan wouldn't destroy Chasm at all. It would just delay another inevitable escape.

"Have you got a better idea?" I asked.

"Oh, no," said Mr. Wong. "I'm just a simple writer, recording stories as they unfold. Only the Universe would know how to destroy Chasm for good."

"If the Universe knows, it must be pretending not to," I said.

"Yeah," chimed Ridge. "The Universe has a real poker face."

"And I'm not counting on it to deal us a very good hand," I added.

"The Universe doesn't have a hand," Ridge said. "It's an intangible force."

"I meant *hand* as in the cards you're holding in a game," I said. "You know what I mean. I was just continuing the poker metaphor."

"*You* are the Universe's hand," Mr. Wong said. "The Wish-makers and their quests."

"If I'm one of the Universe's cards," I said, "I must be the joker. Or maybe a two. After my last quest, the Universe obviously thinks I'm rather small and useless."

"Or maybe you are the ace," said the Genieologist. I stared intently at his wrinkly face. "And maybe this time, the aces are wild."

My hand went into my pocket, a rat climbing out as my thumbnail flicked across the tattered edge of my ace of hearts. Did Mr. Wong know about my single possession?

"I don't know what that means," Ridge said. "But Ace does have some pretty wild dance moves. You should see what happens when he steps on the sidewalk."

"Aces are wild," said Mr. Wong. "It's a poker term. I thought we were dragging out that metaphor."

"Yeah, well, we're just kids," I said, "so we don't really play poker."

"When the aces are wild," explained Mr. Wong, "they can become any card that you need to play."

I shrugged. Mr. Wong was full of confusing phrases that almost seemed like wisdom. But there was only one card I needed to play right now, and that was the one that the Genie-ologist had just stamped.

"You ready to go?" I asked Ridge.

"Yeah," he said. "Time for the jar, I guess."

"Only for a minute." I took hold of the peanut butter container and called him into it.

"Good luck against the Wishbreaker," said Mr. Wong. "Play your cards well, and you might actually survive."

"That's not very encouraging, you know." I flipped open the front cover of *Arabian Nights* and stuffed the stamped checkout card into the envelope.

CHAPTER 18

I unfolded right next to Ms. Gomez, who jumped sideways with a startled "Moooo!"

Ms. Gomez, Jathon, Vale, and Thackary were all standing in a circle on the grass outside the archway entrance to the miniature golf course. A sign hung at the top, displaying the name of the place.

Wish-Come-True Mini Golf Park.

"Seriously?" Jathon said to me. "Ms. Gomez was just about to say something important!"

"Good to see you, too," I said.

"Finish your pointless quest?" he asked.

"Yeah," I lied. I didn't feel like explaining my shattered hopes. What mattered was that I was here now. "Ridge, get out of the jar."

"It's like my entire body is a mosquito bite!" he cried, scratching unceremoniously.

"This is the place from Tina's note?" I unzipped my backpack and pushed aside the sandwich supplies to make room for *Arabian Nights*. I wanted to throw that bread bag to the curb, remembering all the optimism I'd felt about my past when I made that sandwich. I silently vowed that I would never eat peanut butter again.

To me it was all peanut *bitter*.

"Of course this be the right place," said Thackary. "Chasm be hiding somewhere in the golf course."

"The name certainly fits for a genie's hideout," I said. "That's a crazy coincidence."

"We think this is more than a simple hideout," said Vale. "We think Chasm built this place, probably using Tina's wishes." She handed me a promotional pamphlet. "These were all over town. Chasm's got some pretty good advertising."

I studied the bright ad for Wish-Come-True Mini Golf Park. Apparently, the grand opening was almost two weeks ago, before I even opened Ridge's jar.

"Take a look at the prizes." Vale gestured for me to turn the pamphlet's page.

"'Golfing has never been so rewarding,'" I read. "'Complete the course for a chance to have your greatest wish come true! A new car, a three-week paid vacation, a house remodel, anything you can think of . . .'" I looked up. "Why would Chasm be advertising this kind of stuff?"

"Umm . . . guys?" Ridge said. "What do you make of this?" He was standing a short distance away, looking at an electrical pole that ran alongside the parking lot. Stapled to the wooden pole were several papers, fluttering gently in the afternoon breeze.

The rest of us walked over to check it out. I'd seen posters like these before, notifying about a lost pet or stolen bicycle. But these were different.

These signs were for lost people. And there were nearly a dozen adults pictured here!

"What happened to all of them?" Ridge asked.

Ms. Gomez stepped forward, mooing softly as she gestured from one poster to the next, drawing our attention to the dates when each person had gone missing.

"They've all disappeared in the last two weeks," said Vale.

"There's something else these posters have in common." Jathon pointed to the text under each picture. "Last seen: Wish-Come-True Mini Golf Park."

"Chasm is taking prisoners," I muttered. "He told me he was making preparations. That he'd wished to know our plans even before we did."

"Why haven't the police shut this place down?" Ridge asked.

"If the park has any kind of magical components created with a wish," said Vale, "then the Universe will shield it from suspicion. The truth may be obvious to us, but even the best detectives would have a hard time seeing this as anything other than a meaningless coincidence."

"People should at least stop golfing here." As I said it, a young couple exited the course. I couldn't see their faces, but I heard them talking about how disappointed they were to mess up on the last hole.

"People be suckers fer free stuff," said Thackary.

"What is Chasm up to?" I said.

"I'm sure it be nothing serious," Thackary replied. "Perhaps he be lonely, looking fer company other than wee Tina."

That was the most ridiculous thing I'd heard today. Chasm was definitely up to something foul. Thackary was probably just trying to downplay it with hopes that we'd walk into a trap. Then the pirate man would be able to do whatever devious trick I was sure he was planning.

I turned to Jathon. "How much time do you and Vale have left together?"

He glanced at his watch. "Just under two hours."

"That doesn't leave us very much time to complete your quest," I said. "We'd better get in there."

"Looks like we get our golf balls and clubs over there." Vale pointed to a shack beside the arched entrance.

"We're not here to golf," I reminded her.

"Let's just see what that employee has to say," Jathon answered. "Maybe he can lead us to Chasm."

I danced my way across the sidewalk until we were all huddled in the shade of the shack's canopy. Jathon rang a little bell on the counter. It seemed unnecessary, since the building was only one small room and the employee was standing right there.

He was a pimply teen with shaggy hair and a bit of wispy stubble that he shouldn't have been allowed to grow. His collared shirt was fire-engine red, a logo sewn onto the front showing a genie coming out of a golf ball. The pinned-on name tag said *Shane*.

"Welcome to Wish-Come-True Mini Golf Park," Shane said, his tone flat.

"We'd like to speak to the owner, please," said Jathon.

"Mr. Kaz only sees people who complete the course."

"I think he'll make an exception," I said. "He knows us."

"Mr. Kaz doesn't make exceptions to the rules."

"Well, that's ironic, coming from the Wish*breaker*," muttered Ridge.

"If you'd like to play a round," Shane said, "it'll be ten dollars each."

I looked at Jathon and saw that he had come to the same conclusion I had. We could stand here and try to persuade this brainwashed teenager, or we could just beat Chasm's stupid golf game and earn ourselves a face-to-face.

"We'll play," Jathon said.

"Okay," Shane answered. "So, just the two of you?"

To my surprise, he was pointing over my shoulder to Ms. Gomez and Thackary Anderthon.

"What? No!" I said. "We're all going to play."

"Sorry," he replied. "Only people eighteen and older are eligible to win prizes."

"We don't care about the prizes," said Vale. "We just want to golf."

"Mr. Kaz doesn't allow minors on his course," Shane said.

I remembered the posters stapled to that pole. All the missing people were adults, which matched Chasm's exclusive rules.

"What kind of mini golf course doesn't allow kids?" Ridge asked.

"The kind that was created by an evil genie," I answered. "Chasm doesn't want to take the chance that a Wishmaker might play. Especially us."

"Not like Shane's going to stop us," whispered Jathon.

True. The gangly teen hardly looked like a threat.

"Has anyone beaten the game yet?" Vale asked.

"Eleven people, so far," said Shane. He gestured to a whiteboard on the shack's back wall where a list of names was written.

It just so happened that there were eleven missing-persons signs on that post outside. . . . "What did they win?" I asked.

"Nothing yet," said Shane. "Mr. Kaz is waiting until he has a winner for every prize."

"How many does he need?" asked Vale.

"Just one more," Shane said. "And there's a guy on Hole Seven right now who shows some real promise."

I looked at Ms. Gomez and Thackary. "You two have to get in there and stop whoever might be about to win."

"Sounds like you're planning to play dirty," said Shane. "I should warn you that Mr. Kaz doesn't tolerate cheating of any kind."

"He's the cheater," said Ridge.

"Mr. Kaz?" Shane sounded shocked. "He's the most generous person I've ever met. All he wants to do is make people's greatest wishes come true."

Yeah, right. We'd all been down that road on our last quest, lured in by Chasm's promise of giving us the thing we wanted most. What was that evil genie planning this time?

"Mooo!" Ms. Gomez handed Shane twenty dollars.

"Excuse me?" said the employee.

"That, there, be payment for the two of us," Thackary explained, stepping close to Ms. Gomez. As much as I hated being left behind, Ms. Gomez and Thackary might have been able to get in there and learn more information about Chasm's golf course.

Shane took the money. He turned to the wall of the shack and rummaged through a rack of clubs. Selecting two, he returned, slipping them over the counter to Thackary and Ms. Gomez.

"What be the score to beat?" Thackary asked.

"You don't have to keep score unless you want to," said Shane. "To meet with Mr. Kaz and earn a free prize, you just have to complete all nine holes."

"They can hit it as many times as they want?" Jathon asked.

"Sure," Shane replied. "The only rule is that they have to wait until the ball stops rolling before they hit it again."

"That shouldn't be too difficult," I said.

"The course is harder than it seems," said Shane. "If you hit the ball into the wrong place, you won't get it back."

"Moooo!" Ms. Gomez held out her hand, beckoning for Shane to give her something.

In response, he reached under the shack's service counter and came up with two golf balls, one white and the other black.

"I'm going to give both of you a special ball." Shane handed the black one to Ms. Gomez and the white one to Thackary Anderthon.

"These have been specifically designed for the Wish-Come-True course. Once you place your golf ball on the green of Hole One," said Shane, "you are not allowed to touch it with anything but the club for the rest of the game."

"What if they hit it out-of-bounds?" I asked. I'd played mini golf before, and my swings weren't always in control.

"Depends on the hole," answered Shane. "They might be able to hit it back in with their club. Or an out-of-bounds hit might end the game for you."

"If they can't touch the golf balls," said Jathon, "how are they supposed to move them from one hole to the next?"

"The holes are connected," Shane explained. "Hit it into one, and the ball will be deposited at the top of the next course."

This was all good information to help us beat the game and find Chasm, but none of it mattered unless we got to play, too.

Thackary and Ms. Gomez moved out from under the shaded canopy. We followed them to the archway entrance, not sure what else to do. The two adults stopped to face us before entering the course. Tina's mom offered a few moos of advice, but that wasn't very helpful.

"Arrr!" said Thackary. "I always knew it would come down to this."

"A mini golf course?" Ridge said.

He shook his greasy head. "Knew it would come down to

me leaving ye sorry landlubbers behind."

"Just get in there and stop the other people from completing the course, Dad," said Jathon.

"But don't putt it into the ninth hole," I said, fearful of what might happen if Thackary won the game before we figured out how to join them. "It would be pointless to face Chasm alone."

"Pointless fer who?" Thackary asked.

"On second thought," I said, "maybe Thackary shouldn't be allowed to golf."

Before I could stop him, he turned and raced under the archway. Not wanting to be left behind, Ms. Gomez jogged after him, golf club gripped firmly in one hand.

"Shouldn't we go after them?" Ridge asked.

"Won't do us much good without golf balls and clubs of our own," said Vale. "If Chasm built this place, you can bet there will be magical barriers to prevent us from reaching his hideout unless we beat his game."

"We could wish for our own clubs and balls," Jathon suggested.

"I don't know," I said. "That employee mentioned that the golf balls were designed specifically for this course. A regular one might not work with whatever Chasm has created."

"Do you have a better idea?" Jathon asked.

"Well, only adults are allowed to play, right?" I said. The

others stared at me blankly, clearly not seeing my plan. "We just have to wish to grow up."

"I don't really want to be an adult yet," Jathon said. "Too much responsibility."

"Can't be more than being a Wishmaker," I said. "Besides, it would just be for a short time. Once we get onto the course with our clubs and balls, we can turn back into kids."

"It's actually a solid plan," Vale backed me up.

"Great," I said. "But I'm only wishing for Ridge and me." Jathon could take care of himself and Vale. I hoped the consequence would be less severe for me if I only changed two people.

"How long?" Jathon asked.

I shrugged. "Fifteen minutes ought to get us onto the course and out of Shane's sight."

Jathon said something to Vale, but I didn't listen. I had my own wishing to do.

"All right, Ridge," I began, the two of us stepping away from them. "I wish that you and I would turn into adults for the next fifteen minutes."

"I hope I have a cool beard," mused Ridge. "If you want us to turn into adults, your mouth will be full of feathers for the next fifteen minutes."

"Ick!" I said, just imagining it. "How many?"

"Lots."

"Can I spit them out?"

"Yeah, but there will just be more."

Well, it was only for a little while. It would be worth it to get us onto the golf course. "Bazang."

My mouth was suddenly full of small downy feathers. And things looked a little different. For starters, I was much taller. Wider, too. I glanced down at myself. What was I wearing? What was all this padding?

"Ace!" Ridge cried. "You're a woman!"

I gasped, nearly choking on my feathers. I looked at Ridge. But the person in front of me definitely didn't look like the genie I knew. He was now older, with a long white beard and a turban.

"What happened?" I asked, sputtering on feathers. My voice was a woman's voice!

"What happened?" echoed another voice.

Ridge and I turned to see two other adults standing a few feet away. Both looked like they were in their late twenties. The woman had Vale's unmistakable red hair and freckles. And the man seemed strangely familiar.

"You look a lot like your dad," I said.

"Ugh, don't say that." Jathon's usual blond hair had darkened with age.

"Let me guess," said Vale. "Ace wished for you to turn into adults."

"Yeah," I muttered. "Not sure what went wrong."

"Nothing went wrong," Vale said. "You *did* turn into adults."

"But we don't look like ourselves!" cried Ridge. "Even though this beard is pretty awesome."

"That's because you didn't wish to turn into adult versions of yourselves," said Jathon, shaking his head.

"At least my consequence doesn't last too long," I said, wiping slobbery feathers from my round chin. "What was yours?"

"For the next fifteen minutes, I can only walk backward," he said.

"Hope you don't trip," Ridge said.

"Come on." Jathon set off, looking over his shoulder as he walked backward toward the golf shack. I stepped onto the sidewalk, my new body busting a dance move along the way.

The four of us stepped under the canopy shade. We didn't ring the bell this time. Shane was leaning over the counter with a bored expression.

"Welcome to Wish-Come-True Mini Golf Park," the teenager said.

"We'd like to play," said Jathon, turning around to face Shane.

"That'll be forty dollars."

Money! I had forgotten about that little detail. We'd

probably have to wish for it. . . . Ridge reached into his back pocket and pulled out a wallet. Opening the leather fold, he pulled out a fifty-dollar bill.

"This just keeps getting better," Ridge said, passing it to Shane. "Keep the change."

"Where did you get that?" I asked, a downy feather fluttering from my mouth.

"It was in my pocket," he replied. "I guess part of being a grown-up is having a wallet."

"Yeah, but I thought they were usually empty," said Jathon.

Shane gathered four clubs from a rack on the wall, but when he passed them out, Ridge didn't look very happy.

"Could I trade my club for a different one?" he asked.

"Is there something wrong with it?" Shane said.

"Well, no," he answered. "But that one looks really cool." I glanced to where Ridge was pointing. Leaning against the counter was a club with the handle wrapped in red leather.

"Sorry. No exchanges."

The teenager turned to retrieve the golf balls from the corner of the shack. The moment Shane wasn't looking, Ridge leaned over the counter, swiping the red club and replacing it with his own.

"You sneaky old man!" I hissed at him.

"Red is my lucky color," he replied, hiding it behind his back as Shane turned again. He handed each of us a golf ball. Jathon got orange, and Vale got blue. I got a boring brown ball, and, coincidentally, Ridge got red.

"You only have to keep score if you want," Shane said. "Just make sure the ball comes to a complete stop before you hit it again. . . ."

"We know the rules," I said. "Thanks."

The four of us quickly veered away from the shack, Jathon walking backward and me doing a little shimmy as we passed under the archway and onto the course.

Now off the sidewalk, I stopped dancing and surveyed the area. Fake green turf clearly marked each part of the course, with little gravel walkways leading from hole to hole. Classic rock music played through mounted speakers. It was nicely landscaped, with big trees and bushes designed to keep the late-afternoon sun off the golfers.

The tree above Jathon, however, promptly dropped all its leaves on us.

"It's golfing time!" I announced through a mouthful of feathers as I sized up the first hole. It didn't look too complex. Just a jelly bean–shaped stretch of green with the hole at the other end. End-to-end bricks made a convenient border to prevent golf balls from going out-of-bounds.

I tried to decide where to tee off. According to the rules that Shane had explained, once the balls were set down, we wouldn't be able to touch them with anything but our clubs.

By the time I decided where to place my brown ball, Jathon and Vale had already beaten the first hole and were moving on to the second. The redheaded genie had to guide her Wishmaker as he traversed the terrain backward.

I took aim and swung my club. My ball clacked off the

235

brick border, popping into the air and landing in some bark outside the course.

"Seriously?!" I shouted, feathers coming out of my mouth and smoke out of my ears. I ran after my errant shot as Ridge took a swing.

"Seriously?!" he echoed.

"Did yours go out-of-bounds, too?" I asked.

"I got a hole-in-one!" he shouted. "It went right in! One hit!"

"I know what a hole-in-one is, Ridge." I spit some feathers. "But you still have to wait for me!"

I took a few more swings, bark flying everywhere. At last, I managed to get some air under the ball, clearing the brick border and landing it on the turf.

With just two more strokes, my brown ball found its way into the hole. I peered in after it, but there was some sort of underground pipe meant to deliver the ball to the next part of the course.

Ridge and I sprinted along the path to find our golf balls waiting for us at the top of Hole Two.

"This looks a little more complicated," Ridge said.

There was a stream running through the middle, with the hole on the opposite side. The only way across was a narrow bridge with no bumpers or guardrails along the water's edge. One wrong swing and the ball would land with a splash, carried away by the current.

I was pondering my strategy when Ridge's red ball went whizzing past. It lined up perfectly, crossing the thin bridge and rolling down a slight slope. It looped around the hole once and then dropped in.

"Woo-hoo!" cried the genie in his old man voice. "Another hole-in-one! Apparently, I'm pretty good at this."

"Don't get cocky," I muttered.

"Small hits, Ace," said Ridge. "You can hit it as many times as you want, remember?"

Helpful advice. Too much power behind my swing would end the game. I tapped it ever so gently. The brown ball rolled less than a foot. I tapped it again.

"That's a good technique," Ridge said. "We might be eighty years old by the time you get to the hole, but at least it won't land in the water."

"You look like you're pushing eighty already," I commented through feathers.

Seven more taps and I was across the bridge. My brown ball rolled down the slope. A few more gentle hits, and it finally went in.

"Slow and steady wins the game," I said. Jathon and Vale were way ahead of us by now, and I couldn't see anyone else on the course.

Holes Three and Four went about like the first two. I was a dozen swings in when Ridge's ball would shoot past and sink into the hole. I eventually got mine to follow, but it took several minutes and a lot of patience.

We had just stepped up to Hole Five when Ridge suddenly turned back into the boy I knew. I, too, transformed, my plump woman's body replaced with the real me. I patted myself just to make sure everything had changed back properly.

"Oh, man," Ridge moaned, slapping his back pocket. "My wallet's gone!"

"So are my feathers!" I cried happily, running my tongue around my mouth to make sure none of them had lingered.

The music on the course ended midsong, and an announcement sounded through the mounted speakers.

"May I have your attention please . . ." I recognized Shane's voice. "This is a Code Red situation. There are children on the course. I repeat, children on the course."

"I don't see any security," Ridge said, hitting his red golf ball. It zoomed across the fifth hole, bouncing off the brick trim and scoring yet another perfect hole-in-one.

"Not fair," I muttered.

"I don't know." Ridge shrugged. "Beginner's luck, I guess."

"I am putting the course into magical defense mode," Shane said. "This is not a drill."

An alarm blared through the speakers. Suddenly, geysers of fire erupted at random across the green course. This was going to make things interesting. . . .

CHAPTER 19

"I'm guessing the fire isn't part of the regular course," Ridge said. A huge ribbon of flame shot right in front of us, leaving a little scorched mark in the artificial turf.

"Magical defense mode," I said, repeating what Shane had announced over the intercom. "Shane didn't activate it until we turned into kids. Something tells me these bonus dangers were designed specifically to keep Wishmakers away."

"I'm surprised Chasm hasn't shown up," Ridge said.

"I don't think he will. The whole point of having a magical defense system is so he doesn't have to deal with us himself. If we fail the course, we'll never be able to get to him."

"Yeah," Ridge said. "A single blast from one of those fire geysers could melt your golf ball."

"Or your face," I pointed out.

I hit my ball. It raced up the slope, fire exploding on both sides. Apparently, my swing hadn't packed quite enough power, because it came rolling right back, barely missing a spurt of fire on the descent.

"You need to hit it a little harder," Ridge said as my ball came to a stop at my feet.

"Obviously."

I hit again. This one actually did what I wanted. Sort of. At least it made it to the top of the slope and stayed there.

Ridge and I set off across the turf. It was terrifying to run through the streamers of fire. One came so close in front of me that it nearly singed off my eyebrows.

"You'd better finish this quick!" Ridge said. "Every second we stand here increases our odds of becoming a charcoal briquette."

My club came down and the ball rolled forward. There was a flash of fire and my golf ball went careening sideways. It bounced off the brick border and dropped into the hole.

"That was close!" Ridge said as the two of us sprinted to the next hole. We arrived just as my ball came rolling out of the connecting pipe.

"Hey!" I cried. "It got scorched!" One side of my golf ball was smudged black and melted. "Now it's got a flat spot!"

"At least Hole Six doesn't look too bad," Ridge said. "Just don't land in either of those ponds."

There was a pool of water on either side of the course. The

turf sloped down toward them, so it was obvious that I'd lose my ball unless I hit it right down the middle.

I went first. I was pleased with the direction my ball was going. It might have even been a hole-in-one if a giant alligator hadn't suddenly sprung from the pond on the right.

The golf ball hit the animal's front teeth and popped up, landing right inside that massive mouth. The alligator's jaw snapped shut. It swallowed.

My golf ball was gone!

Meanwhile, Ridge took a swing, his red ball zipping expertly down the middle of the course. Two more alligators lunged from the ponds, but his ball barely got past, sinking right into the hole at the end.

"How do you . . . ?" I started. "Ugh!" I pointed at the alligator that had eaten my golf ball. With his magical defensive duty done, he was just turning to slink back into the pond.

"I wish that alligator would throw up!"

I hadn't seen him chew my golf ball. If he barfed out the contents of his stomach, I might have a chance to keep playing.

"If you want that alligator to throw up," said Ridge, "then you'll have to stick out your tongue until you leave the golf course."

"Can I talk with my tongue sticking out?" I wondered

aloud. So I tried it. "This is a test." I sounded like a cartoon character, but it was doable.

"Bazang."

I stuck out my tongue and the alligator threw up. At the center of the disgusting mess, I saw my golf ball, covered in slime. But the other alligators were moving in. Apparently, they had a real appetite for golf balls . . . or throw-up.

Sprinting forward, I swung my club, sending the yucky ball safely to the other side. Amazingly, it actually went into the hole. That was my best yet! Only two strokes. Unless you count the alligator's contribution.

But my celebration was short-lived, as one of the alligators clamped its powerful jaws around the metal shaft of my club.

"Ridge!" I shouted, trying to wrestle it away from the animal as smoke came out my ears. "Give me a hand!"

I thought about transforming him into a polar bear and letting him thump the gator on the head, but that would leave me with my hands on the ground and my head down low. Not a good position to be in with chomping alligators on the loose.

Ridge joined me, and with our combined strength, we managed to work the club out of the alligator's jaws. Both of us fell on our backsides as it came free. But we were on our feet running in less than a second.

It wasn't until we reached the seventh hole that I realized what the alligator had done.

"Look at my club!" I cried, tongue dangling out of my mouth. It was bent in the middle, the bottom half sticking out at a clumsy angle.

"Maybe that'll help you hit around corners," Ridge said.

I sighed, staring down at my half-melted, gator-slimed golf ball. "This really isn't my game," I muttered.

"I think it's going great!" said Ridge. "Only three more holes."

"I can't hit with this." I grunted. "I wish my club would get un-bent." As it turned out, the word *wish* was very hard to say with my tongue out. Go ahead, try it.

"If you want your club to straighten out," said Ridge, "then every time someone claps their hands, your head will spin around once."

"Spin around?"

"Yeah," he said. "It'll twist all the way around on your neck, and back to its normal position."

"Um," I said, "necks aren't really designed to do that."

"Don't worry. It'll be painless," he said. "And it'll only last for a day."

Maybe it wouldn't be so bad. How many times a day did I really hear someone clap? I glanced at my hourglass and then at my bent golf club. This game was hard enough with proper equipment. What chance would I have with a mangled club?

"Bazang," I sighed.

The club in my hand instantly straightened out, just the way it had been before the alligator chomped on it.

My attention turned to the hole ahead. Here, the turf sloped inward to a low spot in the middle, filled with some harmless-looking sand. The only way to avoid landing in it would be to hit the ball along the edge with enough momentum that it would reach the flat area on the other side where the hole was located.

This looked simple as Ridge did it, his red ball arcing around the sand trap and slowly dropping into the hole.

"At this point, I think I'd be more surprised if you *didn't* get a hole-in-one," I said.

"Don't hate the player, Ace," Ridge said. "Hate the game."

I lined up my club and gave a nice swing.

My ball plopped right into the sand . . . and started sinking.

"Quicksand!" I yelled, smoke in my ears as I sprinted down to it. I shouldn't have jumped into the sand, but I wasn't thinking clearly. I needed to knock that ball out before it disappeared!

I swung hard, like I was a pro golfer on a full-sized course.

Sand sprayed everywhere and my ball popped into the air. It rolled up the slope and I thought it was going to go in, but it came to a stop less than one inch away from the hole. A delicate tap would finish it off.

But I couldn't move.

"Ridge!" I called. "I'm up to my knees!"

He scrambled down to the low-lying sand pit. "Is it just me," Ridge said, "or have we had our fair share of sand this week?" He reached out, offering me the handle of his club as a tool to pull me out.

I grabbed on to the red leather wrapping. "Ooh," I said. "This feels nice. Your club's way better than mine! No wonder you're golfing a perfect game."

"I need the extra padding," Ridge justified. "You know I get blisters."

I was up to my thighs now, despite the fact that Ridge was pulling as hard as he could. While we were in this position, a small group of adults walked through Hole Seven. I couldn't see their faces, but they were each carrying a mini golf club.

"That ninth hole was killer," one of them was saying. "Can't believe Brian got it in."

"Hey, where is Brian?"

"I haven't seen him."

"Me neither."

"I bet he ran back to the shack," said another. "Couldn't wait to see what his prize was."

"Prize?" Ridge whispered, eyes locking with mine.

"Chasm got his twelfth winner," I said. "We have to hurry!"

"Hey," one of the adults said when she saw us. "I didn't think they let kids into this park."

"Why's he just sitting there?" asked a man's voice. "Kid, this is a mini golf course, not a sandbox."

"I'm not sitting!" I yelled, speech slurred with my tongue out, smoke streaming from my head. "I'm *sinking*. What did you think happened to my legs?"

"Give us a hand!" Ridge begged them.

In response, one of them gave a round of applause. At the sound of hands clapping, my head spun all the way around. It gave me an interesting view of the golf course, but it sort of made me dizzy, too. The group moved away from us, laughing (which caused me to hiccup).

I knew they weren't trying to be jerks. The Universe's shield prevented them from seeing the truth. To them, there was no magical defense mode. This was just an ordinary mini golf park, with chances to earn some serious prizes.

And by the sound of it, Chasm had his final winner.

"I wish you were strong enough to pull me out of this sand," I said to Ridge. Ahh! So many wishes in such a short time! I was mad at myself for not wishing smarter, but I had to keep going.

"All right!" Ridge replied. "I'm going to be ripped!"

"Consequence?"

"If I get strong," he said, "then instead of running, you'll only be able to skip."

"For how long?" I followed up.

"Until the end of the week."

"Hmmm." Running was very helpful at times, especially when going up against the Wishbreaker. Still, I was a pretty fast skipper, so I could probably manage to get away from danger. I'd just look kind of merry while doing it.

"Bazang," I said.

Ridge planted his feet against the sloped turf, our clubs stretched out between us like a lifeline. Ridge heaved with his newfound strength and I wriggled. I felt like the quicksand was going to suck my pants off and eat my shoes, but I managed to come out fully clothed.

"Come on," I said, skipping up the slope to where my ball was waiting. With a single nudge from my club, I was able to knock it into the hole. Then we were quickly moving to the next part of the course. I was surprised that we hadn't caught up to the others by now. Jathon and Vale must have been doing a pretty good job against the course's magical defense mode.

Hole Eight did not smell pretty. It might have once been an easy, spacious green. Fairly level with only a few rock obstacles. But in magical defense mode, this hole was flooding . . . with *acid*!

The purplish liquid gurgled and hissed, releasing a foul vapor. It was encroaching from all sides, dissolving rock and turf as it spread inward.

Ridge's ball sped forward, and I thought his aim looked slightly off. Then it pinged against a rock and popped into the air, skipping over a little inlet of acid, as it rolled into the hole.

"That was dumb luck!" I said.

"Luck is never dumb, Ace."

I eyed him suspiciously. "Maybe it's that club you stole."

"It has nothing to do with the club," Ridge answered defensively. "It's all raw, natural talent."

I began making my way down the remaining green with small controlled strokes, careful to wait until my mangled ball rolled to a complete stop before hitting it again. I had just made the swing that sent the ball into the hole when I tripped over a small rock.

Flailing to keep my balance, I put my club down to brace myself like a walking cane. There was a loud sizzle, and I realized too late that I had plunged the end of my club directly into the potent acid.

I leaped away, yanking it free. But the damage had already been done. All that was left of my club was the black handle and a short length of the metal shaft. The important end had completely dissolved like sugar in water.

CHAPTER 20

"Let's get to the last hole!" Ridge shouted. "Come on!"

I skipped after him, holding on to my stumpy club and trying to decide if I could still make a hit without wishing to repair it . . . again.

We came around a high hedge and stumbled onto the ninth hole. Everyone was there—Jathon and Vale (who had changed back into kids), Ms. Gomez, and Thackary.

The final hole on Chasm's mini golf course was the classic dreaded windmill. In order to win, we'd need to shoot the golf ball into the small front door of the windmill hut. It sounded simple, but it would require careful timing, passing the ball between the turning paddles of the propeller.

Except, magical defense mode had turned the thing into a deadly windmill of doom. The propeller was now whirring at an impossible speed. And to raise the stakes, each paddle of the propeller was studded with spikes and lined with a grinding chainsaw blade.

"What happened to your club?" asked Jathon.

"I thought I'd make this game a little bit harder for myself," I said.

"You should just use mine," Vale said, offering it.

"What about you?" Relieved, I took her club and tossed my broken one into the hedge.

"One of the gators ate my ball," she answered. "I'm out."

I scanned the area. Jathon's orange ball was still at the tee area with Ridge's and mine. On the left side of the windmill, Thackary was crouched next to his white ball, studying the angle.

"What happened to Ms. Gomez?" I asked. She was seated on the brick border, club lying at her feet. I didn't see her black ball anywhere on the turf.

"Mooo," she said sadly.

"Burned up by yonder acid," said Thackary. "That be where we were standing when the magical defense mode began."

"Those other adults didn't seem affected," Ridge pointed out.

"Aye," replied Thackary. "That be true. But Maria and I be ex-Wishmakers."

That left Ridge, Jathon, Thackary, and me with a chance to beat the game and get into Chasm's hideout. I needed to make sure the rest of us got in there before Jathon's mean dad. If he was planning something sinister (as Ridge and I suspected), then we had to leave him behind. And quickly!

"There's no way we're getting past that windmill," I said. The chainsaw blades were moving way too fast. "I wish that the windmill will stop for five seconds after I hit my ball."

That would only give me one shot, but those were the kinds of wishes that seemed to bring the mildest consequences.

"If you want the propellers to stop for five seconds," said Ridge, "then you'll be stopped for one minute after that."

"What exactly does that mean?" I asked.

"You won't be able to move."

"Just for one minute?"

"Yep."

"Will I be aware of what's going on around me?" I asked. "Will I be able to see?"

"You won't be able to move your head," Ridge answered. "But you can have shifty eyes to see what's happening."

"That's not bad at all," I said.

"Unless the way into Chasm's hideout is only open for fifty-seven seconds," said Ridge. "And you have to stand there frozen and watch it close."

"Why did you have to suggest that?"

"Sorry," he replied. "That probably won't happen."

"Bazang."

I gripped Vale's club and gave my ball a solid putt. As soon as the chainsaw windmill made contact with my golf ball, the deathtrap came to a screeching halt. I watched, my body suddenly frozen stiff. My eyes were trained on my misshapen ball, which actually seemed to be going where I wanted it to go!

Out of nowhere, another ball came speeding in. It bumped into mine just inches away from the halted chainsaw blades.

The enemy golf ball was white. And I knew exactly who it belonged to.

In disbelief, I shifted my eyes to the left. Thackary Anderthon was still gripping his club in both hands, closely watching his shot that had just knocked mine aside.

My poor ball didn't quite have the momentum it needed. It rocked to a stop on its melted flat spot right as Thackary's disappeared into the hole.

I watched in horror as the chainsaw blades fired up again. They came around with frightening speed, tearing into my brown ball and instantly reducing it to shreds.

I had lost! My golf ball was nothing more than bits of scrap. Even if I could move, there was nothing left to hit.

In a silent rage, I shifted my eyes to glare at Thackary Anderthon. But the man was gone.

Thackary had completely disappeared. His club, lying abandoned on the turf, was the only sign that he'd been there at all.

"Dad!" Jathon called. "Where did he go?"

"Into Chasm's hideout," Vale suggested.

There was no way to be sure, but it made sense, since Thackary was the thirteenth person to complete the mini golf course.

With my ball destroyed, I felt my hopes falling. My eyes shifted again as Ms. Gomez leaped up. She had lost, too, but

I could see determination on her face as she raced across the green.

She snatched up Thackary's fallen golf club and held it with her own. Circling past me, she yanked the club out of my frozen grasp. Wielding all three together, she bolted forward and thrust the clubs into the blades of the high-speed windmill, a courageous "Mooo!" leaving her lips.

The force jolted her sideways, but she didn't let go. Bracing both feet against the green turf, Ms. Gomez struggled to jam the blades while her clubs bent, throwing a shower of sparks.

"Mooo!" she called back to us. Locked in such a position, the chainsaw propeller was momentarily stalled, leaving the way to the hole wide open for Jathon, if he managed to shoot the ball between Ms. Gomez's feet.

"Vale!" called Jathon. "Get into the jar."

I saw her disappear into the glass pickle jar as he took aim and swung his club. The orange ball sped forward, ricocheting off the side of Ms. Gomez's tennis shoe, but still managing to clatter into the ninth hole.

Beside me, Jathon's club dropped to the ground and I stared blankly at the spot where he had vanished without a trace.

"What are we going to do?" Ridge asked, nervously gripping the red handle of his club. "We'll be separated if I make the shot. I can't put *you* in a jar."

Ms. Gomez let out a bovine groan, casting an anxious glance at the two of us, as if wondering why we weren't doing anything. Then her three clubs snapped and she was thrown backward, the chainsaw windmill grinding to full speed once more.

My frozen minute must have been up, because I suddenly lurched forward, helping Ms. Gomez to her feet.

"You're going to have to wish for a new ball," Ridge said.

Ms. Gomez let out a moo, shaking her head.

"I don't think that'll work, either," I agreed. "Shane said the golf balls were specially designed for this course."

Ms. Gomez looked at me earnestly and pointed at the ninth hole. "Mooo!"

"I'm sorry," I said, "but my cow-talk isn't any better than my chickenese. Besides, there's nothing we can do."

Ms. Gomez pulled the peanut butter jar from my backpack and handed it to me. She mimed a few more things, and I think I understood her plan.

"She wants you to take the swing," I said to Ridge. "I can call you into the jar once the ball is in motion."

"Will that work?" Ridge asked.

"It worked for Jathon and Vale," I said.

"But that was the other way around," he said.

"Still, they must have both been allowed into Chasm's

hideout," I reasoned. "Otherwise, the pickle jar probably would have been left behind with Jathon's golf club."

Ms. Gomez nodded, mooing.

"You'll have to make another wish," Ridge said. "There's no way I can hit it past those blades."

Ms. Gomez shook her head, pulling the red-handled golf club out of Ridge's grasp. For a moment, I thought she might use it to stall the propeller again, but instead, she made a few gestures, punctuated with moos. Suddenly, we were playing charades with a lady who talked like a cow.

Ms. Gomez held her hands into a T, and then pointed at the club.

"Time-out?" Ridge said.

"Tee time?"

She let out a frustrated groan and shook her head again. Ms. Gomez pointed at herself with a questioning expression.

"Who are you?" I said.

"Ms. Gomez. Um . . . Tina's mom," Ridge started listing. "A really bad opera singer?"

"The Trinketer!" I said.

She nodded, pointing once again at the club Ridge had been using.

I slapped a hand to my forehead. "The club is a trinket?"

Ms. Gomez let out a long, satisfied "Mooooooo," which I

257

interpreted to mean, "Yes! I'm so glad you two dummies finally figured that out. Did you really think Ridge was *that* good at mini golf?"

"But who wished for it?" I asked.

Ms. Gomez flipped the club upside down and pointed at the striking end. It was engraved with a fancy font that said *Mr. K.*

"Who's Mr. K?" Ridge asked. "Sounds like a brand of cereal."

"Chasm," I said.

"Isn't that spelled with a *C-h*?" asked Ridge.

"He must use a different spelling when he calls himself Kaz," I said. "Otherwise, people might call him Mr. Chaz."

"Mooo!" Ms. Gomez interrupted, passing the red-handled club back to Ridge.

"Why would Chasm have a club that lets the user score a perfect hole-in-one?" Ridge asked.

"If this is the only way into his hideout," I said, "then Chasm would have to golf every time he wants to go inside. This trinket would make that a lot easier for him."

Ms. Gomez nodded furiously, pointing at the windmill.

"It also explains why there's still a chance to beat the course even when it's in magical defense mode," I continued. "If Chasm had made the course completely impossible, he could end up locking himself outside."

Ridge licked one finger and held it up.

"What are you doing?" I cried.

"I'm testing the wind," Ridge said.

"Don't pretend like you're some expert," I said. "There is literally no way for you to mess this up as long as you use that club."

Ridge shot me a disapproving glance and clucked his tongue at me. "Don't ignore the talent."

He took the shot, red golf ball zipping across the green.

"Ridge, get into the jar!" I called. He disappeared as his golf ball somehow zipped through the twirling saw blades and shot into the ninth hole.

Another hole-in-one.

CHAPTER 21

Everything suddenly changed. The bright daylight of the mini golf course was swapped for immediate dimness that made it difficult to see. The padded turf under my feet was replaced with solid stone.

I could tell we were inside a spacious room. Wait, not a room—this was a big cave. Of course, Chasm had made his hideout in a giant underground cavern. It was a setting he was familiar with.

Someone grabbed my arm and I nearly jumped out of my skin. "Get down!" Jathon whispered, pulling me into a crouch. Vale was next to him, but there was no sign of Thackary.

"Where's your dad?" I asked.

"I don't know," Jathon answered. "He must be hiding some-where in here."

As my eyes adjusted to the dim lighting, I realized that this

260

cave was actually much different from the one where we'd orig-
inally found Chasm's jar. Elaborate chandeliers hung from the
ceiling. There was framed artwork on the walls, huge tapestries
that looked modern and hip.

We had appeared on an upper ledge of the cave. Now the
three of us were crouching between two large potted plants.

An illuminated escalator appeared to be the only way down
to the main floor. A man was riding the long moving staircase,
almost to the bottom. Must have been Brian—that talented
golfer who had been the twelfth person to complete Chasm's
mini golf course.

The main floor of the cave had been decorated like some
kind of extravagant party. One wall sported a glowing aquar-
ium, exotic fish swimming in hypnotizing patterns. There
were lounge chairs scattered across the open space, with tables
overflowing with food. Music pulsed through unseen speakers,
all bass and rhythm with no real melody.

Several people were milling around below. All of them were
adults, so I could only focus on their feet, but they didn't look
like they were trying to escape. They relaxed on the chairs,
lingered around the appetizers, socializing.

At the center of it all was Chasm.

I could see him clearly, even from a distance. He towered
above everyone else, his fedora hat tilted stylishly on his bald

head. He walked around, greeting people with a warm hand-shake.

Then I saw Tina. She trailed behind Chasm like an injured puppy on an invisible leash. I couldn't see all her consequences from here, but I could tell they were painful just by the way she walked.

"How did I do?" Ridge's voice floated up from the peanut butter jar in my hand. "Did I beat the ninth hole?"

I almost fumbled the container, feeling bad that I hadn't pulled Ridge out the moment I arrived.

"Ridge, get out of the jar."

The boy appeared beside me, and I instantly pulled him down beside Jathon and Vale.

"Whoa," Ridge whispered. "This place is fancy."

"Would you expect anything less from Chasm?" I asked.

The man on the escalator finally reached the bottom. He stepped off the metal staircase, standing awkwardly, unsure of what to do.

Chasm noticed him at once and clapped his broad hands. My head spun completely around, and the music stopped, everyone quieting for an obvious announcement.

"Welcome!" Chasm said. "Bienvenido! Willkommen! No matter how you say it, I want you to feel right at home here. Mi casa su casa, as they say."

262

The newcomer stepped forward and Chasm took him in a warm embrace. "Can we hug? I'm the hugging type. Let's hug."

Chasm released Brian and turned back to the others in the cave. "Great news, all around!" he cried. "Our friend here is the final winner of the Wish-Come-True Mini Golf Park contest!"

There was a smattering of applause and cheering that sent my head spinning a few more times.

"You know what this means, right?" said Chasm. "The moment you've all been waiting for has finally arrived. I've tried to keep you happy and comfortable. Some of you have waited more than a week. Am I right, Eric?" He pointed and winked at one of the men, the gesture winning some good-natured chuckles from the others on the floor. I hiccuped.

Chasm swung a thin leather strap off his shoulder. I hadn't noticed it before, as it blended in with his suspenders. The strap was connected to a small bag, the top flap clasped shut with a buckle.

"Is Chasm carrying a purse?" I whispered.

"It's called a man-purse," replied Ridge. "Some call it a murse."

"That's not a thing," I said.

"Guys need somewhere to store things, too."

"I thought that's what pockets were for," I said. "Or backpacks."

"Does it look like anything would fit into the pockets of those skinny jeans?" Ridge replied.

"Good point." Chasm's pants were so tight, I doubted he could squeeze a stick of gum into one of those pockets.

Chasm unclasped his man-purse and reached inside. I squinted to see what he was pulling out and gasped when I recognized it.

It was the spool of string.

Only, now the spool was much, much smaller, the wooden dowel showing where string had once covered.

Chasm began unspooling it, the white string coiling at his feet. He pinched the end as the string slipped off the dowel. Then he held up the empty wooden spool, as though showing it off to everyone present.

"When the string runs out . . ." Chasm said. "That's when I promised to make your greatest wishes come true." Ceremoniously, Chasm handed the end of the string to Brian. Then the big genie turned to face the waiting group of adults.

"It's finally time for everyone to tie on."

"What?" Ridge shrieked. "Tie on? What's he talking about?"

All around the floor, the adults were pulling items from pockets and purses. As they held them out, I realized what they were.

Chasm had given each person a length of the string. And

now, in an almost rehearsed manner, they all began tying one end around their wrists.

"What are they doing?" Jathon muttered.

"Chasm must be making sure that we can't use the string," said Vale. "It's useless if it's already tied onto someone."

"That's all of it," Ridge said.

"Tina . . ." I muttered. What hope did we have of rescuing her now? Maybe we could use Jathon's dagger to cut a piece of string away from one of those adults. But Ms. Gomez had explained that it wouldn't work unless it was a full tether length.

"Now," Chasm said, extending one arm. "Step on up! You've only got forty-two feet, so you'll need to stay close. But once you tie the other end of that string to my wrist, I'll be able to grant your wish."

I suddenly felt cold as I realized what was happening. It was bad enough that Chasm had used up all the string. But his plan was far worse than simply stopping us.

"He can't do that . . ." Jathon said. "The string can only be used to make a tether become visible. . . ."

"No," I whispered, thinking back to the specific wording Ms. Gomez had used when describing the wish that had created the trinket. "The string can be used to create a visible tether between a genie and whoever is tied to the other end."

"I know," snapped Jathon. "A visible tether."

"Don't you realize the difference?" I said, struggling to keep my voice down. "We've been thinking that the string can only be used to make an existing tether visible. But that's not it at all. According to the original wish, the string will *create* a tether. That could work on anybody!"

I heard Ridge gulp in fear. "Chasm is about to get twelve new grown-up Wishmakers."

CHAPTER 22

Our attention was fixed on the floor below. Chasm was striking an arrogant pose, one hand on his hip, with the other outstretched. Tina cowered behind him, shaking her head, voiceless mouth agape so she couldn't warn the others.

The dozen winners of the mini golf game stood in a half circle around Chasm. By now, each of them had knotted their piece of string around their own wrist. Several were moving forward, the other end of the string looped and ready to cinch around Chasm's thick wrist.

"We have to stop them," I muttered. "I wish . . ."

But my mind went blank as the first person tied onto Chasm. As soon as the knot tightened, the length of string between the genie and the new Wishmaker lit up like a glow stick. The magic rippled along the white string, forming that steadfast tether that the Universe required of all Wishmakers.

The next person tied on, and I thought of Ms. Gomez, waiting for us on the mini golf course. With each new tether that formed, her ankles would get bound for an additional hour. She'd be helpless out there!

"Chasm's going to be unstoppable," Vale whispered.

"This was his plan all along," I said. "He basically told me that the string would give him the power he needed to conquer the world."

Three more people had tied on, each stepping back as soon as the task was finished.

"He's going to destroy Tina," Jathon said. "Once he has these other Wishmakers, she'll only slow him down."

It was probably true. Tina had been Chasm's one limitation. Being tethered to her was the only thing keeping him out of his jar. He'd made some extravagant wishes with terrible consequences, but he couldn't harm Tina too much.

All that was about to change. With multiple people tethered to him, Chasm could make some severe wishes, even if the consequence brought death to one of his Wishmakers. What would it matter when he had a dozen more to choose from?

"I wish that Chasm won't be able to leave this cave for the next half hour," said Jathon.

His unexpected wish made me turn in surprise. "Just a half hour?" I cried.

"Trying to lessen my consequence," answered Jathon. "Besides, that's all the time I have left with Vale. I figure we'll either beat Chasm or the world will end in the next thirty minutes."

"Well, ending the world would be one way to stop him," Ridge said. "But it's not great for us."

"Chasm might still get his way," said Vale. "At least for a little while."

"What do you mean?" I asked.

"The big consequence doesn't always happen immediately," she said. "Eventually, the air will turn into chocolate sauce, but it might not happen for a few months, even years."

Jathon impatiently tapped at his hourglass watch and looked to Vale for an explanation of the consequence.

"It's a bad one," she said, "since trapping Chasm here is directly tied to your quest."

"I'll decide how bad," Jathon said. "Just tell me."

"If you want Chasm to be stuck in this cave," said Vale, "then anytime you go outside, it will rain on you."

"Just on me?" he asked.

She nodded. "Like in the cartoons. It'll be a narrow stream of rain that will follow you anywhere you go."

"How hard is it going to rain? Just a drizzle?"

"Torrential downpour," Vale said apologetically.

"Can I use an umbrella?"

"Yeah," she said. "Or a poncho. But you'll need to take them everywhere you go or you'll get soaked."

"How long will this last?"

"Forever."

I saw Jathon scowl, shooting a glance to the floor below. Brian, that newcomer we'd seen on the escalator, was just tying on the final piece of string. If Jathon didn't accept the consequence in the next few seconds, it wasn't likely that Chasm would stick around.

"Fine," he said. "I guess I'll just stay inside for the rest of my life. That would be better than letting everyone in the world choke on chocolate sauce."

"You'll be the pastiest kid in America," I said.

"Probably the whole world," Ridge added.

Jathon glared at us. "Bazang."

The final tether flared brightly, and Chasm lowered his arm, a dozen strings stretching from his wrist like strands of web from a spider.

"All righty, then!" the big genie shouted. "We'll be out of here in no time. On to world domination. But first, I believe I owe each of you one free wish." He reached up and took off his hat as though showing respect. "Tell me the greatest desires of your hearts. Let's start over there with Emily and go clockwise.

Sound fair?" Chasm pointed to the woman on the far left. "You're up, honey."

Emily's voice sounded small compared to Chasm's booming baritone. "Anything?" she asked.

"Anything," answered the evil Wishbreaker. "And I mean anything."

"Well, I wish that my dog hadn't died, but you probably can't do anything about that," she said wistfully.

"Aww," said Chasm. "Poor pooch. When did she die? Well, let's see if we can't get little Fluffers back for you." He leaned forward. "Could you do me a favor and say the word *bazang*?"

"Uhh . . ." Emily stammered. "Bazang?"

I heard barking. There, yapping at Emily's feet, was a little white dog. She screamed, stooping to pick up her pet. "It's her! It's really her! Oh, thank you, Mr. Kaz! How did you—"

"That's enough from you." Chasm held out his hand. "Please save all questions and comments until the end of the presentation. Anthony!" He pointed at the next man in line. "Your turn, bud."

"Oh, wow." The man named Anthony fidgeted nervously before saying, "I wish for a million dollars."

"Basic, and rather boring," droned Chasm. "No real imagination, but that's to be expected among a group of adult

271

humans. Anthony, my friend, your wish will come true as soon as you say 'bazang.'"

"Bazang," he replied.

"Very nice," said Chasm. "You are now a millionaire. Go ahead. Check your bank account."

Anthony pulled a mobile phone from the jacket of his sport coat.

"Not now!" said Chasm. "We're in a cave. You really think you've got service down here? Next!"

"Thank you, Mr. Kaz," said the next man. "It's an honor to be one of the winners of your mini golf contest and I—"

"Save it for someone who cares," Chasm cut him off.

"Okay," said the man. "I wish for *two* million dollars."

"Really?" Chasm chuckled, causing me to hiccup. "You're going to one-up old Anthony? I mean, I thought you looked dull, but I never . . ." He trailed off with a sigh. "Say it."

"Bazang," said the man.

"My turn?" asked the next woman. "I wish to be a famous actress."

Chasm yawned. "And . . . there it is. Fame. When you walk out of this cave, don't be surprised if the paparazzi are waiting. Your latest movie was a smash success."

"I've never . . ." the woman stammered. "I've never been in a movie."

"Oh, get over yourself, dollface!" answered Chasm. "Just say the magic word, and you're a star."

"Bazang!" said the woman.

"We've got to do something," Jathon whispered as the conversation carried on below.

"This is like a bad reality-TV show," Ridge said. "Money, fame . . . Chasm's right. These people don't have much imagination."

"You shouldn't agree with Chasm," I said. "He's the bad guy."

"I'm just saying, I don't think we can count on any of those adults to wish for something that could slow Chasm down," Ridge explained. "They're just going to waste their free wishes."

"Ridge has a point," Vale said. "We've got to go down there."

"You have the dagger?" I asked Jathon.

In response, he flashed me the ancient blade. "I'll need to slash through all of those strings," he said. "The only way we can get Chasm to go back into his jar is by severing every one of his connections."

"What about Tina?" Ridge asked.

"We'll have to figure something out," I said. "If we can cut one of the strings close to the person's wrist, maybe it'll be long enough that we can reuse it on Tina."

"Chasm isn't going to like us interfering," said Jathon.

"At least your wish will stop him from leaving the cave," I said.

"Still, with thirteen Wishmakers at his command, Chasm will be able to make some pretty big wishes, regardless of the consequences."

"Then you'll have to use the element of surprise," I said. "Cut as many people free as you can before Chasm notices."

"We'll need a distraction," Jathon said.

"I'll take care of it," I answered.

"You've got something in mind?" Vale asked.

"It had better not involve me wearing a hula skirt and coconut bra," said Ridge.

I shook my head. "Oh, I've got a distraction that Chasm won't be able to ignore."

The four of us turned our attention back to the floor. The final person was stepping forward to make his free wish. I could see him wringing his hands together nervously.

"Do you know Julia Johnson?" he asked awkwardly.

Chasm took an impatient breath and said, "No."

"Of course not," the man muttered. "She's from my work. She's in HR. . . . She doesn't know me, but I . . . I wish that Julia Johnson would fall in love with me."

"There's the lovesick fool I was waiting for!" cried Chasm. "You know the drill. Let's hear the word."

"Bazang," said the man.

"Exactly," Chasm said. "Julia Johnson will now follow you to the ends of the earth, which may actually be necessary by the time I'm done with this planet."

Chasm clapped his hands, causing my head to swivel. "I hope you've all had fun here. I've made your greatest wishes come true, but I've been saving the best part for last. You see, as the Wishbreaker, I'm not allowed to force people to be my slaves. You all had to come willingly, lured in by the opportunity to see your greatest dream fulfilled. I tried standing on a street corner and offering free wishes, but apparently everyone thought I was crazy."

"I still think he's crazy," whispered Ridge.

"I'm actually quite sane," Chasm went on. "I'm just a magical guy, and the Universe has a way of shielding regular people from my real intentions. So I had to create some sort of test to get people excited about coming to me. Hence, the whole golf park thing. I tried to make it as easy as possible for regular people, but I seriously overestimated human hand-eye coordination. Anyhoo . . . Now you're mine, and I can do as I please with you."

"That's not fair!" shouted one of the men.

"Who do you think you are?" cried a woman.

"You'll be hearing from my lawyer about this!" yelled another.

Chasm held up a finger. "Cue the bickering," he said. "Ugh. The grown-up humans are even worse than the little ones. But then, that's another reason I made the mini golf course exclusive for adults. You see, you never know what a child will wish for. I couldn't take the risk that one of them would use their free wish for something that would complicate my plans. But adults . . ." He waved his hand dismissively. "You guys pretty much stick to love, fame, and fortune. So predictable."

"Hey!" called one of the men. "Why can't I get this string off my wrist?"

"You're a Wishmaker now, sonny," answered Chasm. "That means we're inseparable. I know. It's kind of the pits, being all tied together." He raised his arm, gesturing to the strings trailing from it. "I'm counting on you guys not to get all tangled up, okay?" Chasm sounded kind of like a teacher laying down rules for a new school year. "I should probably force one of you into making a wish for that. . . ."

"You have to let me go!" cried a woman. "I don't want to play anymore!"

"You know what?" said Chasm. "I don't want to play anymore, either. So, let's get down to business. The twelve of you have another wish to make. This time, you all wish for your voices to be silenced in my presence."

This was met with a chorus of complaints and shouts. I saw

Chasm's red hourglass pop open as he began to explain the consequence.

"If you don't want to be able to speak," Chasm said, "then your mouths will permanently hang agape while you are with me. Don't worry!" He held up a hand. "They'll be able to close your jaw when you're lying in your coffin."

This was exactly how it started for Tina. Chasm had made this same wish, coupled with this same consequence, as a way to silence Tina and take control.

The shouts of protest rose even louder, but Chasm sang over the top of them, his voice echoing through the vast chamber. "Ba-ba-ba-zang!"

The cave suddenly went eerily silent. I couldn't focus on the faces of the adults below, but I saw several of them fall to their knees in despair.

"See, I like this better," Chasm said to his silent slaves. "Much more interesting when I'm in charge. Now, as much as it grieves me to leave this place . . ." He reached out to a corner of the room. "I'll miss you, minibar and Jacuzzi. But it's time to take over the world."

Chasm twirled his fedora and deposited it perfectly on his head. "Where should we go first? Somewhere with a lot of people. Make a big splash. Maybe I'll start by making myself the president of the United States."

He spun around, pointing a finger at one of his newly tethered Wishmakers. "Eeny, meeny, miney, Allison. Your turn! You wish to instantly transport us all to Washington, DC."

Allison held up her hands in fear, but Chasm suddenly went rigid, glancing around the big cave. "I can't?" he muttered. "Why not? Someone wished to keep me here? Who?"

Time to make my big debut. I patted Jathon on the back for luck and then stepped onto the top step of the escalator.

"Hello, Chasm!"

CHAPTER 23

Chasm whirled around, his gaze falling on the descending escalator where Ridge and I were standing one stair apart from each other.

"Why, hello, little Ace," Chasm said with an unintimidated grin.

I instantly dropped to one knee on the moving staircase and bowed my head. "I am at your service, my liege," I recited, forced into the saying since Chasm had greeted me.

"Interesting," said Chasm. "You've come to be my servant? I must admit, I did not see that coming."

I rose to my feet. "That was a simple slip of the tongue," I said to Chasm. "What I meant to say was, 'I am *not* at your service, my *whatever-the-opposite-of-liege-is.*'"

"Ah," replied Chasm. "So, you're the one who wished to keep me in this cave."

"Yep," I said. "That's right." The whole point of this confrontation was to draw Chasm's attention away, allowing Jathon to sneak down and cut the people free.

"You're not going anywhere, Chasm!" I continued. "Because you have an appointment."

"An appointment?" Chasm raised one eyebrow curiously. "Let me guess, with destiny."

"No," I scoffed. "Not with destiny."

"Were you really going to say destiny?" Ridge whispered.

I shrugged at him. "It's a good line."

"Did you really have a plan for a distraction?" Ridge said quietly. "Because it seems like you're just stalling."

"Stalling *is* a distraction tactic," I pointed out. "But that wasn't my plan."

"Well, you'd better get to it," Ridge said. "Once we reach the bottom, I fully expect Chasm to squash us."

I cleared my throat and shouted to my enemy. "I challenge you, Chasm!" I pointed at him for dramatic effect as smoke vented out my ears. "To a battle!"

Chasm threw back his head and laughed. "I would crush you like a potato chip, puny human."

I hiccuped. "Not just any kind of battle," I went on. "A *rap* battle!"

"Now, this just got interesting!" Chasm answered. "I accept!"

Ridge grabbed my arm. "That's only going to buy us, like, two seconds," he whispered. "You heard Chasm rap at the library. There's no way you can keep up with him."

"I'm not going to do it without help," I said. "I'll make a wish."

"When?" Ridge cried. "We're almost to the bottom. If Chasm hears you wish for it, he'll think you're cheating. You know he doesn't like cheaters."

"Good point," I said. "Walk with me."

I turned around and began walking up the escalator. This didn't take us anywhere, but it kept us from reaching the bottom. We hovered about ten feet above the landing, padding over the steps as quickly as they came.

"I wish to be a great rapper," I whispered. But what if Chasm was still better? What if he used Tina's wishes to be the best? "Not just great," I added. "I wish to be an *unstoppable* rapper."

"If you want to rap," said Ridge, "then anytime you stand still, you will slowly sink into the ground."

"Will I be able to get myself out?"

"As long as you don't sink too deep," said Ridge. "The ground will be like goo under your feet. Keep shuffling and you won't sink."

"What about when I'm sleeping?"

"It only happens when you're standing," he said. "So, don't sleep standing up."

"I usually don't," I said. "How long?"

"Rest of the week."

I nodded. "Bazang."

We stopped walking, turned around, and let the moving stairs carry us down to the floor.

"Did you get a little confused on how an escalator works?" Chasm asked. He was waiting near the landing, a sneer on his broad face. His group of Wishmakers stood behind him, many of them stretching their new tethers to the full forty-two feet. I spotted Tina sitting on the stone floor, not fifteen feet behind the Wishbreaker. She looked bad. Even worse than when we'd seen her at the library.

"I was getting ready for the rap," I answered. "Just had to ask Ridge what rhymes with *Chasm the loser*."

"Easy," answered Chasm. "Battleship cruiser. Library user. Bus ride snoozer. Textbook abuser. Broccoli refuser."

Wow. He was fast. "Let's do this." I stepped off the moving stairs, but I didn't hold still out of fear of my new consequence. Instead, I hopped side to side, my feet skimming back and forth so I wouldn't sink into the floor.

"Hey, bud," Chasm said. "I see you shuffling there. Do you need to go potty? I'm okay to wait. The restroom is just past the ping-pong table."

"I'm fine," I said. "So, how's this going to work?"

"We'll have Teeny lay down a beat," Chasm said. "You and I will rap back and forth until one of us gets stumped."

"Sounds fair," I said.

Chasm snapped his fingers without looking back at Tina. The girl slowly rose to her feet and began stomping her magical shoe in rhythm, an impressive array of sounds resonating through the cave.

"You go first," I said.

"Happily." Chasm closed his eyes, focusing on the beat that Tina was laying down. Then the battle started.

"Let's pick this up where you and I left off,
I led these people here, like a horse to the trough,
And now you understand why I needed your string,
I got a dozen wishers from a mini golf swing.
You never even thought that I could multiply the tether,
Now I'll be making wishes and I don't care whether
Anything should happen to these poor pathetic losers.
They chose to come to Mr. Kaz, so pickers can't be choosers."

Okay. Now it was my turn. I started speaking a sentence, feeling terrified. But the words flowed off my tongue with excellent rhythm and rhyme. It took a bit of focus, but it wasn't very hard.

"You think you're something fancy with your little man-purse,
It's time for Mr. Kaz to answer to the Universe.
You'll end up in a jar, without a reassignment,
And you'll be getting old in solitary confinement.
You told me yourself, there was a trinket with power,
Capable of taking you down, in half an hour,
Or less. And I know you really want me to leave,
But the Universe is waiting with an Ace up its sleeve."

Nailed it!

I glanced at Ridge, who seemed to be equally impressed with my performance. Not only had all of my sentences rhymed, but I thought I'd managed to shake Chasm a bit with their meaning. He was feeling so secure about stealing the spool of string that I felt like he could use a reminder about the second trinket—the dagger that could bring him down.

"A mediocre rap from a worthless boy,
Your life is so depressing. Nothing to enjoy,
A lonely little orphan kid who doesn't know his past.
You, the hero. Me, the villain. So typecast."

As Chasm insulted me through his second verse, I tried hard not to stare at the flash of movement I had seen on the far

284

wall. It was Jathon, I was sure of it. He must have made some kind of wish that allowed him to crawl along the ceiling and descend behind Chasm on the opposite side of the cave. I had no choice but to jump into another verse of rap and try to hold the evil genie's attention a little longer.

"Keep your eyes on me, you maniacal genie,
You're nothing but a dirty-rotten, good-for-nothing meanie.
I'm a rapping distraction, with a heavy dose of swagger,
'Cuz my friend is standing right behind you holding a
dagger!"

Shoot, I might have just spoiled the fact that Jathon had snuck up behind Chasm. But hey, at least it rhymed!

Chasm's eyes grew wide, and he spun around in shock. Jathon had gathered the Wishmaker adults behind him. Vale held all twelve of their glowing tethers, the strings gripped tightly in a bundle between her hands. Jathon lifted his right hand and I saw the dagger glint in the blue lights from the fish tank.

"No!" Chasm screamed.

Jathon brought the old blade down, slashing through the dozen strings in a single blow. With the adults cut free, Vale only needed to hang on to one of the thin strings to try to reuse it on Tina.

But as the dagger sliced through, something unexpected happened. The strings seared like a flash of fire. Vale gave a shout and pulled her hands away. In the blink of an eye, the magical pieces of string had been reduced to little more than ash, falling through the genie girl's fingers.

Apparently, the string was a one-time-use kind of trinket.

I saw the knots flake away from Chasm's wrist as he brought his arm up. The twelve civilians, now ex-Wishmakers, stumbled backward, rubbing at their wrists where the strings had once held them.

"Run!" Jathon shouted, waving at them. "I created a door on the upper landing! Make your way up the escalator and get out of here!"

"What have you done?" Chasm wailed. He swung his arm, knocking Jathon heavily across the back. The boy hit the ground, trinket dagger falling from his grasp and skidding across the stone floor.

"Ridge!" I yelled, ears smoking. "Balaclava!"

He instantly morphed into a penguin-winged polar bear and leaped at Chasm's unprotected back. The attack knocked Chasm to his knees, preventing him from hurting Jathon with a second blow.

Meanwhile, I was down on my hands and feet, bear-crawling across the floor to the place where Jathon's dagger had fallen. I scooped up the ancient blade and craned my neck to look for Tina.

I spotted her in a huddle on the ground next to a lounge chair. Vale was already at her side, attempting to speak to the mute girl.

Over my shoulder, I heard Chasm yell something unintelligible, pinned under Ridge's huge polar bear bulk.

"I've got my paw in his mouth!" Ridge proudly announced.

"But he's biting down pretty hard. You guys had better do something soon!"

"Tina!" I said, crawling awkwardly over to her. "We're going to cut you free with this dagger." With my elbow locked stiff from my pay-as-you-play consequence, I started slashing the blade through the air like a madman, hopeful to connect with Tina's invisible tether.

"Forget it," Jathon said, rubbing a bump on his head as he came up behind us. "The dagger can only cut the tether if it's visible. I don't know what we're going to do."

"I couldn't hold on," said Vale. "The string burned away as soon as Jathon cut it."

Jathon laughed when Vale said his name. I hiccuped. "Chasm wasted the whole spool!" Jathon moaned. "All five hundred and . . . *however many feet* there were!"

I stopped my hapless air-cutting. Something didn't add up. I thought back to when we'd measured the string in the ski lodge. It had been enough to go between Vale and Jathon *thirteen* times.

"Thirteen times," I muttered. "Chasm ran out of string, but he only tied on to twelve people."

"What are you saying?" Jathon asked.

"I'm saying that a forty-two-foot piece of string went missing between the ski lodge and here." And I suddenly had a very good idea of where it might be.

"Thackary Anderthon!" I hissed, tilting my head to scan the hideout. There he was, finally emerging from whatever corner he'd been hiding in. The despicable man was walking slowly toward the spot where Ridge had pinned Chasm. In his right hand, he held a piece of white string, loosely coiled as he approached the captive genie.

Thackary must have been planning this all along! That was why he acted so defensive every time someone mentioned the string. He had always known of its power to create a new tether, and now he planned to use it for himself!

I couldn't reach Thackary in time. Not while forced to remain on all fours. And Chasm was an easy target, gagged and pinned by the shaggy polar bear. There was only one way to stop Thackary. One way to buy us a little more time to get that final piece of string and tie it onto Tina.

"Balaclava!" I shouted. More smoke out my ears.

Ridge transformed into a skinny kid, and Chasm bit down on his fingers.

"Yeooooow!" Ridge howled.

Chasm sprang to his feet, swatting at the smaller genie as though he were a bothersome insect. Ridge tumbled onto one of the couches with such force that it tipped over.

"Yarrr! I be humbled to speak to the great Chasm!" cried Thackary, not even shirking away as the Wishbreaker turned to him.

"You look familiar," Chasm said. "Have I had the misfortune of looking at your face before?"

"Aye! We met when ye first emerged from yer jar," said Thackary. "I pledged meself then, and I pledge meself now." He held out the coiled piece of string. "Make me yer loyal servant!"

"Hmm . . ." Chasm said. "You do know that I enslave people, take away their wishes, torment them with serious consequences, and make them do whatever I want?"

"Aye," said Thackary.

"Okay, cool," said Chasm. "Just checking."

"I'll do anything to shake the consequences I now carry," said Thackary, glancing at Jathon.

Sure, he had some pesky problems lingering from his time as a young Wishmaker. No one wanted to carry consequences. But tethering himself to Chasm was not the way to get rid of them. The Wishbreaker would only assign him *worse* consequences. And besides, Tina needed that string!

"You're one weird little dude," Chasm said. "But I guess I could use you to take over the world." Chasm reached out to take the string.

Tina suddenly appeared out of nowhere, coasting forward on her roller-skate foot. Her sock-covered hand darted out and grabbed the coil of string, yanking it from Thackary's unsuspecting hand.

"Arrr!" The angry man lunged, grabbing on to the back of

Tina's shirt and halting her escape. But he only held her for a second before he fell back, howling in pain. "Yarr! Ye've got a hive of bees swarming yer midriff! Fierce little stingers!"

As Thackary rubbed at his fresh bee stings, Tina kicked, coasting toward me with a determined expression on her face as I shuffled my feet.

"Bad Teeny!" Chasm shouted, thrusting out his foot and tripping her escape. Tina flew toward Ridge and me, and I braced to catch her. Our silent friend toppled all three of us to the floor. Chasm pounced on us, but we were suddenly shooting sideways.

What was this? We had landed on a rug, and now the Universe was pulling it out from under me. Chasm hit the floor where we had been, as the three of us tumbled off the rug, finally rolling to a stop.

It was a rather painful experience, and I sat up, rubbing my shoulder. Ridge was strewn across my legs, and Tina was a few feet away, already stumbling to her feet.

"Well, little Teeny," Chasm said, cracking his knuckles as if preparing for something dreadful. "Why don't we remind your friends what I'm capable of? I'm feeling a little fiery sensation coming on." He tapped his chest. "Compassion?" he mused. "No . . . Heartburn? No . . ." He snapped his fingers. "Oh, I know what it is!"

Tina's eyes went wide and she looked right at me. As Chasm

291

opened his mouth to say something, she made a quick decision and tossed me the coil of string.

"It's *abracadrizzle*," said the Wishbreaker.

I imagined that Jathon and Vale were pretty confused by Chasm's statement. But Ridge and I knew exactly what that word would do.

In a flash, Chasm transformed into a dragon. His arms were now stout forelegs ending in hooked black talons. Well, that was going to complicate tying the string around his wrist.

The pay-as-you-play consequence instantly took effect on Tina, a wall of flames leaping up around her. I suddenly realized why she had tossed me the string. With Tina surrounded so closely by flames, it was too risky that the delicate string would catch fire and burn up.

I needed to convince Chasm to transform back into human form so the defenses around Tina would drop.

Thackary Anderthon was nowhere in sight. I assumed he had slunk back into whatever corner he had come from. Jathon and Vale were racing toward us, but Chasm's long tail suddenly snaked out, knocking them backward. His thick neck turned, and dragon Chasm let out a gush of flames.

I braced myself (and by bracing myself, I mean shutting my eyes in absolute fear), but the fire didn't touch us. I felt the heat of the blaze all around, and I gripped tightly to the dagger and the coil of string in my hand.

"Abracadrizzle." When I heard Chasm's voice, I finally dared to open my eyes. The dragon had ignited a ring of fire all the way around us, like the one that had surrounded Tina, only much bigger. With this new border, Ridge and I were the only ones trapped inside with Chasm, while Tina, Jathon, and Vale were shut outside the new wall of flames.

Returned to his regular form, Chasm straightened his bow tie, one hand behind his back and an obnoxious grin on his face.

"Aren't you boys missing something?" Chasm asked.

"I've got everything we need to take you down right here!" I brandished the dagger and the string, proud that I hadn't dropped them in my fear of getting burned alive.

"I'm not talking about your trinkets," Chasm said, whipping his hand out from behind his back and showing off the item he was holding.

It was Ridge's peanut butter jar.

"How did you . . . ?" I muttered.

"Oh, is this important?" Chasm asked with fake concern. "I just saw it sticking out of your backpack, and I thought . . . Gotta have it. You'd be surprised what you can steal while your opponent stands there with his eyes shut."

"You're a pickpocket?" I cried.

"Technically, he's a pickbackpack," Ridge said.

"Well, it doesn't matter, anyway," I said to Chasm. "There's nothing you can do with that jar. Those things are magically enhanced and totally unbreakable."

Chasm broke the jar.

He smashed the peanut butter container against his forehead like a tough guy crushing a soda can. There was a blinding blast of magic, and Ridge's jar exploded into tiny fragments.

Ridge screamed. The boy genie looked like he was on the verge of panic.

"I didn't think that was possible!" I muttered.

"Puh-lease!" said Chasm. "I'm the Wishbreaker. Emphasis on *breaker*. I can steal people's wishes, force them into consequences. . . . Did you really think I couldn't break a genie jar?"

"It's okay, Ridge," I said. "You're still my genie. This hasn't changed anything."

"Don't you know what this means?" Ridge cried, bordering on hysteria.

"It means he dies," said Chasm. "He has nowhere to go when this quest ends. Your poor widdle genie will fizzle out of existence forever."

Now I understood why Ridge was panicking. Wouldn't you panic if you had less than a day before "fizzling out of existence"?

"I will break you down, boy," Chasm said. "I took Tina. Now I've taken Ridge."

"I'm not giving up," I said. "We know how to free Tina. And I'll figure out how to save Ridge."

"Are you sure?" asked Chasm. "It's hard to save other people when you are lost yourself."

"What are you talking about?" I said.

"I've got a great idea," Chasm said, "and I want you to hear me out. Okay?"

"You're the bad guy!" Ridge shouted. "You've got *bad* ideas!"

"That's just not fair." Chasm's voice was dripping with pretend hurt. "Sometimes bad guys have good ideas. Like this one: Use the string for yourself, Ace."

"That *is* a bad idea," I said. "You seriously thought I'd fall for that?"

"Think about it!" cried Chasm. "Everyone who ties to me gets one free wish. This is finally your chance to find yourself. Don't you want to know your past? Aren't you curious about where you came from? Who you were?"

Of course I was curious! But I'd given up on that after my failed attempt to meet Samuel Sylvester Stansworth's parents. There was another cause far more important than learning who I used to be. I was here for Tina!

"You can't ask about your past with a regular genie." Chasm gestured to Ridge. "But I can give you that wish with no consequence attached."

"Yeah, yeah, yeah," I said. "And then I become your eternal slave. Not happening."

"You've got the dagger!" Chasm pointed at the weapon in

my hand. "The minute you get what you want, I'll let you cut yourself free. I promise."

"I don't believe you," I answered. "You'll steal my voice, just like you did to the others."

"Even if I was lying," said Chasm, "making a wish to steal your voice would take a couple seconds. You'd have plenty of time to cut the string before I can spit it out."

He'd actually made a good point there. It was just a tiny piece of string and I'd seen how easily the dagger had sliced through it.

"Ah," Chasm said. "I can tell you're thinking it over. You realize that I'm a reasonable fellow with reasonable ideas."

"Taking over the world is not a reasonable idea!" Ridge said. "And, by the way, I can't tell if you're trying to rule the world or destroy it."

"I think of it as a nice mix," said Chasm. "Maybe sixty-forty. Destroy the people I can't control. I mean, if I destroyed *all* the humans, there will be no one left to see me on Broadway."

"Nobody's going to see you on Broadway!" Ridge said.

"I'll make them," said Chasm. "And they'll like it."

"Come on, Ace." Ridge turned to me. "You can't possibly be considering anything this guy says. You know it's a trap."

"It's not a trap!" Chasm said. "It's a fair offer, with an easy escape clause. Use the string to connect us. Cut yourself free with the dagger."

"What's in it for you?" I asked, shuffling back and forth so I wouldn't sink into the floor.

"I've decided I prefer my tethers invisible." He gestured at Tina outside the fire wall. "You get to learn your past, and I make sure that the string gets used up."

For one final moment, I let my mind linger on the idea of learning my past. I daydreamed about getting the answers I'd spent years seeking.

And then I looked Chasm in the face and said, "No way." I took a deep breath. "There is only one piece of string left, and I'm using it to save Tina. You can't tempt me anymore, Chasm. You know why?"

"Enlighten me," said the big genie, folding his arms.

"Because I don't care," I replied. "I'm done chasing my past. I don't care who Ace was. All that matters is who I am."

"Very poetic," Chasm said, awarding my speech with a slow clap that made my head turn around. "But I can see the lie behind your brave words."

"I'm not lying!" I said. And I meant it. Seeing Tina bravely striking out to steal the string from Thackary only confirmed my feelings. Once and for all, I was ready to move on from the questions that had bothered me.

"If you truly don't care," said Chasm, "then why do you cling to the one thing from your past?" He pointed at my hand. "I know about your little card."

The ace of hearts card was pinched between my fingers. I must have pulled it out of my pocket without realizing it. That explained why there was a rat on the floor. The card was my nervous habit. My link to the past.

"Oh, this old thing?" I unfolded the card and held it up for Chasm to see. "Actually, I'm kind of tired of it."

I ripped the card in half—and that was when things got really interesting.

CHAPTER 24

Samuel Sylvester Stansworth looked at his genie, despair on his face. "Only one hour left," he said. "I guess that's goodbye to all silver cars."

"I don't know," Dune replied. "A lot can happen in an hour."

"Yeah, like getting pulverized by angry gorilla chefs," said Sam. The creatures pounding on the bathroom door had appeared the moment Sam picked up the saltshaker trinket. There were at least a dozen gorillas, each wielding a fiery spatula of doom. Sam had done his best to wish their way out of the restroom, but the ex-Wishmaker who owned the diner apparently had other trinkets in place to prevent such magical escapes.

"We'll have to fight our way past them," said Dune. "But we'll have to move that boulder you wished for." The huge stone was doing a decent job of blocking the bathroom door.

"They'll destroy us!" Sam cried. "You know how many wishes it'll take to get out of here alive?"

"Well, those guys aren't going to give up until we complete your quest," Dune reminded him.

The gorilla with the floury apron had said as much. Yeah, it talked. Not great, but it got the point across by saying, "We smash Wishmaker. We stop quest."

"Finish your quest and the gorilla monsters go away," Dune encouraged.

Sam threw his hands up hopelessly. "Even if we get out of this diner in the next hour, the Grand Canyon is halfway across the country. We'll never get the saltshaker emptied unless I wish for it directly."

"That's usually not a great idea," warned Dune.

Sam shrugged. "Maybe worth a shot if it keeps us alive." He took a deep breath. "I wish that my quest would be complete." The hourglass popped out on his wrist, but he didn't even glance down at it.

"If you want your quest to suddenly be completed," said Dune, "then everyone we know will have their head replaced with a soccer ball."

"What?" Sam shrieked, his voice echoing through the empty diner bathroom. "Won't that kill them?"

"Strangely, no," Dune answered. "They'll still have a functioning brain in there. But they won't have eyes, ears, mouths, noses. . . ."

"That's horrible!" cried Sam. "Everyone I know?"

"Everyone we know," corrected Dune.

"But, I know a lot of people. My mom and dad. My little sister. My grandma and grandpa. And what about my teachers and my friends? And then there's everybody in the neighborhood. . . ."

"I don't think you can list everyone you know in thirty seconds," Dune said, pointing at the hourglass on his Wishmaker's wrist. "It's been awhile since I've been out on a quest, so I really only know you."

"So that means my head will get replaced with a soccer ball, too?!"

"And mine," said Dune. "Since you know me."

"I can't . . ." Sam mumbled. "I obviously can't accept this. Better for everyone to lose their cars than their heads. No way." His hourglass folded out of sight.

Dune sighed. "Too bad you know so many people. That consequence wouldn't have been so bad if you didn't know anybody."

Sam stared at his genie, a wild idea striking him upside the head. "I think we can get around this," he whispered. "I think I can trick the Universe!"

Sam crossed the diner bathroom, searching for something. He stopped next to a frame on the wall by the paper towel dispenser. The Wishmaker smashed the glass with his elbow and withdrew the contents of the frame.

It was a playing card. An ace of hearts.

"Vandalizing the artwork is your big idea?" Dune asked. "That was probably signed by someone famous."

"It's just a random decoration, I think." Sam held out the card for the genie to inspect it.

"Oh, so you're going to do a card trick?"

"Sort of," answered Sam. "And I hope it works." Carefully pinching the corner of the card, he looked at Dune. "Trinket. I wish that this card would store all of our memories as soon as it is folded and release our memories once it is ripped."

"Now, that is a good trick!" Dune said. "As a consequence, you will have your back stuck to the ground for an hour after the card is folded or ripped."

"What if we fold it more than once?" Sam asked.

"You'll only take the consequence the first time it's folded," answered Dune. "That's when the magic will kick in."

"So if I happen to unfold it and refold it a bunch of times, nothing new will happen?"

Dune nodded. "You can only lose all of your memories once."

"Well, that's reassuring," Sam said. "I wouldn't want to keep forgetting what I was doing." He tapped his chin in thought. "Bazang."

For a brief second, the ace card shimmered magically in Sam's fingertips. "Great!"

"Wait, I'm not sure I see your plan here," said Dune.

"Once I fold the card, we won't know anyone," Sam explained. "And if we don't know anyone, then I can wish for my quest to be completed and dodge the consequence."

Dune grinned. *"If you don't know anyone, no one's head will be replaced with a soccer ball."* Then he frowned. *"But I see a big problem. How will you remember to make the wish for your quest after you fold the card?"*

Sam scratched his head in thought. *"I'll make the wish first,"* he said. *"Then I'll fold the card right as I say, 'bazang.'"*

"You'll have to time it just right," Dune said.

"I can do it," he answered. *"Now I wish that my quest would be complete."*

Dune's eyes went wide as the hourglass appeared again. *"You're not going to like this."*

"What?" moaned the Wishmaker.

"If you want your quest to be completed," Dune said, *"then everyone you* don't *know will have their heads replaced with a basketball."*

"Why?" Sam cried. *"Why did it change?"*

"The consequence isn't always the same," answered Dune. *"If you make the same wish more than once, sometimes the consequence changes to something equally awful. Probably the Universe's way of stopping you from doing tricks like you were about to pull."*

"This is stupid!" Sam yelled, throwing the ace card down on the hard floor. *"I guess we're just going to get cooked up by the gorillas!"*

"Hey," Dune tried. *"Don't give up. You've still got wishes."*

"No!" he said. *"I'm done making wishes. I'm done taking*

consequences. This has been the hardest week of my life. Just look at me! My shoes are too small, and my shirt is freezing cold. Anytime someone clears their throat, I have to slap the bottom of my foot. I smell through my ears, and I break every chair I sit on. I have to do five pushups each time I go outside. If anybody screams, I fall asleep, and when I try to whisper, it sounds like I'm yelling. I've got crumbled-up potato chips in my socks, and my legs got stuck facing backward for a whole day. Hot water feels cold to me, and cold water feels hot. The wind blew my hair off, and I had a slice of onion stuck to my forehead. Every time I yawn, a bug flies in my mouth!"

He sat down, right there on the bathroom floor. Dune nodded sympathetically. "You forgot about when your hands got replaced with hooves."

"Ha!" Sam cried. "Of course! How could I forget about that day?"

"I know it's hard," Dune said.

"But you don't know. You're a genie. You don't have to make the hard decisions and live with the consequences."

"It's not that great being a genie, either," Dune rebutted. "I might actually like to make my own choices."

"It doesn't matter," Sam went on. "Now we're going to get smashed because I wasn't clever enough to get us out of here."

"Technically," Dune said, "the gorillas are only going to smash you." He changed his voice to imitate the sentence that the gorilla chef had spoken. "We smash Wishmaker."

Sam looked up, his eyes suddenly glinting with hope. "That's it!" he said. "They're only after me because I'm a Wishmaker."

"Aha!" said Dune. "Once our time runs out, I'll disappear and you'll no longer be a Wishmaker. The gorillas should leave you alone. All you have to do is survive another hour."

Something suddenly burst through the bathroom door. Dune turned abruptly. It was a hairy hand clutching a burning spatula, dangerous flames dancing in the dim bathroom light. Sam's defensive boulder wasn't going to help if the gorillas punched through and climbed over the top.

"Survive another hour . . ." muttered Sam. "That'll take too many wishes. Too many consequences. I can't do it. Unless I wish . . ." He took a deep breath and looked directly at his genie. "I wish I wasn't a Wishmaker. I wish I didn't have to make any more wishes."

Dune looked up sharply. "Sam," he whispered. "That's crazy. You'll fail your quest."

Sam just waved him off. "I basically failed it already. Losing some cars isn't the end of the world. I'd rather stay alive. What's the consequence?"

"It's . . . it's unknown."

"Unknown?"

"The Universe isn't telling me anything about it. I don't know, Sam. This has never happened to me before."

"Is it going to hurt people I care about?" he asked. *Another gorilla arm punched through the door.*

"I don't think so," said Dune. "From what I can tell, you'd be the only human affected."

Dune bent down and scooped up the fallen ace card. There was no practical use for it now, but they had to be careful not to let it bend.

"You're not seriously thinking about accepting the Unknown Consequence, are you?" Dune asked, *seeing Sam seated in the middle of the bathroom floor, staring at the sands pouring through his hourglass.*

"I don't want to wish anymore," *whispered Sam.* "I'm done." *And then he said the magic word.* "Bazang."

CHAPTER 25

The torn halves of the ace card fluttered to the ground, and I suddenly knew exactly what I needed to do.

"Umm . . ." I said to Chasm. "I changed my mind." I tossed him one end of the string. "Does your offer still stand?" I took the other end of the string and tied it in a simple knot around my wrist. "I'm ready to be your Wishmaker."

Chasm stooped and picked up the loose end of the string while I held my breath in anticipation. The wall of fire around us was beginning to dwindle, but it was still enough to hold back the others. I wondered if they could see what I was doing.

"I thought you'd come around," said Chasm, holding out his wrist. "But you know I can't tie the tether around my own wrist. It must be your choice. So, come let old Kaz make your greatest wish come true."

I must have been holding still, because my feet had sunk

into the floor. Squirming, I pulled them out and stepped forward, taking the end of the string from Chasm's hand. I made a simple loop and cinched it tight around Chasm's wrist, a ripple of glowing magic passing down the line between us.

"Yes," Chasm said. "Yes! You were every bit as foolish as I expected."

The genie's big hands shot out. One of them snatched the dagger from my grasp, while the other shoved me backward.

"Hey!" I called. Guess I should have realized that getting close enough to tie the tether on Chasm would also be close enough for him to steal the dagger.

"Oh, you feel betrayed? Tricked?" Chasm laughed. "Boohoo! What did you expect? I'm the bad guy!"

"Ace!" Ridge's voice called out from behind me, but I didn't turn to look at him. I was still invisibly tethered to Ridge, but now I had a second genie. The Wishbreaker.

"Can we move things along here?" Chasm said. "I've got other stuff to do today. Let's take care of this free wish nonsense." He held out a cordial hand to me. "Go ahead and make your wish, Ace. You should know that you can't wish to have more wishes without consequences. I wished against that when I was created three thousand years ago."

"I'm not interested in more free wishes," I answered. "I only need one."

"Right," said Chasm. "You want to find out your past. . . ."

"No," I said. After what I'd just learned from tearing my ace card, I knew that this wish had to go to Ridge to save him and to make things right. And glancing at Vale beyond the ring of flames, it occurred to me that I shouldn't stop there. I remembered asking her how she liked being a genie.

"We're just pulled along because we have to be here."

Well, it was time to change that.

"This one is for my genie friends," I said to Chasm. "I wish for Ridge, and Vale, and all the other genies to turn human. To no longer be genies."

"Really?" Chasm said. "I see what you're trying to do here, and it's not going to work. Sure, this will save your little genie friend from fizzling out of existence, and give all those other weakling kid-genies a chance to live like pathetic humans. But it won't stop me. I am not a common genie. I am the Wishbreaker, and my power cannot be wished away."

"Bazang!" I said.

From behind me I saw a blinding flash of light as my wish was granted, turning Ridge into an ordinary human kid. Another burst shone across the cave as the wish reached Vale. I knew it was happening all around the world, young genies suddenly popping onto Earth as regular kids.

I felt a little smile creep onto my face. I'd done all I could for them. Their service as the Universe's middlemen was over. Now they'd see what it was like to live free and choose their own fates.

But Chasm was right about the Wishbreaker. My free wish hadn't stripped away his power. I hadn't expected it to, and I was okay with that. You see, I had a special ace up my sleeve for this guy.

"Ha!" shouted Chasm. "Now you're mine! You wish to have no voice. And the consequence is . . . Wait a minute. I can't wish that? Why can't I take away your voice?"

"Even the Wishbreaker can't wish against a wish," I said, a knowing smirk on my face. "If you took my voice, you would stop me from rapping. And I specifically wished to be *unstoppable.*"

And with that kind of lead-in, I pretty much had to finish this off in style.

"Let's start by thinking back to what the Universe
 told you,
The trinkets we were seeking could bind you and hold you,
The first was unmistakably that spool of string,
But you were kind of clueless 'bout the second thing.
We thought the ocean blade would catch you off guard,
But all this time the second trinket was my ace card.

By tearing it to pieces I have learned about my past,

The memories returned in blast, at last,

Let me spell this out, I hope it's not too soon,

Ridge is Samuel Stansworth, and my name is Dune."

Chasm stared at me in thought. He reached up and stroked his chin. "I'm sorry," the man said. "I've been calling you Ace this whole time. But your name is actually Dune?"

Chasm was puzzled. I, too, had spent three years utterly confused. But the Unknown Consequence wasn't unknown to me anymore. You see, I used to be Ridge's genie and Ridge used to be Samuel Sylvester Stansworth. When he'd accepted the Unknown Consequence in that bathroom, it had caused us to switch places. That was the Unknown Consequence. It turned the genie into a human. And it turned the Wishmaker into a genie, taking away his or her ability to make choices, fulfilling the wish for no more wishes. It just so happened that the ace card had been in my hand at the time, and the force of the switch had caused me to fall and bend the card, accidentally deleting all our memories.

At the same time, I must have hit my head hard enough to knock me out for a couple of days. I woke up in the hospital. Still not sure how I got there, but that's where my new memories began. You pretty much know the story from there on.

311

To think I had carried the answers in my pocket all these years.

The Genieologist's words suddenly made sense. *"Sometimes, if you give up what you always wanted, the Universe gives you what you truly need."*

That ace card had meant everything to me. But only when I was ready to give it up, did I find out who I really was. And with that came the knowledge I needed to take down Chasm for good.

I tossed my backpack to Ridge. "Eat up," I said. "We've got a pointless quest to complete."

Still lying on his back, paying for the trinket consequence, Ridge reached into the pack and pulled out the peanut butter and jelly sandwich I had made in that parking lot. It wasn't in great shape, the bread totally smashed and peanut butter leaking out the sides.

"Do I really have to eat this?" he asked hesitantly.

"For the good of all red roses," I replied. Ridge began to chow down and I knew that Jathon and I had both completed our quests. Yes, Tina was still captive, but Jathon had done what the Universe had asked him to do. Using the dagger, he had forcefully separated not just one but twelve Wishmakers from Chasm.

"Quests complete!" I announced.

The Wishbreaker stepped toward me. "Why are you wasting my time?"

"Because," I said, "Aces are wild."

"Anything you wish against me will come with a steep consequence to you!" shouted Chasm.

"That's what I'm banking on," I replied. "Consequences are part of making choices. Part of being human. You'll see." It was time to finish this. I knew I was doing the right thing, even though my heart ached a little at the thought of it. "Now I wish for no more wishes."

"What?" Chasm cried. "What a foolish idea! And the consequence . . . It's completely unknown."

"Not to me," I said. "Samuel Sylvester Stansworth and I know exactly what will happen. Bazang!"

Chasm jolted, his man-purse slipping from his shoulder and spilling open. His red ceramic genie jar rolled out, the open top venting crimson smoke.

The dark plume swirled around my waist, pulling at me. Now that I had my memories back, I remembered seeing this same thing happen to Sam when he accepted the Unknown Consequence. He'd been sucked into my salsa jar on the floor of that diner bathroom.

I was now standing far enough from Chasm that the glowing string was taut between us. A blast of magic carved

through the air, and we were suddenly trading places. It was like snapping the tether, except instead of returning us both to one central location, this simply shot us past each other. The string came untied from our wrists, falling limply to the floor as Chasm was whipped off the end and sent tumbling.

The smoke was all around me now, and my feet never even touched down. I cast one last glance across the room. Then I was pulled headfirst into the red ceramic jar.

It was dark and quiet.

I couldn't tell if I was floating or falling. It was actually very relaxing in there, and I felt myself getting very sleepy.

Hopefully I had set everything right. Tina would be free, since Chasm was no longer the Wishbreaker. Vale and Ridge were free. My friend could take up his old life as Samuel and finally return to his family.

By making that fateful wish, I had made the last decision I would ever make: to become a genie again. I certainly wasn't happy about becoming a simple middleman to the Universe, whose only real responsibility was listening to the choices of a Wishmaker—but I had to take one for the team.

I sure would miss being a human. My ability to choose. My freedom.

My friends.

BUT WAIT, THERE'S MORE. . . .

I emerged from the jar in a puff of smoke.

This was going to be my first new assignment. Another cave? Seriously? Well, I guess it was time to meet whatever unfortunate kid had become my Wishmaker while on some spelunking adventure.

I turned around and came face-to-face with Thackary Anderthon.

"You?!" I shrieked. "What?" He was the only other person in the cavern, and he was holding a jar. The man was definitely my new Wishmaker. But how was that possible?

"Ha-ha!" Thackary cried. "It worked! After all this time!"

His voice! Something was different. Thackary Anderthon no longer talked like a pirate. Since he was now tethered to me, all the consequences he had carried from his youth were finally erased.

"How did you break the rules?" I demanded. "Adults aren't supposed to be able to open a genie jar."

"But you're not just a regular genie, Ace!" Thackary said. "You took Chasm's place! You're the Wishbreaker!"

I got chills. I had swapped places with Chasm; I had been sucked into his jar. I wasn't bound by the regular rules of the Universe. But this also meant I was stuck with Thackary . . . *forever.*

"Where are we?" I asked. "How did you find my jar? Where are the others?"

317

Thackary held up a hand. "It's a long story," he said.

"How long have I been gone?"

"One week."

Really? A whole week? It felt like I had barely dozed off!

Thackary's face broke into a broad smile. There was something less despicable about his appearance. "That was a brave thing you did, kid."

"It worked?"

"Chasm turned into a pathetic weakling without his powers," answered Thackary. "Ms. Gomez punched him in the nose and he ran off crying. Taught him to mess with an angry mama. Although she is a good deal shorter than she used to be, since Jathon used the dagger to cut all those strings."

"And Tina?" I asked.

"Safe," said Thackary. "Although she still carries those terrible consequences from her time with Chasm. I suspect you'll see her shortly. She's waiting just outside the cave."

"What?" I cried.

"They're all out there," explained Thackary. "Jathon and Vale, who is quite enjoying her human freedoms, thanks to you."

"What about Ridge?"

"He's with them," Thackary said. "But he actually goes by Sam these days."

My friends were just outside? "Why didn't they come in?"

"They wanted to, but the four of them are currently tied up."

"More bad guys?" I asked. "Who got them?"

"I did," answered Thackary.

I clenched my fists at him, but he held up his hands defensively. "It was the only way," he explained. "Tina and her mom have been using trinkets to try to locate you, with Sam, Jathon, and Vale helping where they could. I followed the group here and took them by surprise before they could enter the cave. I knew it would make them hate me, but that's the only reason I was able to do it."

"Ugh. You're a terrible person," I muttered.

"You're right. I was. For so many years," he answered. "But that's not who I am anymore."

"What do you mean?" I said. "You don't just turn into a nice guy overnight."

"Not overnight," said Thackary. "For me, it happened in the blink of an eye."

"Yeah, right."

"Haven't you ever wondered *why* I was so mean?" he asked. "Why I named my own son something that would encourage other kids to make fun of him?"

"There's a reason?" I asked.

"I was fifteen years old when I first became a Wishmaker," Thackary explained. "That's about as old as they come. Ms. Gomez and I crossed paths while pursuing our separate quests. I finished early, but I stuck around with my genie to help Maria."

I raised a suspicious eyebrow. It was hard to imagine Thackary helping anyone.

"She introduced me to her best friend, Lisa," Thackary continued. "For me, it was love at first sight."

"Wait a minute," I cut in. "Is this a romantic story?"

"That night, Lisa was hit by a car."

"Yikes," I said. "Now it's a tragedy."

"She was taken to the hospital, but the doctors said she wouldn't survive," continued Thackary. "I only had a few moments left with my genie, and I wished to save her life."

"I'm guessing that had a pretty steep consequence?" I said.

"By saving Lisa's life," said Thackary, "I was doomed to spend the rest of mine doing things to make everyone else hate me."

I felt the heaviness of the conversation settle on me. Thackary's behavior suddenly made a lot of sense. All his life, the Universe's consequence had forced him into doing cruel things.

"Lisa made an instant recovery, and I was waiting by her side," continued Thackary. "Eventually, years later, we got married. But she was the only person I was ever allowed to be kind to. I became a monster to everyone else. Including my own son."

"What happened to Jathon's mom?" I asked.

"Lisa passed away six years ago," said Thackary. "And everyone still thinks I'm a monster." He suddenly looked up, his eyes glimmering with hope. "But now I don't have to be the villain anymore! I can finally be the father that Jathon deserves."

"Why didn't you tell him?" I asked. "Why didn't you just explain that being mean wasn't your fault?"

"I couldn't," he said. "The consequence wouldn't allow me to explain it, because that would be a contradiction. Knowing the truth would make Jathon hate me less, so I've had to keep it in all these years."

"What about Ms. Gomez," I said. "Did she know about your consequence?"

"Yes," said Thackary. "She was there when I made the wish to save Lisa's life. But before she could tell anyone the truth, I wished that Maria Gomez would never be able to share my secret. It has made her mad at me all these years, but that was exactly why I had to do it."

"I'm sorry, Thackary." I never thought I'd have reason to say those words.

"No, I'm sorry," the man replied. "I've done terrible things in my life, and it's time to set everything right. I get one free wish, don't I?"

"I . . ." I didn't know what to say. As the Wishbreaker, I could grant it. "Yeah. I guess."

"I'd like to set you free," he said. "I'd like to do for you what you did for all the other genies."

I shook my head as the Universe told me that couldn't happen. "I'm afraid it doesn't quite work like that. I'm the Wishbreaker. My powers can't be wished away." Just like Chasm had said.

Thackary shrugged. "Well, it was worth asking." He rubbed his hands together in thought. "Guess I'll have to use my backup plan." He reached into his pocket and withdrew a small item. As my eyes focused on it, I realized it was a familiar piece of string, tightly coiled.

"Where did you get that?" I asked.

"It was left behind when you and Chasm switched places," Thackary said. "It untied from your wrists without any damage, so I gathered it up, figuring it could come in handy."

Next, Thackary reached behind him, his hand reappearing with the weathered dagger that Jathon had used to cut Chasm's Wishmakers loose.

He stooped, setting the two items on the stone floor in front of him. "These are for Tina," Thackary said. "She can use them to get a fresh start."

Then he stood up tall. "As for my one freebie, I wish that my genie jar will go straight to my son, Jathon Anderthon."

"*Your* genie jar?" I asked. "You're a mortal. You don't . . ."

"Bazang!" Thackary shouted. "Now I guess it's time for consequences." He looked me right in the eye. "Here's a little something I learned from a wise kid. I wish for no more wishes." Thackary didn't even pause for me to explain. "Bazang!"

The red smoke came curling out of the ceramic jar, but this time, it flowed around Thackary. Next came the surge of magic, blazing brightly between us. We swung sharply through the air, and I was deposited right where he had been standing.

As for Thackary Anderthon, my sworn enemy, he was sucked into the ceramic jar in his hand. It fell to the stone floor, but didn't shatter. I watched a red lid appear out of the smoke, sealing over the jar's opening.

Then, without a sound, the genie jar disappeared.

I looked around the empty cavern. I was completely alone. Human again, thanks to the sacrifice of Thackary Anderthon.

The sound of shoes scuffing on rock caused me to whirl to the cave's opening.

Tina. Jathon. Vale. Ridge (or Sam, I guess). My friends sprinted toward me, nearly tackling me in a giant group hug. Jathon still sported a few lingering consequences from his time with Vale, but it was nothing compared to Tina's sad state.

"Where's my dad?" Jathon asked, the first one to pull away.

"He's . . ." I began. "Well . . . he should be here any second."

"Big jerk," Sam muttered.

"Actually," I said, "I think he's kind of a hero in his own way."

"My dad?" Jathon said.

"Yeah, right," said Vale.

"You'll see," I said.

"What do you mean, I'll see?" Jathon asked.

"Your dad traded places with me," I explained. "He used my same trick and got sucked into Chasm's old jar."

Jathon looked like someone had punched him in the stomach. "Seriously? My dad's a genie?"

"Not just a regular genie," I said.

"A pirate genie!" Sam said.

"Thackary Anderthon is the all-powerful Wishbreaker now," I reminded him. "Your dad had one free wish before he got sucked into the jar. He's coming for you, Jathon. And when you open that jar, the two of you will be tethered together forever."

Jathon looked panicked. "I don't think I'm going to like that."

I thought about telling him of Thackary's sudden change, but the jar would be here soon. It would be better for Jathon to hear it directly from his dad.

"Trust me," I said. "Everything's going to be okay." I reached down and picked up the old dagger and coiled length of string. "These should get rid of your consequences," I said to Tina. "Once Thackary shows up, you can tie onto him and then cut yourself free."

She accepted the items with her sock-covered hand and a hopeful look on her face. "I never should have opened Chasm's jar," Tina whispered.

"You saved the world three times over, Tina," I said. "There is no reason to be ashamed of the choices you made. You were very brave."

"And *you* were very clever," Vale said to me, grinning. "Setting all the genies free like that . . ."

"I hope it was the right choice," I said. "I couldn't ask all the genies. I don't even know how many of you there were."

"Trust me," replied Vale. "I'm sure none of us are sad about not being genies anymore. Being human is way better."

"I think everyone is forgetting about how brave *I* was, too," Sam chimed in. "After all, I was the one who had to eat that sandwich Ace made."

I turned to him. "All this time, *you* were Samuel Sylvester Stansworth. . . ."

He sighed. "Sorry about what happened at the diner three years ago."

"I should probably thank you," I said. "If you hadn't made that wish, I never would have been able to experience what it was like to be a real human. I would have been stuck as a genie forever."

"Being a genie wasn't all bad," Sam said.

"But there are some real perks to being a regular mortal kid," said Vale.

"Like being able to choose where you want to go and what you want to do," I said.

"Like having people that care about you," said Sam.

"I cared about you," I said. "Even when you were a genie."

"I was talking about having a family," he replied. "But thanks."

"Speaking of family," I said, "have you been back to find your mom and dad?"

"Yeah," Sam said. "They're actually much nicer than they were when you met them. By the way, wasn't it obvious that they were *my* parents and not yours?"

"It would have been a real giveaway, if I had been able to see their faces," I said. "But I guess the Universe needed me to figure it out a different way."

After all that had happened, it did make me a little sad. I'd never had a family, and I never would.

"Well, we'd better get going," Sam said. "My parents told

me to be home by dinnertime and we're still halfway across the country."

Vale pulled a bouncy ball from her back pocket. "This ought to get us there."

It had to be a trinket, although I had no idea what it did. "What about me?" I asked. "Where am I supposed to go?"

"You're coming home with me," said Sam. "Mom and Dad want to meet you."

"That sounds nice," I said. "I'd like to look your parents in the face and have a chance to explain why I acted so weirdly that day."

"They're used to having weird kids," Sam said. "One time, my sister and I had a competition to see who could act like an animal the longest. I was an Australian emu. My sister was a cat. She got a dry spot from licking her own arm."

"Eww."

Sam nodded. "Like I said. Weird kids. You'll fit right in."

"What do you mean?"

"Face it, Ace. You're not the most normal kid."

"That's not what I'm asking," I said, shaking my head. "What did you mean, I'll fit right in?"

"Oh," Sam said. "I thought that was obvious. I'm going to adopt you."

"You can't adopt me. You're just a kid."

"Fine. My parents will adopt you," he said. "I'll ask them very nicely."

"What if they say no?"

"You'll have to impress them."

"How?" I asked.

"Well," Sam said, "I wouldn't start by making them a peanut butter sandwich. . . ."

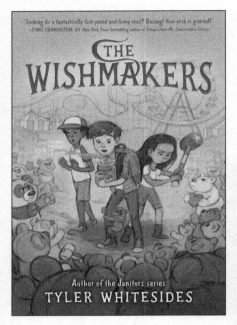
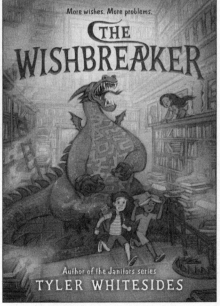